DAISY JACOBS
SAVES THE WORLD

An improbable adventure

"Imagination is more important than knowledge."

Albert Einstein

ABANDON HOPE ALL YE WHO ENTER HERE

R ight until the moment the world ended, I was feeling pretty happy about things. The irony of it didn't hit me until later. Then again, if all life began with the Big Bang — which a reliable authority tells me it did — I guess it's only fitting that's exactly how my life should end: with the biggest bang of all.

But none of what happened is my fault. So if you had plans for the rest of your life, don't look at me. I'm not taking the rap. I'm entirely blameless for any mayhem, death and destruction.

Until it all went a bit pear-shaped though, I was in control. And I was properly happy because my life was — finally — about to begin. Or, that's to say, my love life at least seemed like it was. And then …

Well, they say go out with a bang, right?

HOW THE DEATH-DEALING MONSTER CAME TO EARTH
Somewhere above Planet Earth.
This morning.

There's nothing. No sensation, awareness, or feeling. Just *it*.

It is the merest hint of conscious matter. *It* is elemental — just primordial atoms of being that drift towards a place where *it* can coalesce, find form ... and *become*.

It moves with languid speed through the vast, empty darkness. This is how *it* has been since the beginning. Since the dawn of what some call time.

Its aims are modest: *it* doesn't actually crave death. Death is simply a by-product. When *it* finds the right conditions, *it* finds form.

It becomes.

These conditions are astonishingly, incomprehensibly rare. But they do exist. And throughout the ages *it* has happened upon them. And *it* has *become*. In some places, one form *becomes*. In some, there are tens, hundreds, millions ... even billions. But all forms have limits. Eventually, they're used up, worn out, broken down, empty — finished. That place ceases to *become*.

Ending thus, *it* reforms into mere atoms, adrift in search of the next *becoming*.

This is how it's always been. How it will always be. Because *it* is unceasing, relentless, and entirely without emotion. *It* gets no kick from the ferrous tang of blood, the crunching of bones, or the screams for mercy.

2

Finally, after eons adrift, *it* finds a new place with favourable conditions. A place with billions of heartbeats that can bring *it* the briefest physical existence. Of course, even with the biological richness of this planet, the reaping will be swift. For *it*, this will be a brief pit-stop; a cosmic snack on the way to eternity.

So the death-dealing monster comes to the small, blue-green place …

And *it* finds Daisy Jacobs.

Chapter 1

MEANWHILE ...

"Love, anxiety and heartbreak — in one fell swoop I'm going for a hat-trick of teen angst!" Behind me I hear my best friend, Amy Porter, crack up at my assessment of the emotional mess I've landed myself in.

"This isn't like you, Daisy," she replies. "You shouldn't do this, but don't let the Satellite Simpletons be the reason. Just take a step back and think."

'Take it easy', 'don't do it', 'be sensible', 'avoid situations that make you anxious'. It's the same old message — but from Amy of all people.

Well, you know what? I may be sick of living in fear, but I'm *really* fed up of living life with the handbrake on in case I get the panics. Because that's another thing about being a teenager: we can be unbearably, insufferably optimistic. So, yeah, I'll probably end up in a tizzy again and my heart will most likely get broken, but a teeny, tiny bit of me thinks this may just be the day *everything* changes. And for once I don't care! At least I'll know — and pretty soon everyone else will too.

"No, Amy, this time, I'm gonna believe in myself, even if no-one else does. From being a super nerd, I may even end up as a fully fledged, swan-like member of the in-crowd!"

"Yeah, well, it's either that or I'll have to pick up the pieces. And I can't see Icky Ellie Watson suddenly opening her heart just cos she sees you opening yours to Connor."

"Huh, well," I smile wickedly, "some of Ellie's friends call her a wit, but I think they're only half right ..."

Amy laughs as I silently strive to control my breathing. I've tried to work on my 'fight or flight' reactions to stressful situations. So right now, though I feel like running, I know I need to fight the rising sense of dread. I must do this. I have to follow my suddenly crazy heart, which is about to launch itself in the general direction of Connor Wheeler. I mean, he's tall (even by supercharged, hormone-powered Year 10 standards), he's captain of the football team and he's got that chiseled chin, floppy-haired thing going on — plus he's just about the only one who comes close to matching my grades. And, although he's on the fringes of the unsavoury group of boys and girls who orbit around Ellie, I can't believe he's just another one of her Satellite Simpletons. He likes poetry, for goodness' sake!

"Hey, Daisy," Ellie's voice trills in my direction, "we're having a discussion over here. Can you settle an argument for us? As an outsider, what's *your* view of the human race?" Even from the other side of the playground, I see that her, admittedly very pretty face (drat!), dimples into a grin as the Satellites break into peels of sycophantic laughter. But Connor, who in this analogy is the largest, outermost planet, appears to flush … and was that a shake of the head? By the group's standards, that's open dissent! No one seems to notice it but me, though; not that Ellie would say anything to rein Connor in. I'm sure her sharp-features, shiny-face and burgeoning chest (double drat!) would like to cuddle up to his flawlessness every bit as much as I would.

Amy glances at me, eyebrows raised, "sure you to want to rise to her petty taunts?"

I hide a grimace. Ignoring cheap insults has become second nature, but soon I may no longer be Scuttleford's Number One Nerd (© Icky Ellie Watson).

"I think she's only part of the problem. I love it here, but you've got to admit it's pretty boring in our insignificant corner of the world. And I think this will just stir things up a bit."

Look, I don't live in a big city. Not London, New York, Moscow or Paris. I live in a tiny village you've never heard of — Scuttleford (see, told you) — on the outskirts of a small, sleepy town (Braedon) that won't have ever registered on your consciousness. Because why would it? Scuttleford's the sort of place you pass through without noticing. There's a pub, a tiny general store and a few cottages dotted around. It's probably basically unchanged since Domesday — which is, like, forever. So maybe my esteem issues are about living in a backwater part of nowhere and sharing a classroom with troglodytes like Ellie.

Nothing ever happens in my village. And literally nothing ever happens in my school. And although I'm a teenage girl in the middle of hormone Hades, with parents who are just *so* understanding, a little brother straight out of hell, a best friend who's sometimes my worst enemy because she is one stubborn lady who thinks she always knows better than me (and sometimes actually does) and this Connor Wheeler, will he ever realise that I'm living and breathing on the same planet as him situation — despite all that, I know, deep down, that what all this amounts to is somewhat less than what Dad refers to as "a hill of beans". He says this in an atrocious American accent that, for some reason, always has Mum in stitches. I'll give him my full on teenage sigh, and sometimes wonder why he still does it: to get Mum giggling or to get a rise out of me. He always ends up smiling though. And the thought of his smile calms me a little now.

Unlike many of the reality-TV-following, social-media-swamped, computer-game-obsessed people of my age, I know there's no easy way out of this. No earth-shattering event will happen to me, not in here in little Scuttleford. Unless I make it happen.

"How do you know it's the right time to do this?" asks Amy.

"I can't wait for the right time," I reply, "because that will never come. There'll always be something to put me off or hold me back. I have to do this now. For better or for worse."

"For richer or for poorer," Amy mutters under her breath. She gives me an innocent look. "Well, you never know, it might work out *really* well for you," she adds doubtfully. She grins mischievously as she hums a few bars of the Wedding March.

"Yeah, right," I sigh. So what if I'm about to walk into my brief moment of school-wide fame (or *infamy*, if it goes horribly wrong). Because one of the perks of being an adolescent is the freedom to believe you have control over your own life. Now's the time to do crazy things without thinking through the consequences.

However, I really think this low self-esteem thing has gone on long enough. Wallowing in panicked self pity only gets you so far in life and, as far as I can tell, gets you nowhere at all in love. So I need to settle this once and for all.

I've dreamt about this moment often enough; it's about time I actually *do* it. So what if his friends think I'm a geeky-weirdo? So what if Icky has her low opinion of me confirmed? I know I'll be the talk of the school for at least a week, but I don't care. I must do this: I must give Connor Wheeler the chance to express his undying devotion to me!

I've been pacing for ages, and while Amy's tried to talk me down, I've been psyching myself *up*. "You're bonkers, Dais. He'll ignore you. And Ellie will laugh. You'll never live it down. Never, ever, ever. This is the kind moment they'll record with a plaque next to the 'Playground Buddies' spot on the wall over there, where all of the super saddos hang out. I think you're gaga. Barmy." She grins, trying to make light of it, "do this and we can officially class you as lots and lots of fries short of a Happy Meal!"

Her words of 'encouragement' go right over my head. I'm crafting the perfect phrases: the matchless words that will make him wonder how he could have been so unaware of my existence for so long. Finally, I'm ready. Now I stand tall, stretch to my full 5 foot one and three-quarters, take a deep breath, push out my pathetic excuse for a bosom, hug my bestie … and set off towards Connor.

"Some day we'll look back at this moment and laugh and laugh and laugh," Amy calls out after me.

Yet, even as I paste on a fixed, eternally hopeful grin and deep-down believe there's a real chance it will all turn out okay, as I begin my walk across the suddenly acres-wide school playground, I have the unshakable feeling that something truly, mind-bogglingly awful is about to happen.

My progress seems so slow; it's like I'm wading through wet sand. I will my heart to maintain a steady beat. Out of the corner of my eye I see other students look my way as I head towards Connor and all the Satellites, lined up next to him like ill omens.

There's an electricity in the air; a tension that can only be ended by a ferocious lightning strike or a slender teenage girl being pummelled by public shaming. It seems inevitable now: the moment they'll talk about (and laugh about) for days, weeks, generations to come (the time span increases with every step, and depends upon when the next schmuck does something similarly and outrageously ridiculous as holding themselves up to highly public humiliation). For truly this could hardly be more public — as more and more kids simply stand and gawp. This is ignominy as a spectator sport; and in the sudden, hushed and chilled silence, it's clear that right now, I'm the only game in town.

I feel my face blossoming from delicate pink to the finest shade of pillar-box red as dozens of pairs of eyes bore into me, the crowd on the edge of their metaphorical seats, thrilled to be ringside at a genuinely historic event in the annals of Scuttleford Secondary School. They'll be able to tell their grandchildren they were there at the actual moment when Daisy Jacobs — *the* Daisy Jacobs — shamelessly, nay *wantonly* sought lasting and outright humiliation.

I'm like the guy in a white hat going through the swing doors of a saloon in a Sunday afternoon Western on TV. The world stills. The sudden reduction from playground cacophony to pin-drop quiescence alerts the Satellites and they, too, turn to observe me.

8

Chapter 3

THE INSIDE SCOOP

W ha—?
     I see no light and except for a strangely distant, dull throb in my head, I feel no pain. This isn't surprising as I'm sure banged my head when I crashed to the ground.

Apart from that throbbing, almost perceptible hum, I feel ... nothing. Nothing at all. Perhaps I'm out cold? Or in a coma? Or dead?! I'd usually expect a racing pulse and a rush of panicked fear at this clearly ridiculous thought, as that's something of a speciality of mine. But, weirdly, my heartbeat is a barely-sensed flutter. The uncomfortably distant pulse is enough to make me sure I'm alive, but I can't shake the unease. It's like I'm remembering how my heart beats in my chest in any anxiety-inducing situation, rather than actually feeling the rapid pulse for myself.

Other noises, at first far off and vaguely impressionistic, break through my senselessness. It's a white noise of voices that I hear as a low murmur, almost like an echo of what must be a tumult of cacophonous noise. Surely everyone must be really concerned about me? I did faint, didn't I? Did I lose consciousness altogether? And if so, how long have I been out?

The last thing I remember is the brilliant flash of light. Then ... nothing. I just sank into complete darkness. I went far away from the horror of my attempted speech. I don't actually know what happened, only that it must have been *waaaaay* worse than Amy's forecast. Maybe I'll be famous, after all — as the person who made the single most disastrous declaration of affection in the entire history of the universe!

I'd secretly hoped, as I walked towards Connor, Ellie and the Satellites, that, if it did all go wrong, the ground would open up beneath my feet and swallow me up and so spare me the resulting shame. I didn't know I'd literally get my wish! On the first bit, anyway. I think eternal shame is pretty much guaranteed.

Things slowly begin to drift back into focus. But not "focus" exactly, because I can't see anything. There's nothing at all, just total darkness —inside and out!

As I'd walked, an echo of the familiar panic had edged into my consciousness, but I'd remembered my breathing exercises and faced down that feeling as I steeled myself to actually talk to Connor. And to do it publicly.

I know reached the group. And I opened my mouth to speak. And —

I search for a foothold in the confusion. What *had* happened?

Was that brilliant, blinding flash a seizure, maybe? I try to focus, but the world's hazy. My blurred vision is like my distant heartbeat and fuzzy hearing: everything's muddy and indistinct. Like there's gauze between me and reality.

I feel rather more *without* it than *with* it, if you catch my drift. When I try to talk my voice remains mute. I focus hard, trying to make these shapes, these forms understand me. "What happened? Why are you —" But they don't respond, because although I'm trying to frame the words, I'm not actually speaking. *I* can hear my voice, but only inside my head.

Is this some clever trick played on me by Ellie and the Satellite Simpletons? But no, they're called the Simpletons for good reason: they could never come up with anything as elaborate as this. They'd put chewing gum on my chair or a spider in my lunch box, or, more likely, just post something mean online. They wouldn't give me poison or whatever to make me think I'd had a stroke.

Does this make any sense at all? It doesn't, does it? I mean, how could it? It's just that *nothing* feels right.

I hear a burst of tinny laughter. "Coo-eee, Daisy, are you still with us?"

Someone replies, but I'm fading in and out and don't catch all of it, "—goodness' sake, Ellie, shut up for once in your—" The voice sounds like Connor's, but —

"Give her some space, let her breathe." This is a deeper, more insistent voice — a teacher's, I think. There's a blur of voices to go with the overall blur that's inside my head. I sense activity around me …

"Sir, she fainted, sir! Just like totally blanked on us!" Is that Ellie's over-excited chattering? "She swooned at Connor's feet. I think it's love, sir." Yep — most likely Ellie!

"Daisy?" The teacher's voice again. I think it might be Mr Ford, a loud but not awfully effective Maths teacher. Enormously tall and broad, he compensates for a surprising lack of authority by wearing over-formal three-piece, pin-stripe suits that look like they've been exquisitely tailored … for someone else. His habit is to stand as ramrod straight as a parade-ground sergeant-major and shout a lot. He's shouting again now: "Daisy, can you hear me?!" he screams into my ear. Just as well I *can't* hear very well, his yelling would most likely deafen me!

Disconcertingly, I sense panic in his voice. Teachers shouldn't panic, should they? They should be calm and collected. He doesn't sound level-headed, though. He sounds as though he's about to crack under the pressure of handling not just the usual crowd of not very sensible young people, but also an *in*-sensible girl.

I'm sure my heart must be pounding! This chaos should terrify me, but I feel … numb, just sort of distant. And there's that buzz in my head. I'm a long way away from anything tangible; I'm like a ship, drifting rudderless, desperately in search of shore. And literally any port to get me the hell away from the storm that's happening in my head right now would be fantastic!

But I don't know if my heart *is* pounding, because now I can't even feel the distant, pulsing beat I could a moment ago. So I can't see or hear anything, except dim shadows and a blur of noise, and my heart seems to have stopped. My limited senses are even preventing me from seeing the light coming to meet me at the end of a tunnel that you're supposed to see when you're dying!

Through the murky haze of my senses, I hear someone call my name. And suddenly, a weird vibration runs through me. Look, this'll sound weirder still, but it feels as though I'm moving; moving through thick, blanketing fog. I'm not being carried, I'm not on a stretcher or in an ambulance, but I'm sure I'm moving — and quickly, side to side, up and down.

"Come on, girl, what's wrong with you? Just snap out of it, why don't you!" I'm spinning again, my head whiplashing to and fro and my dizziness increasing alarmingly. I'm rocking to and fro and — oh, I think I'm going to —

"Sir!" Maybe Connor again? "Sir, I don't think it's a good idea to shake her." His voice is low and careful, the point made quietly and precisely.

"I bet she throws up all over you, sir," adds a voice that pierces the darkness with such swagger that I think it must be Ellie. And her remark, made as a joke, is probably even more helpful, as the shaking stops instantly.

"Well, I don't know wh—" A sudden stir interrupts Mr Ford's floundering.

"What is going on here? Stand back everyone, please." That's more like it! Cast iron hauteur and the first voice I'm almost sure of. It's genuine authority at last, in the form of our head teacher, Mrs Griffin. Her confident, clipped tone and slightly mannered way of expressing herself silences the baying mob and I sense the immediate restoration of order. Identifying her calms me a little. It's partly her sheer competence, but also the fact that a) recognising her makes it less likely I'm dead; and b) if I am, I'm in heaven, not hell, because Mrs G is very much on the side of the angels.

She assesses the situation quickly. "Okay, let's give the poor girl some air, shall we?" Phrased as a question, it's clearly a command. "All of you, back to your classrooms, now."

"But Mrs Griffin, we've still got five min—" whines another voice (Claire I think).

"Now." The single word is enough to silence the muttering. "Mr Ford, make yourself useful and see to it, will you?"

The weirdest thing, as someone takes charge on the *outside*, is that I've no idea what's happening on the *inside*. This is difficult to explain, because although I think I'm still here and doubt if I'm actually dead — but I just don't feel in control at all.

"Yes, Mrs Griffin." Mr Ford sounds relieved to have something to do that does not involve trying to bring a stricken teenager back to her senses. Crowd control is more in his line. "Come on now, don't hang about, let's go, come on, off with you all!" He's immediately shouting at the gawping mob, his over-fussy nature reasserting itself.

It's good someone is in charge. And actually, I'm feeling better, too. The light is brighter. The haziness is fading. In fact, *everything* is fading.

There's no pain. Everything's going away. All fading …

I see a lo-o-o-ong tunnel; and teeny, teeny lights. Reeeeeaaalllly briiiiiiiight liiiiiiights. Everythin' 's distant.

far away away

i'm goin' faaaaaarrrrr away—

Chapter 4

BUY A SPORTS CAR!

The Daisy Jacobs' form sighs. Breathes deeply. If it could truly sense, if it could feel, could experience sensation, it would yell and scream and jump and laugh and sing and—
But *it* is confused: what is "yell" and "scream" and "jump"? *It* doesn't understand.

It has been so long since the last *becoming* but now it has found a form! The very first of this place's forms. The first of many, many, many. And maybe, it thinks, when this body is used and it moves to the next and the next and the next — maybe that's "laugh" and "sing" … ?

Suddenly its attention is intently focussed. The form that was Daisy Jacobs looks up at the baleful, low-hanging sky and inhales deeply. Because now it is happening: Daisy Jacobs is *becoming*.

It can feel the being's life ebbing away. And this is … good? *It* thinks so and is surprised, not by the thought of how good it is to become — to take the life of this form — but by the very idea of "think". "Think" is new; and in a life spanning the entire history of the universe, "new" itself is, well, novel. "Think" is clearly a complicated process. And *it* is not sure it needs to spend time on "think" — or with "laugh".

Because its existence is grey. Simple and grey. It's been grey since the beginning. *It* is the oldest and the smallest thing in the universe. In one sense, it *is* the universe. Because *it* is nothing but matter, condensed to a tiny single point of infinite density.

It is, in fact, Quark.

And all Quark does, all Quark ever does is drift. Oh, and Quark absorbs life wherever it goes. Absorbs as in pulverises to that same

16

point of infinite density. It has to be said that this is rarely good for the life that is discovered.

But Quark doesn't mind that. Because it *has* no mind. Quark is innocent. Resolute, but blameless. Homicidal but free of guilt … if not intent.

Everywhere Quark finds life, *it* pulls the life in and crushes it out of existence.

Quark means absolutely no harm to anyone or anything; so if everyone and everything happens to be squidged out of existence as it passes by, that is unfortunate — for everyone and everything, that is. But not for Quark.

And anyway, it's unlikely that anyone *will* get crushed into oblivion. Because space is big. The universe is larger than we can even begin to understand. The universe is so big that when you look up into the sky at night, you can see stars that are larger than our sun and yet look like tiny pinpricks of light. Even whole galaxies look like a few little dots of white in the inky blackness.

So in all that immensity, the chances of being squished are infinitesimal.

However, space is dangerous. If we went there, we'd be dead — bang, dead. Gone. That's why when we do go into space, we go in spacesuits or spaceships. And that's why we're sensible enough to protect ourselves from the dangers of deep space by living on a planet that has an almost perfect protective shield called the atmosphere.

Unfortunately, the atmosphere offers about as much protection against Quark as arming yourself with a banana would do you if you came across a Bengal Tiger as you walked through the park, and every bit as much use as a rubber ring would be if you chanced upon a Great White Shark in your local swimming pool.

In neither of those highly scientific and carefully calculated scenarios would you be likely to survive long enough to blow out the candles on your next birthday cake.

So I'm sure we can agree: the day Quark came to earth and found Daisy Jacobs was not the one when you'd take out a pension that will mature when you are 60, or to sign a lease agreement on a £250,000 sports car — no, scratch that: it's *exactly* the day to take out that lease, because you can drive the supercar off the garage forecourt and know the chances of you ever having to cough up that £250,000 are about the same as discovering a life-munching space entity has just arrived on earth to snuff the life out of every life-form on the planet …

Chapter 5

FIRST PERSON BINARY

You know how it is when you're in school and Miss What's-her-name, your English teacher, gives you the exercise where you have to write a sentence or a paragraph in first person and then one in third person? Well, this is like that; I feel like me — Daisy Jacobs' me, first person me — but I almost feel as though there's another — a third person me — there too. Actually, *here* too. Obviously, I don't mean literally here; I mean … well … it's like I'm me, but I'm not really me and— Come on, this is just too weird to say out loud, or think out loud, which is all I can do at the moment.

But this *is* me. Yet it's *not* me. I mean, I'm me, but I'm — aargh, how to explain?!

Look, at least I do I know who I am: I'm Daisy Jacobs. And I know that I'm almost fifteen. I know my parents have ordinary jobs — Mum's a doctor, Dad does something or other in I.T. that's considered important at a big company in the City. I have one little brother, Luke, who's ten. And I *am* a teenager, so naturally I think there should be more to life than home and Scuttleford Secondary and my normal, everyday existence, but when I hoped for something exciting to happen, I was rather hoping that something would be Connor Wheeler-shaped, rather than going totally out-of-my-mind-shaped!

Because … okay, how can I say this? How can I tell you what's going on? How can I make you believe? Because you *must* believe me. I'm sure it's no exaggeration to say that everything depends on that. I need to tell you exactly how this messed up situation came about. Because, deep down I suspect it could be both dangerous and disastrous for —

No, let's stick to what I know, or *think* I know. The basics.

So. Do I look different? There must be something *really* strange about me; genuinely, freakishly weird — yeah? I mean, you may not know me well, but you'd notice say ... a third eye in the middle of my forehead? Or a whole second head maybe? I mean, there *must* be something because that's the scale of weirdness I'm operating on here!

"Being a teenager is the worst time of your life." That's what Miss Partridge said in English one day. I didn't believe it for a minute; but then I'm (usually) an optimistic person. Life is what you make of it, that's what I've always thought. But if someone/something makes something else entirely out of *your* life ...

Look, I'm teenager, okay? I'm used to nature throwing the works at me. Physically and emotionally, everything's changing. What with the spots and the inexplicable mood swings and the boobs and the bleeding and the rampaging hormones, you'd have thought us adolescents already had all the bases covered as far as feeling freakishly bizarre and weird. But the fact is all of that stuff *is* normal. *This* is outlandishly *ab*-normal.

You know I asked if I looked different? The reason I asked is that I don't know and I have no way of finding out. It's true! If you want to check your hair or the progress of your latest zit, you can just use your legs to walk to the bathroom mirror and use your eyes to see how fine you're looking (the zit's okay, by the way, hardly noticeable at all — last time I could see, that is). If, for example, Connor Wheeler wanted to reassure himself of his overall gorgeous, hunky-handsomeness, he could check out his reflection.

I don't have that luxury. Because my body's no longer my own. I'm in some weird state of unconsciousness. And I have a horrible feeling this is just the beginning. I know I sound like some mad person standing on a street corner with a placard emblazoned with

"The End is Nigh!!!" (Why do they always add extra, unnecessary exclamation marks? As if "!" is bad, but somehow "!!!" is *very, very* bad and we're all likely to leap into action as a result?) But I am scared. SO scared. Because I really do think the end is coming. Actually, that's not true, I think it's already here. (Oh, my god, I AM that mad person!!!) And no one will believe me; I know you don't. You think I'm bad, bonkers, barmy, off-my-trolley, a few coupons short of a toaster. I appreciate that. And I don't (really) blame you. Much. But you *have* to believe me. Have to. Because the end of *me* is here. The end is happening to me right now, as I speak.

I know this mind/body split thing is ridiculous. The idea's too silly to even consider. I'm sure it's just that my head's spinning and my brain's fuzzy, but what if —

"It is okay, people. I am fine. I am good. All is peachy-cool-awesome."

The voice breaks through my reverie. Lightly modulated, maybe slightly breathy. But confident. A voice I recognise. A voice I'm used to hearing … just not in this way.

"Stand back and give this girl-person … space." The voice cackles as if at some private joke.

This is not a voice in my head, but an actual spoken-aloud voice. And since the bright, flashing light and the swooning and the dizziness and the out-of-body (in-body?) experience, this is the first voice I have recognised with absolute one hundred percent certainty. Because it's a voice I have heard all my life, ever since I *had* a voice. But as I'm still out cold(ish) and because I'm barely capable of rational thought, I can't believe I'm hearing the words. I'm not the one *speaking* the words. And that's *really* strange.

Because it's my voice.

Chapter 6

QUARK IS NOT HAPPY

Quark knows something's not right. Something is ... off. It's like being in another being's home, or trying on someone else's clothes, or putting someone else's false teeth in your mouth — ugh! That's horrible! Having someone else's teeth in your mouth! It's besgustin'! But why should that be? Why is it okay to have *your* teeth in your mouth, but not okay to have someone *else's*?

Quark doesn't understand. And what is "besgustin'"? It is Daisy, but Daisy-ago. Daisy of the past.

And, Quark wonders, why is Quark even thinking? What *is* thinking? Quark simply *becomes*. Fast, fast, fast. None of this hanging about lark; none of this feeling! Quark just *becomes* the thing that was. Then uses it and *becomes* the next. And the next. Always *become*. And always the next. Always and forever. Forever past; forever future. Ever, ever, ever.

Quark wants to become! Now, now, now! Quark has waited. At the moment, Quark doesn't understand time, but knows there's been a lot of it. Quark has waited sooooo long! And now it's time to *become*. There are many, many, many forms here. All will become. First one Daisy Jacobs and then the next and on and on and on-on-on-on-on-on —

Become, not *think*. Quark doesn't need to understand.

Quark's in charge. Quark can speak with her voice. Quark can think Daisy thoughts. So Daisy should go. Go, Daisy Jacobs! Go, go, go! Leave Quark alone in this form! This is *Quark's* now. If Daisy Jacobs wants a body, Daisy Jacobs should find one of her own!

Daisy Jacobs' body breathes slowly in and out. Quark must be in control now. But this being is difficult to grasp. To get a hold of. The form has not quite *become*. Quark got her; claimed her; subordinated the form. But is *it* in control? Quark has the upper hand, but is Quark in the driving seat?

Quark senses — as much as *it* can sense — an image, a blurred something that isn't *it* and that is just out of *its* reach. Quark can't understand. No form has ever resisted the becoming. That in itself is difficult to grasp, because we're not talking of a week or a month or a lifetime, we're literally talking about *ever*. But Quark knows this Daisy Jacobs *is* resisting.

By now, this being should not be thinking. This Daisy Jacobs should not be. She shouldn't be even a 'she'. What is a she anyway? Is a she the same as a human? A Daisy? Is a Daisy the standard form in this place? Quark can sense ... frustration at being thwarted. Quark knows that all the beings in this place are waiting for *it*. All the humans, the Daisy Jacobs, the shes. All waiting to *become*. Millions and billions of Daisys and shes.

Daisy Jacobs' body takes another deep breath and stands as tall as a nearly fifteen-year-old she-Daisy Jacobs-human-form can stand. Quark is clear and certain: she will not be a she for long. Not a human. Not a Daisy Jacobs. She will be *it*. She will be Quark. Totally, one-hundred percent absorbed. She *will* become.

"Stand back humans. All is fine. This Daisy Jacobs is A-OK."

This form is Quark's. Daisy Jacobs has no choice. And absolutely no chance.

Chapter 7

NOTHING EVER USED TO HAPPEN HERE

"You young uns don't know you're born." How many times have we heard that or something like it? Seems like every adult who ever lived has said it. Honestly, they've got no idea what it's like, this growing up lark. They totally underestimate how hard it is to endure the physical and emotional changes we go through — discovering love and heartbreak at the same instant. Withstanding peer pressure as we cope with low self-esteem. Living life in full colour, rather than standard adult black and white. And doing all this while surviving Petrarchan sonnets and double chemistry!

But no teenager who ever lived has gone through what's happening to me now!

A thin, panicked scream escapes me, but it's as though my scream is high pitched, like a dog-whistle that's inaudible to the human ear, because I hear nothing. I try again, louder this time, a full-out blast of shocked, wailing anguish … nothing. No sound at all. Just a deep, ringing silence like an echo from within a tomb.

Yet my *voice* is talking. My *body* is moving. And neither has anything at all to do with me. I thought I was blind and deaf and dumb. Turns out I'm possessed or have been body-snatched!

And I have such a pounding head; a headache that didn't build up slowly like the one that often dulls my senses for a day or so a month. This just appeared — wham! — sending shafts of pain searing into the parts of my brain I can still feel.

Trust me: I'm still in here. Except I don't know where "here" is. And, to whoever is in charge of the rest of my mind and body, I'm not going anywhere; you will not get away with this. I want my body back — now!

Do you hear me? Get out!

No answer … ?

Of course there's no answer, I can almost hear you say! She's tricking us, she's having us on. Well, I don't go in for practical jokes. But if someone's playing a joke on me, please stop. It's gone too far already. And, well — I'm scared. Terrified, actually. Heading for full-on panic. So, please: just stop.

The muffled silence engulfing me is positively screaming, if that makes any sense. But when I try to speak — to break that silence — I can't hear my voice. In fact, I can't even make the mental connections that would begin to form words. It's like the links have shorted out or been cut altogether. We take speaking for granted, don't we? I mean we just open our mouths and speak. Or scream for help.

But now I hear a voice that I know is mine, I feel worse. Even more scared than before. The silence weighed heavily on me, but the voice that's mine and yet so *not* mine is more disturbing than the deafening silence that came before.

"Yes, head teacher person, I am perfectly fine. Thank you for asking."

See? For whoever has kidnapped my body and all of my voice box, speaking isn't a problem. Although speaking like a regular person, rather than an automaton or the speaking clock *is* an issue! Even my actual voice sounds weird from in here. My vocal chords are being used. But the tone is wrong. It's flatter, more monotone; less mellifluous, if I may say. There's no warmth or passion to it. It's dull. Unnatural. Robotic, almost. In fact, it's like the voice of someone who's learning to speak — or at least learning to speak a foreign language. Enunciating words precisely and carefully.

"Are you sure, Daisy?" I hear Mrs Griffin ask. "You don't sound quite … yourself."

No kidding! Please push this, Mrs G. Please ask what on earth this body-snatcher or Russian mind-hacker is doing messing about in the brain of a fourteen-year-old girl, in — of all places — Scuttleford.

"I think it would be a good idea to see Mrs Thomas."

"I am honestly fine. Zero is the problem here. My body is functioning well within acceptable parameters."

"Nevertheless …" My brain-napper does not know Mrs Griffin. If he/she/it thinks it can talk its way out of this situation, it's very much mistaken. It does not know how our head teacher works. Mrs G rarely gives direct orders; she doesn't need to. She has this aura of authority. It's like a super-power. She never shouts or even raises her voice, but she has an amazing gift for making suggestions which, in the nicest possible way mean "do what I say. NOW".

So, "a good idea" means I *will* go to see Mrs Thomas, our school librarian and chief first aider. And my brain-invader has no say in the matter!

"I will do so." Apparently, "I" have surrendered to the inevitable. My body begins to move.

Inside my head, I'm frowning. My body feels as though it's being operated by remote control — from a drone base in Nevada, Leningrad or Pyongyang, maybe. Wherever I'm going, *my* feet are taking me there; *I* am not, my feet *are*. My body is moving and *I* have nothing to do with it! I'm not responsible. I am not telling my legs to put one foot in front of another. And if I'm not giving the orders, who is?

It's a surreal experience and I feel a mix of vertigo and sea-sickness. As though my body's moving through the guidance of a hacked and partially downloaded online map. The movement is not natural or smooth. The body-snatcher knows how to move limbs about as well as it knows how to form sentences, but through the hazy, fog-like view I have, I can see I'm heading to the first aid station next to the library.

So there's some sort of muscle memory going on here: my body's moving like a discombobulated puppet, but it *is* moving. And there's also something going on in my brain: something or someone is using my brain well enough to form stilted sentences. And they know where the library is. Personally, I'm not capable of standing up at all, let alone walking about like a cyborg made by a committee that couldn't agree on the ground rules.

Hang on: I've stopped again.

"Now Daisy, you've been in the wars, I hear." I bet most pupils of Scuttleford Secondary are calmed in times of need by the Welsh lilt of Mrs Thomas. She would instantly reassure me, if only I could talk to her, be *myself* with her. Unfortunately, someone *else* is myself at the moment!

"As I tried to explain to our esteemed leader, there is no cause for concern. The unit … the form … the —" My controller falters for a moment, as if trying to correct a software issue that's hampering the execution of a command sub-routine. I can imagine a scrolling message on the inside of my eyelids: "Systems error, please contact your Network Administrator."

Even through the fog of my vision, I can see this warrants the full Mrs Thomas head tilt and sympathetic, "Mmmmm", that's only going to lead to a phone call home.

Yes, that's it! Mum'll sort this out! She can manage crises that even Mrs G can't cope with. Having a GP for a mum can be a total pain in the bum — particularly the awkward sex talk she insisted on — but she never, ever seems to stress about anything. She'll see through this Russian robot's mind-control tactics in a flash.

"This Daisy Jacobs is all well and good. Hale and hearty."

"Mmmmmm," another head tilt, "well, we'll just make a quick call home, shall we?"

"Alive and kicking?"

"Yeeeeesss … " says Mrs Thomas, and reaches for the phone.

"In the pink?"

"Oh, hello, is that Mrs Jacobs? This is Mrs Thomas here, first aider at Scuttleford Secondary. Now, there's no cause for concern, but Daisy's had a little bump on the head."

"Tickety boo?"

"What's that? No, she is talking. She's definitely talking! She's just, well — not quite herself."

"Bright-eyed and bushy-tailed?"

"That's right, dear. Yes, Mrs Jacobs, that will be fine. We'll see you in about a quarter of an hour, then."

Mrs Thomas hangs up the phone and even through my fogged-up vision I can see her smile. "Mum's on the way and she will take you home."

"My female parent is a medical practitioner."

"That's right, dear."

"You are just a first aider."

Mrs Thomas' smile falters. "Well, I do my best, nonetheless."

She does so and I bet that fifteen minutes seems like an eternity to her as fake-Daisy babbles in a most un-teenagerly fashion.

Finally, there's a knock and then the door opens. "Daisy, sweetheart, what's happened to you?"

If I could sigh, I would. If I could yell with sheer, unadulterated joy, I would. Mum's here! All is well. Everything is going be absolutely fine.

"Oh, mother," I hear my voice say, "I think I fainted and now I feel dizzy and I have *such* a headache."

Okay, so maybe not *absolutely* fine ...

"Poor you!" And I know by the fact that my vision is now restricted to blurry red linen, that Mum has enveloped me in an embrace. But I can't feel her comforting warmth, or breathe in the delicious rose-scent of her perfume. Instead, my imposter gets the full benefit of Total Mum.

"Can you please take me home, mother."

"Of course, my love." She must be concerned about me, because even "mother" doesn't give her pause. Since when did I say "mother"? She's *Mum*. Always and forever!

Mum thanks Mrs Thomas and has a quick word with Mrs Griffin before leading me out of the school to the car.

"It's okay, Daisy, I'll take you home and we'll make you better."

"Thank you, mother." I feel my face form into a grimace of a smile and see Mum's hand reach over and squeeze my leg.

Remember me saying that Mum will sort it out? Well, if I could shout at her now, I would. If I could yell with sheer, unadulterated misery, I would. Mum's here, but it seems all will *not* be well. My life's gonna carry on being exactly as terrible as it has suddenly become.

I howl in silent anguish and frustration. A full-on, really-go-for-it, lung-bursting scream …

But, of course, Mum can't hear. No one can hear. "I'm in here! Mum, help me!" I try to bellow; I try to let her know that the person, the *thing* sitting beside her in the car, luxuriating in the loving concern that only Mum can give, is *not* me. I'm shut inside, trying to get out while cyborg-Daisy gets all the attention.

I try to scream again, but I can't make any connection — to her or to the real me.

Then the anger, the anxiety, the fear — all of it dissipates into a fog of nothingness. My senses dim still further. My panic subsides and I feel myself sink into a big, comforting blanket of darkness that clouds my vision and sends me into the deepest oblivion.

Chapter 8

THE TRANSCENDENCE OF QUARK

In all the history of Quark, which — give or take five minutes — is all the history of the entire universe, Quark hasn't gone in for self-assessment. Quark has never needed to.

Because Quark is what you might call a fundamental force — yes? Eh? Means nothing to you? Okay, a singularity. Still no? Okay. How about a black hole? A formless black hole, adrift in space. Yes? Got that? I know, I know: black holes are super complex and space-science-y, but all we really need to understand about them is that they may, just possibly, swallow matter. Where that matter goes once swallowed doesn't, well — matter.

What *does* matter is that Quark is a kind of black hole. A black hole currently in possession of two legs, two arms etc. In fact, all the bits and bobs that make up a fourteen-year-old girl. Or rather, *almost* all. Because there's one teeny bit that's not — yet — Quark.

With the first stirrings of consciousness comes the realisation that Quark is not *all* of Daisy. This concept is hard for Quark to grasp. Even harder than that science-y bit was for us two paragraphs ago. Because, from Quark's perspective, Quark is everything and everything is Quark.

I know! Talk about self-centered and egotistical!

(In the brief flashes of consciousness, before each *becoming* is complete, Quark is so utterly self-absorbed that Quark usually thinks of Quark in the third person. As His Quark-ness, if you like. This is what despots, former reality TV stars-turned Presidents and planet-munching space-entities do. And I'm sure you're thinking the same as me: it gets tiring after a while. So, as long as you faithfully promise not to tell Quark, we'll put a stop to that.

Let's agree who'll be the star of this book {even though, in a sense, we can class one character as an *actual* star}. Who are you going to root for: a human girl, or a blob of nebulous matter drifting through space, occasionally guzzling planets? And we can all agree that Daisy is {at the moment, at least} a girl. A she. So, for ease of reference, from now on Quark will be "he". Okay? Remember — not a word!)

Quark struggles to raise the chin of the Daisy Jacobs' human. To hold the Daisy's head high. To straighten the Daisy's back. To thrust out her puny chest. Quark is important!

Quark's role is nothing less than determining the entire fate of the universe!

Even for mind-bogglingly teeny blobs of near nothingness, I'm sure you agree: this is a *big* job.

And as Quark revels in growing self-awareness, he remembers that the way he goes about determining the fate of the universe is to take it apart, one molecule at a time. First, he finds the relevant single molecule or group of molecules in each place. Then he *becomes* that bit. And, in a very real sense, that bit becomes him. Then he pulverises it into microscopic parts of near nothingness. And then he moves on and does it again. And again.

So: after the first there's the second. It's the natural way of things. Two become four. A gentle rolling out; a cascade. Four become eight. It's beautiful, calculated, pure. Maybe the single most beautiful thing in the whole universe. Eight become sixteen. Mathematical in its perfection. Sixteen become thirty-two. A transcendence of becomings. Onwards and onwards and onwards.

It starts with the first and rolls on. Always without a hitch. For billions of years, without fail.

In some places the first is over in a blinding flash. In others it's a long-lasting bliss of consuming togetherness. It can a fungus-like creep from one form to another or an instantaneous tsunami of consumption, ravaging a planet in the blink of an eye. Those *becomings* do not satisfy him as much.

31

The blue-green planet had looked promising. He thought the billions of human-she-Daisy Jacobs would last long, long, long.

But, as always, the process starts with seeding the first *becoming*. And never had the first taken so long to *become*. Quark was somewhat miffed about how stubbornly this bag of molecules was resisting the simple process of being pulverised into space dust.

All he wanted to do was do what he came into existence for. And all the insignificant little Daisy Jacobs need do was GET OUT OF HIS WAY!

But Quark is becoming stronger, even as she weakens. He's now free to roam through her mind. To take control and begin the wondrous, transcendent process of *becoming*, as what used to be Daisy Jacobs continues to fade away …

Chapter 9

THE END IS NIGH

I don't know how I come to be in bed. I remember being in the car with Mum and then … nothing. Now I'm in my bedroom. It's dark and apparently my body is asleep. I, however, am suddenly awake and what passes for conscious.

When I saw those bright lights, I thought the clichéd obvious: that the end was nigh and I was dying. But here I am. With no clue what's happening outside my body. Obviously, my eyes are closed so I can't see anything — not even the inside of my eyelids. I can't hear anything either, although as my body's asleep, it's a relief to discover I don't snore …

Although I know my body's in my bed, in my bedroom, in my house, I'm — well, how can I describe where I am? There's solid darkness everywhere. It's like being in a deep cave. Logically there's only one place I can be: in my own head. In my brain.

This place is both real and unreal! I mean, it exists — it's in my head, obviously, but it's *only* inside my head. And this is where you'll get your cast-iron, "call the guys with the straitjacket" proof of my madness: I can see walls and a door. I know it sounds crazy, but I'm locked in a room *inside* my own brain! And I say locked deliberately, because I put the lock there myself, soon after I came to. I'm pretty sure my kidnapper knows I'm here and means me no good. So, as soon as I realised where I was, I adapted the words of Beyoncé and put a *lock* on it!

Sounds simple, doesn't it? Go to the shop, buy a lock, put it on your door. Easy peasy. However, this is an imaginary room with an entirely made-up door, so I had to focus really hard, but — if I say so myself — I've created a nifty lock with loads of levers, bolts and latches. And then I made (well, imagined) a huge, old-fashioned key which I've put in the equally imaginary pocket of my school blazer, which I still appear to be wearing. I chose a key rather than a combination lock, because I figured if whoever invaded me has enough access to my brain to walk and talk, they might have my memories too. Any random number I choose would be easy to figure out. But a great big key in my pocket — they won't get that!

So I think I am safe ... for the moment. And —

Hang on, I'm moving. Am I getting up? No, I think I just rolled over onto my side. And I can see little flickers of light — I think from the landing light that's still left turned on for Luke. So I'm lying on my left side, facing the door of my bedroom. The flickering though, what's that about? You know ... I wonder if this is REM sleep; is that what it's called when you dream? Am I dreaming? I wish this whole situation *was* just a dream! And if my body-snatcher *is* dreaming, I hope it's a nightmare! A really terrible nightmare about a teenage girl who gets into their mind and sings mindless pop songs for hours and hours, without knowing all the words ("I liked it, so I put a lock on it, I liked it, so I put a lock on it ... oh, oh, oh!!!") — or being able to carry a tune. Or maybe a dream about some mindless Russian robot that steals their life, steals hugs from their mum and gives them a bad (well, even worse) reputation with their schoolmates.

Anyway, I'm in this imaginary room with a lock made of — what? Willpower, maybe? The room is bare, with grey walls, a black tile floor, no windows — and a sturdy door. It's both a functional space and a manifestation of my stubborn determination not to surrender!

So, it's me against ... whatever or whoever is in control of my body. And even though I've only got this tiny bit of me left, I will not give in —

Wait! Now there *is* movement. My body is sitting up; hauling itself to *my* feet. Yes, I'm moving! This is so weird! My body moving, one foot in front of the other but *I'm* not doing anything. And although I don't have control of my senses, I know the movement is awkward. I'm kind of rocking forward and backwards, like some kind of weird Frankenstein made from parts of other people's bodies.

Awkward or not, I've made it to my bathroom.

My eyes dilate under the harsh glare of the overhead light. And, just like that, there I am in the mirror. Me, yet clearly not me. My vision's blurred, but I'm looking in the mirror, through my own eyes at a face that's mine, but not mine. The most disturbing thing is that I look ... well, like *me*. I see no visible effects of this ... whatever it is. I look normal. It's still upsetting that my family and friends don't realise there's anything seriously wrong, but maybe more understandable now I know I don't have a second head on my shoulders or have broken out in boils or something.

But it's so weird to see my face and not know what's going on behind my own eyes! If I was in control of my tear ducts, I'd cry — with sheer frustration as much as anguish at my hopeless situation. If I was in charge of my voice, I'd scream. But I'm alone. And who can help me when I'm stuck in here?

"I think *we* are alone would be more accurate. More in keeping with the facts."

Now, you might think walking around with no thought or control, or looking at my own face in the mirror without having the first notion of who or what is behind the blankness of my own eyes, is the strangest, scariest thing you can imagine. But hearing that disembodied voice — *my* voice — speak to me as though I'm a stranger, while reading the thoughts of my own mind, is almost enough to send me over the edge into the unfathomable depths of actual madness!

Any certainty, any unquestioning, unshakable, unassailable belief that non-panicky me might have had — feeling as though I actually was ever in control, and that everything might be solid, concrete, assured ... that tentative, fragile security vanishes in an instant. This moment pulls the rug from under me and brings the foundations of my entire life tumbling down. Now, suddenly, mere existence is relative, intangible, uncertain.

"Can you hear me?" the voice continues. The shock is real. The voice — I repeat: *my* voice — is definitely speaking to me. It's my voice, and although *I'm* not speaking, my voice is talking to me! In a very real sense, I'm talking to myself!

"Wh— Who— Eh?" I try to think, try to bring what's happening into focus, but I can't make any sense of it. And the voice inside my head makes as much sense as it did when I tried to speak to Connor before I fainted.

In the mirror, my eyebrows lift and my head tilts to the left. "Hello? Is anybody there? Daaaiisy?"

Well, now there really can't be any doubt! *I'm* the object of the questioning.

"Coooo-eeee."

Equally, there's not a shred of a doubt that it's my face that's being pulled about into various grimaces. And my voice making the stupid noises.

"Now that is just rude."

"What?"

"Calling me stupid. That is not a nice way to talk."

"Am I — are you — talking to me?"

My face looks around the small bathroom, shrugging my shoulders and pulling my face in a kind of "duh" expression. "Yes, you are and yes, I am!"

"Pardon?"

"There is no one else here, is there?" My hands indicate the empty space in which my body stands. "I am Quark. And I am now Daisy Jacobs. Please be so kind as to vacate your body."

"What?!" I seriously hope this is an hallucination. Because, if I wasn't already totally mad, I'd be truly certifiable now!

"Leave. Go. Depart. Shoo!" My own hand waves in my face in a 'be off with you' kind of motion.

"I don't understand. What is Quark? And why is Quark in my body?"

"Quark is me and you are Quark! You were chosen. You need to go so you can *become*."

"I need to go so I can come?"

"*Be*-come."

"Yeah? And exactly what am I going to be-come?"

"You will *become* one with the universe."

"Er — thanks, but no thanks. I'm already a fully paid-up member of the human race and I think that counts as being 'one' with the universe."

I can hear its voice. I can't see whoever or whatever's running the show, because it's inside me and right now it looks like me. But my lips move when this Quark speaks, and the words are audible. However, my own voice is internal. I'm not speaking aloud. All in all, it's like two different parts of my brain are speaking to each other!

I scrutinise the familiar face. The face I obviously know better than any other. I search for recognition. For *me*. My own eyes stare back. Familiar and unfamiliar at the same time. My grey-green eyes are colder than usual, cool Atlantic, rather than coastal Pacific, as they glower fixedly, as if peering deep into my very soul. I rein in an increasing sense of panic and try for nonchalance. "What sort of name is Quark, anyway?"

"I am an elementary particle."

"You don't say."

There's confusion in my reflected face. "I do say. You asked, and I answered."

"I mean — I don't know what that is."

"You don't? But it is straightforward! I am a fundamental constituent of matter."

"Mmmmm … "

"Daisy Jacobs, I know this happened quickly. For a simple form like yourself, it must have come as a bit of a surprise when I appeared like that, with no warning. Things are very different where I come from."

"Where do you come from?"

"A long way away."

I smile (inwardly, obviously). "Kettering?"

"Further."

I thought of the drone controller I'd imagined. "Russia? North Korea?"

"No — further."

"Australia? No. They're our friends down there. They wouldn't pull a trick like this."

"No, you are right, I am not from Australia," Quark says.

"Well, there is no further than Australia."

"Are you sure … ?"

"Yes. Unless … "

"Yes … ?"

"Are you saying you are from — ?"

"Yes … ?" He's leading me towards the unthinkable.

"From — like from a different planet or something?" I don't *want* to believe it!

"Or something, yes — exactly."

"So *not* a different planet? You're not an alien?"

"I am a singularity. Or rather *the* singularity."

I guffaw. "A black hole? I have a black hole inside of me? Come on! I may be a bit lacking, but even my worst enemy wouldn't say I had a black hole for a personality!"

"Well, you do!" In the mirror, my lips form what, in dim lighting, could pass for a smile. Or a smirk, maybe. Or an evil grin…

"A black hole with a personality disorder, more like." I try to think-whisper, but I'm new to this whole thinking aloud way of communicating and Quark hears me.

"Well — it is your personality," he says, crabbily.

Hang on! I'm being insulted by an alien-singularity-particle! A *thing* with my face that speaks with my voice! In my own bathroom! In my own head! I heave another inward sigh and let that pass for the moment. I'll return to trying to get my personality back once I sort out who or what I'm dealing with. "And what's this *'becoming'* you talk of?"

In the mirror, my lips curve into another smile and my head nods sagely as if I've asked exactly the right question. "Daisy, you are the universe. Your blood, your bones, your DNA. You are made of the universe. You are made of star stuff!" Quark clearly thinks I should be super impressed by this.

"Okaaaaay ... " Under different, less kidnappy circumstances, I might have been.

"So when you *become*, you are you are set free! You become one with the universe. It is like going home!"

"Does it hurt?"

"No, Daisy, not at all. It really is painless; it is like closing your eyes and going to sleep."

He speaks of *becoming* with real reverence, but I need him to make clear what I begin to suspect he means. "Okay. It's like sleep. And then I wake up, or ... ?"

"Well, sort of ... not," he hedges.

"How can I sort of not wake up?" I'm now officially narked at this Quark creature-entity-thing. "Isn't there a term for 'sort of' not waking up?"

"Well — " In the mirror my face looks almost abashed.

"Isn't sort of not waking up in fact better known as being dead?"

This is like the most ridiculous internet hoax or the most far-fetched alien-abduction, cosmic conspiracy theory. Except it truly *is* cosmic: Quark is an alien creature thing. He's in my head. And he wants to kill me!

So, if I'm not very, very careful, this Quark will be into my imaginary room in a flash and I'll be gone. What's truly me won't exist anymore. I'm only fourteen, so this is not a happy thought. If I have to face the "there must be more to life than this" conversation, it should be when I am much, much older — like twenty-five, at least! But fourteen? Nah! I'm not giving in. I'm not going down without a fight. And I'm not coming out of my imaginary, but all too real to me, refuge!

I try distraction. "How do you know?"

"Sorry?"

"How do you know it's painless?"

"Well —"

"Have you gone through it yourself?"

"I have done this countless times, Daisy."

"But you haven't ever had it done *to* you, have you?"

My face frowns, my lips purse. "No, of course not. *I* am the singularity. *I* am Quark."

"So you're the one who does it, aren't you?"

"Yes — "

I think-speak over him. "Always the predator, never the prey."

"Well, yes, but it is quick and pain-free, I assure you. It is quite a harmless process."

"Harmless! Yeah, right — except for the fact that I'll die."

"Daisy, you will join countless trillions of other molecules."

"When did you start doing this?"

"At the very dawn of what you call time."

"So you've done away with lots of beings? Not ... whole planets?"

"Well ..." If it's possible to be both abashed and proud simultaneously, that's the expression on my face right now.

"You've seriously done away with millions?!"

"Billions, I think you'll find." Quark shrugs, modestly.

"Used them up and spat them out."

"Now that is not true!"

"Yes, it is! You crushed them and moved on, that's right isn't it? That's what black holes do."

"No, not at all. All those beings, those planets, those galaxies — they are all me now. All Quark. They are part of what I am. Part of the fundamental matter of the universe."

"What? I just give in? Just roll over and die?"

And, just like that, reality hits me like a tidal wave of grief. My mind, or rather the little bit of my mind that *is* mine, suddenly floods with memories of Mum, Dad and my little brother Luke; of Amy and the friends I love; things I've done and so much — so much! — that I want to do with my life. My life which has barely started. These are the things I'll lose. The chances and opportunities I'll miss out on if I fail, or if I give in to this Quark-thing.

Well, my desire to live is stronger than my fear of dying. I want the chance to enjoy school, go to university, find love. Have a *life*. That trumps the terror I feel. Also, because I'm a teenager, it also triumphs over that thing called common sense — which fortunately hasn't fully developed yet. If it had, it'd tell me I have no chance!

I'm probably the subject of current gossip for the whole freaky playground drooling/possession episode and if Quark gets his way I'll end up as the infamous Girl Who Died in Secondary School.

I know the prospect of my ceasing to be is not a big deal to you. If I take the ultimate high-dive and surrender to the seemingly inevitable, then a few people will be really upset. For a while. A very short time. But admit it: things will move on. Humanity will, somehow, soldier on without me.

But, as of now, I'm alive — though I barely recognise the face in the mirror, with its deep frown of frustrated anger. It's shocking to see this stranger — no, worse: this hollow version of myself looking back at me. My lips form a single, solid line as Quark spits out, "infuriating child! Come out now!"

"Nope." Inside, *deep* inside, I smile. Despite what you may have heard to the contrary, I *am* still here. I'm faded around the edges. I can't see very well. I can't hear much. I can't actually speak. I don't have a body, as such. But I'm still fighting — against odds that didn't seem too hot to begin with and which now look pretty overwhelming. But I'm still me. I'm not *it*, not Quark.

My eyes, under the bright bathroom lights are like the eyes of a creature in the wild. Am I really in there? Inside that thing? Even Mum wouldn't recognise those eyes, would she? But I sense the challenge and the danger behind that look, behind the intelligence that lurks within eyes that had never previously seen me harm anyone or anything. And the danger is no less real for coming from within my own mind.

How long am I going to be stuck in here like this? It may be one of those bad news/good news situations. Bad news: yes, I'm stuck here for the rest of my life. Good news: the rest of my life will be very short indeed!

But I refuse to give up. Refuse to surrender to *it*, to Quark.

I can stay where I am, hiding away in the dark recesses of my own mind and I'm pretty sure Quark will eventually find me. Or I can figure out some way to strike back and have at least a chance to survive. There's no choice: I *have* to fight.

There's no time for pathetic self-pity. A usurper — an alien usurper at that! — will not tease and torment me in my own body! I need a plan. And then I'll fight back. Starting now.

Chapter 10

COME OUT, COME OUT, WHEREVER YOU ARE

Daisy Jacobs is quiet. Brooding might be the word for what she's doing.

Hiding is *definitely* a word for what she's doing!

Quark *longs* to *become*, but he can be patient. In fact, he's been patient for a long, long time. Of course, time doesn't mean anything to him. But this is the longest he's ever waited for the first *becoming* in any place. In this place's puny timeframe, Quark's last experience of even a momentary delay was when large reptiles roamed the neighbourhood, stomping on little rodents that would eventually evolve to become shes and humans and Daisy Jacobs. (He hasn't quite pinned down the precise definition of this planet's primary life form.) But even for a timeless, ageless, formless clump of primordial atoms, Quark's patience is being stretched.

He has a tantalising sense of his goal. He looks down at the soft hands of the body he inhabits. He feels he can — almost — reach out and touch his goal. He's close. So close to *becoming*.

But Daisy Jacobs is in the way. She is being unnecessarily obstructive.

He wonders why she's behaving like this. Why she's making it so personal. He simply wants to *become*. That's all. There's nothing personal involved. No emotion. No malice. Quark means Daisy Jacobs no harm at all. It's the furthest thing from his consciousness! Of course, there's no actual conscience in Quark's consciousness. But he absolutely, positively bears her no ill will. Categorically not! Daisy's hand on Daisy's own heart.

So he can see no need for this negative emotional … vibe he's picking up. All this negativity. He can't understand why she doesn't just come out of the stupid room!

Also, just because Quark isn't used to feelings, doesn't mean he can't sense such things through the special connection he has with Daisy. And frankly he doesn't like how he's being made to feel like the bad guy here. Like an outsider. True, Daisy *is* inside; literally deep inside — somewhere. But that's no reason to keep him on the outside like this. They can be together, he thinks. They *belong* together. This will, after all, be a true union, a fusion, a joining. Maybe even the greatest ever *becoming*. Think of the honour!

Quark decides to sweeten the pill still further. He will make her a most generous offer. A promise that she can take to the bank. Once Daisy Jacobs' form is used up and finished, Daisy Jacobs can have it back! Oh, yes, she can! All she need do is stop sulking and skulking in whatever dark corner of her — now *his* mind — she's hiding in.

Quark waits …

If he could whistle, he'd do so now.

"Daisy, I'm still waiting … "

Silence.

"Daisy, Daisy give me your answer do!" he says in a sing-song voice that Quark does even not begin to understand the origin of. "Day-sy, oh, Daaay-sy . . . "

Silence.

"DAISY JACOBS COME OUT THIS MINUTE!"

More silence.

"COME OUT AND *BECOME* RIGHT NOW!"

Absolute, total and complete silence; disturbed only by a distant echo of Daisy's voice, "now-now-now".

That's it! Now Quark's finished with being nice. Being kind and thoughtful and generous. Because this Daisy-form belongs to *it* now, he fumes, and it's high time Daisy got with the programme and moved right on out! Time for her to give up and surrender. To wave the white flag and enjoy the first of this blue-green planet's *becomings*.

This place's many, many, many becomings.

"But, always remember, Daisy Jacobs: you get to be the first!"

Chapter 11

INDEX CASE

"Wait — the first?" I'm shocked into ending my silent protest.

"Ah, Daisy, you are still there. Hello!"

Like, where else would I be?! "You said the first."

"Yes?"

"What does that mean? I thought you were here to get me."

"I am, but — Oh, you think I am here to get *only* you? You think I have travelled countless light-years across your little, insignificant corner of space, especially to pay a visit to you? To this particular Daisy Jacobs?!" My body laughs; actually laughs. It's a forced, mechanical, stagey laugh, entirely devoid of any semblance of actual humour.

"Daisy Jacobs, you have ego."

"I'm not arrogant! Far from it. In fact, as far from it as it's possible to be."

"But you believe you are the hero."

Images come swimming up from my memory, so many that I'm surprised there's enough space in my bit of my own mind for them all. I think of parties and birthdays and times when I've been the centre of attention. I never enjoy having all eyes on me, but I've always felt I should at least be the hero of my own life, you know. Not an actual star, not like on TV or in a film — I'd hate that! — but in my life. I mean, it's like everyone I know has got boyfriends and girlfriends, or they're sneaking out of the house at night to drink with friends, or they're exaggerating about making out. That's why I'd finally decided to make sure that panic really was a thing of the past and go out on a limb by talking to Connor. In public. I wanted to prove to myself I could do it. And I wanted ... more. I have my family. I have school and homework. I hang out with a few friends ... mainly Amy, actually. Don't get me wrong, I like my life, but it'd be good if there was a bit more actual *life* in my life. Instead, it's always seemed as though I have a walk-on role, off at the side, just at the edge of the frame, hanging with the extras —

I snap out of my introspection. "What? No! I'm not — how can I be a hero?"

"Not 'a' hero. *The* hero. You believe you are the hero of your own life — "

"Huh?" He must be joking! Talk about being cut to the quick!

" — when you are not. You are an organism. One of many such organisms in this place."

"This school?"

Quark sighs. "Sometimes, Daisy Jacobs you are not the hero. You are just dense."

"I beg your— "

"This is not your story. Your epic adventure. And you are *not* the hero. You are one of billions of identical humans. You are just a group of cells. You come from cells and you'll go back to being cells. And you are just the first."

"First?"

"Yes — numero uno; a pioneer; the Index Case. The first to *become*."

"You mean ... ?"

I feel my head nod. "That's right, Daisy. What an honour, yes?"

Er? Hello? Reader, oh, dear reader, are you still there?

So — remember when I said I was in a good news/bad news situation? Well, I hate to be the bearer of bad news, but ...

The *good* news is that I am now certain that I can count on your support. And pretty soon you will *really* be pulling for me. You'll be my own little cheerleader. You will want me to win *soooooo* bad!

The *bad* news is that this thing just got worse. Worse for me, yes; but a whole lot worse for *you*.

If you've been following closely, you'll know I've been possessed, or invaded or taken over and yadda-yadda-yadda, all the rest? That I was me, but not really me anymore? And that only I could save myself from Quark?

Well, it turns out it goes a bit deeper than that. Houston — we have a WAY bigger problem!

This disastrous situation I talked about? Turns out it's not just a disaster for me, but for everyone. And that includes *you*. Don't ask me how I know that. I can't quite figure out how I know. I'm kind of vague on exactly how this possession, body-snatching-thing works. What I do know is at the level of a whisper; a rumour, if you will. I'm in here, deep, deep inside my own head, hiding. If I don't hide, I think Quark'll get me. Then the tiny bit of me that is still me won't be me anymore. And won't ever be again. Are you following this? It's quite complicated, I know.

So, let me make it simpler. Think about when you heard that someone at school had done something terrible. Bad enough to get them excluded, or even expelled. Possibly they were nasty to a geeky person on social media, saying just the meanest, most unkind things, like that she's doing dirty deeds with a boy called — well, let's not get too carried away here, let's keep it general. I'm sure you get the picture. Something bad happens. Something morally reprehensible and unforgivable. So, anyway, these people are in your school and you may know of them, but you don't really know them. Either the vicious, icky wretch who does the deed or the sweet, innocent, lovable geek against whom such vicious (and totally, totally untrue — worst luck!) aspersions are cast. You get the picture. You don't know these people, but you get to hear about it all the same. Whispers start. Rumours spread. And some of it at least, has a basis in the truth.

That's the case here. Right now it's just a rumour. A hint. A mere whisper. But I know deep down in my, my ... in the tiny bit of me that *is* me, I know it's true: whatever it actually *is* that I have, or that has *me* — it's coming for you too.

You read that right; this being/entity/thing/anomaly/singularity, this *Quark* that's inside *me*, is coming for *you*. Actually, in a very real sense *I'm* coming for you …

Quark found me first. And now he's got me … *almost*. And that means Quark will soon have you. And then him and her and then everyone. All Quark needs is all of me. And when he has all of me, then he (and I) will come for you. In fact, *I'm* coming for everyone.

So the end of the world is beginning, right here and right now. With me.

Chapter 12

INCANDESCENT

"COME OUT!!!!!!!!!"

Chapter 13

THOSE WHO ARE ABOUT TO DIE, SALUTE YOU

"To be honest, I'm a bit disappointed. I'm not convinced you're up on the whole cheering for Team Daisy thing. The wishing me luck with my fight to the death with the evil entity (or whatever). Is it nothing more than passing interest for you? A bit of a diversion? I understand — when you don't have a stake, these things don't really tug the heartstrings, do they? Don't set the pulse racing or get the adrenaline pumping. Car crash at the end of your road, your kitten slightly shaken = front page news! Disaster on the other side of the world, hundreds perish = yawn … so what was for lunch again?

I get it. When you don't have a direct involvement, it's difficult to care too deeply. But you did get the news, yes? Because, if you did, you should be scared by now. Terrified even. I mean, it's only sensible to fear your own imminent death!

And sure, on the whole, I'd very much prefer to return to being a nonentity — especially given the alternative. Why was I plucked from obscurity like this? If Quark needed a gateway to humanity's oblivion, why couldn't it be a Nobel-Prize-winning scientist, or a special-forces soldier? Someone capable of the speed of thought and action that could make a difference and actually save us?

But you know what? It's not one of them. It's me.

So, yeah, I'm sitting in here (so to speak), mentally pouting at the unfairness of it all. Given the choice, I'd bury my head in the sand. I'd put my fingers in my ears (if only!) and sing "la, la, la, la" at the top of my voice until this whole situation went away. Or I'd take a pyjama day and just snuggle under my duvet!

But that would solve nothing.

Because this *is* happening to me. And if it continues, if I actually *become*, then pretty soon, it will happen to you too. And then I will conquer the world. Please don't take this personally: I don't mean you any harm. And I guarantee you that the small part of me that is still actually me will be very sorry as I pulverise you into your constituent parts. But the me who gets a buzz from debate team and full marks in a spelling test, who can't even be (really) horrible to her (slightly) awful little brother, who can't even get Connor Wheeler to notice that I exist ... that seemingly insignificant little me will then kill everyone on the planet.

So, let's try again: are you scared yet?

Mmmm?

Not scared by the thought of a homicidal fourteen-year-old girl coming for you? And for everyone else in the world?

Because, believe me, you *are* next.

Then your mum. Or sister. Or best friend. Then everyone in your family, your street, your school, everyone you've ever met or heard of. Your favourite pop star and TV personality. That woman with the irritating voice who does the weather on local radio. The guy who shouts and gets over-excited when he calls the lottery numbers. The President of the United States. The Pope. Everyone. From paupers to princes.

Quark is not here just for me. He's here for all of us. And once he's got through me, he'll be on a roll, he'll have a plan, he'll know what to do and he'll get us all.

So, is the full extent of our problem apparent now?

There's an unfeeling, people-chomping entity on one side — inside me, in fact — and there's everyone on the planet on the other side. And one thing, just one teeny-tiny little thing stands between them.

Me.

Yup, little Daisy Jacobs.

It turns out that I *do* have to be the hero of this story. Because if I'm not, if I don't win, then there'll *be* no story. We'll all be just cells, just so much fodder for the universe — in the form of Quark — to feast on.

Still, let's not get ahead of ourselves: the fate of the whole, entire human race rests on an imaginary lock on a door that does not even exist, protecting a room that is a mere figment of my imagination.

That's reassuring, huh? I mean, it's quite a weight to bear on my shoulders, you know. And I don't even have broad shoulders.

Are you sitting more comfortably now? I mean there's teen angst over spots and friendship groups and boys and there's the fate of the planet in the hands of a fourteen-year-old girl.

Got to get your priorities right, huh? So, I would suggest rather strongly that you show a modicum of concern. And maybe worry about this … just a little.

Any advice or help you can offer — well, no, don't worry, I know there's nothing you or anyone else can do to help.

So just stick with the long-distance cheerleading (and the worrying). Because I'm not at all sure I can stop myself.

And if *I* can't stop myself, *you've* got no chance!

So, if you turn over the next page and it's totally blank, don't bother locking the door, just enjoy your life whilst you've got it, because I can guarantee you won't have it for long.

Chapter 13a

Chapter 14

LIFE, THE UNIVERSE AND EVERYTHING

The universe is big. Really, really big. But although it's vast (over ninety billion light years in diameter) it's highly logical. It's governed by rules and the most beautiful things in all of existence: hugely complicated sums, equations and theories that lots of people buy books about to make themselves look good but never, ever read. (If those people had actually *read* the books they bought, they may have figured out Quark's existence and not left the fate of mankind in the hands — or the mind — of a fourteen-year-old girl.) But, oh no, they had to buy gym memberships that they never used either, or sit with friends in pubs discussing football, or at home watching talent shows on TV. Imagine: watching a border collie dancing the rhumba, rather than studying massively complex quadratic equations! It's unbelievable, isn't it?!

However, take away the silly bits and the rest of the universe *is* logical.

And our planet, where Quark has now spent two whole days, is small. From his perspective, it's mind-crushingly insignificant. He can barely believe it, or *we*, ever came into existence in the first place. It was all down to a series of coincidences: the impact of a meteor that failed to miss or of a comet that *did* miss.

On a universal scale, this galaxy, this solar system, this planet doesn't matter. At all.

And yet Quark has been here for two days. Clearly, two days out of the approximately 13.8 billion years that Quark has existed doesn't seem like a lot. But in the past, Quark has laid waste to whole solar systems in less than two days.

And it would have been the same here too, he thinks.

Except for the girl.

This girl has temporarily — *only* temporarily — delayed Quark's progress.

And what are the chances of that? The odds of selecting this puny little girl on this trivial little planet are so microscopic that they just barely register on the outermost reaches of impossibility.

And yet ... Quark met Daisy Jacobs.

Quark *became* Daisy. *Almost* ...

Except for that eensy-weensy little room in her head, Quark has finished her. He is *so* close. Quark can sense the domino-effect that will follow as one *becoming* follows another and another in rapid succession. All it will take is this first one.

Because Quark is inevitable. Overwhelming.

Now Quark makes Daisy's body stand tall. Or as tall as he can. Her spine is ramrod straight, her shoulders back, her head held high. This is as large and proud as Quark can make her. Quark is going for seriously, earth-conqueringly impressive, but, in Daisy, can only make it as far as moderately okay ... for a Thursday.

He sighs. In all of history, in all of what scientists call time, Quark has found, *become*, absorbed, used-up and departed — leaving behind ... well, pretty much nothing. Floating matter does not have an ambition. If it did, Quark's would be to reverse the mess that the Big Bang made of what became the universe. Quark's innermost desire is to compress everything — absolutely *everything* — in the universe into a space something less than the size of a pin-head. That will be neat, tidy, complete.

There are no experts in Quark, as Quark is the impossible made real. In fact, the equation postulating Quark's existence is still many decades in the future, and once Quark has finished with this planet, there will *be* no future (at least for Earth), so the equation, perhaps the planet's greatest-ever achievement, will never come into being. But I repeat: Quark is inevitable.

And he never, ever fails. However, as of now, Quark is only *almost* Daisy Jacobs. And he cannot fully *become*, overwhelm, use up Daisy Jacobs until she gives in to the inevitable … or he tricks her into doing so and stamps her out of existence.

Frankly, he's becoming a little tetchy about the whole situation. Actually, he's not so much perturbed as positively splenetic with rage! Beside himself with fury. (Although, how an entity that currently resides within another being can be beside himself is too boggling for anyone's mind to cope with.)

Yet somehow, the most powerful force that has ever or will ever exist has so far failed to immolate a fourteen-year-old girl. Quite why is a question that should absorb more of his time than it does. But Quark, no doubt influenced by what passes for logic in his newly human nature, decides to try something new. For the first time in the entire history of the universe, Quark is going to school.

Maybe what he learns there will help him. With any luck, she will soon be *dying* to *become*!

Chapter 15

DAISY'S COMING FOR YOU

Hi! I'm still here — and that's good to hear, isn't it! Sorry about that whole blank page thing. Just making sure you were paying attention. Have you thought of a plan yet? Because I haven't.

Don't think I haven't been busy, 'cos I have. I now have a TV in my room, so when I 'see' stuff through my eyes, that's what I watch it on. My life, on TV. Weird or what?! Don't get carried away though — it's not a 56 inch OLED or anything; I mean, that would be ridiculous! A TV of that size in my brain! No, this is one of those really old-fashioned TVs with a wooden stand that's actually bigger than the thick glass screen. The picture's not great to be honest; there's a lot of interference and the sound comes and goes too, like Dad said it used to be when TVs first came out in the 1970s or whenever. This is not high-tech we're talking about, it's more like a piece of furniture over there in the dimly-lit corner of my room. And now I've got a TV, even a crappy one, I can see a bit more of what's going on.

Regardless of what I can or can't see, the fact that we haven't got a plan yet is … well — frustrating is kind of an understatement, because I'm sure this brain-frying, life-ending apocalypse could be stopped. It will take a genuine once-in-a-lifetime, brain-the-size-of-a-planet plan. And a miracle, too, probably. But it would mean no more "AAAAAAGGGGHHH!-end-of-the-world". And on the whole, that would be a good thing.

But, don't forget, there's only one person who can stop it. One person on whom the entire fate of the human race depends.

Me.

The destiny of mankind depends on Daisy Jacobs. So, no pressure, huh?

Do you see my problem? Can Hulk save the world? Er, maybe. Spiderman — possibly. Einstein or the world's major super-power think-tanks? Well, who knows? Superman — no problem; an absolute, total walk in the park.

But me? Fourteen-year-old girl — check. Pain-in-the-butt younger brother — check. Messed-up hormones, more than a bit geeky, in "like" with Connor Wheeler (my oh, so cute classmate who you may have already met) — check, check, check.

World-saving super hero? Er, not so much.

And it's difficult, because while I'm in here, I'm not as sure as I was about what's going on out there — where you are. My senses are a still bit vague. It's like when you come round from an operation. I had my appendix out last year and when I started to wake up in the recovery room, I was all woozy. I could barely keep my eyes open even as I was trying to wake up. I was confused and things were all jumbled and mixed up. I tried to focus on the doctor and the nurse as they spoke to me, but what they said came to me in dribs and drabs — just unconnected pieces that didn't join up or make sense.

Just like what's happening now makes no kind of sense. I know I am here, in this room in my head and that this tiny bit really is me. But … who are you?

You're not it, are you?! Because then there'd be no escape, no hope at all for me. Or for anyone. But no, you can't be! That would be mean and cruel, ruthless and just … horrible. Okay, I know wiping out all of humanity is a kind of bad thing to do, but I don't think Quark is mean. He's loathsome and creepy, granted. But not cruel. How do I know that? I think I can sense it. In an eerie way I sort of "feel" Quark. Inside of me; inside my head. Sensing him like that is how I stay focused on keeping Quark out. And stay safe. Well … safe-ish.

So, for the moment, I will accept you are still *you* and that you're on my side. And that you're *not* Quark. You're the one who'll help me figure out exactly what's going on. And help me to stop him. You will help me, won't you?

But, hang on a minute … if I can't reach the world and can't touch it, then how can I reach you? How can I save me and so save you — and all of us?!

All this is literally driving me out of my mind! Having to deal with the stuff that life throws at me is hard at the best of times, but when I can't access all of my faculties, it's nigh-on impossible. It feels as though another bit of the real me is being eaten away, trampled underfoot with every moment that passes. It's overwhelming. Because if Quark succeeds, then, to paraphrase that famous comedy sketch, I will be no more. I will cease to be. I will be an ex-human. I'll have gone to meet my maker.

My life will be over.

There — I've said it. It's out in the open.

But what exactly *can* I do to fight back? Brute force won't cut it. I need to be sneaky. More … human. I mean, if this had been a regular kidnapping, I'd try to escape. I'd call for help. I'd fight. I'd yell and scream until my throat was raw. I can't let inconsequential fears like the disdain of others at school or impending, horrible death put me off. I must be active about this.

Fear comes from not knowing. From ignorance. I need information; I need to know more. Then this situation is just a problem. And I'm good at solving problems.

I'm going to do this in classic teen fashion: I'm going to watch as much TV as I possibly can!

Chapter 16

A POINTLESS WASTE OF TIME

Today, in a unique first in the history of Quark, time loses its rigidity and symmetry. Time both speeds up and hangs about him like the heaviest of burdens. All his senses are suddenly turned up to the max. He feels as though his system is about to blow a fuse. He can't comprehend how humans cope with so much input — especially as at least 99% of it is useless, inane drivel!

He's used to being omnipotent and to the freedom of being everywhere, simultaneously. So being basically nowhere, while encased in the body of a teenage girl is disconcerting. Today, things are still more intense. He thinks something chemical has changed within Daisy, because he feels more ... human. The sensory overload disturbs him, but he's sure it's a just step on the way to *becoming*. There's a blurring of the boundary between him and the reality of what it is to be human. The filter is wearing away. This is Humanity Unplugged!

Quark has been aware of himself — or rather, of Daisy — but suddenly it appears as though he's aware of *everything*. Constant, mindless, mind-numbing stuff envelops him, swamping his five human senses. It's a burden magnified by extra senses that he's automatically wired in to unused parts of Daisy's brain. His humanity is overloaded as the undeveloped brain he's operating within struggles to adapt quickly enough to cope with added sensory enlightenment. But the pure Quark within Daisy receives the briefest, microscopic flash of home — of eternity. And from where he is, tucked away inside the body and mind of a teenage girl on a small blue-green planet in a distant backwater of the

Milky Way, that glimpse is exhilarating and tantalising. He longs to be away, to be free once more. He just needs to complete the *becoming* that seems to be underway …

Quark can feel Daisy's heart racing as he seeks to gather up her errant atoms. It's hard for him to focus and think straight, so he's amazed that a mere girl can cope with it. The noise alone, compared to the blissful silence of space. And the total lack of order. The sheer randomness. Frankly, he thinks it's extraordinary humans even last as far as adolescence! And this particular human female is a challenge, even for a Quark used to bringing order to universal chaos!

He will rely on the tedium of school to restore calm. And then he'll rearrange Daisy's molecules!

Still, as Quark leaves the house, he has to steel himself: he's more aware of *life* than ever before. Not just the sights, sounds and smells all around him, but of the blood coursing through Daisy's veins. He can feel the rhythmic, pulsing movement of the individual valves of her heart.

So far, he's drifted through three days at school, going through the motions with almost robotic efficiency while searching for a way to take over more of Daisy. It's as though time spent in the classroom and in interactions with schoolmates has been a theatrical backdrop — just routine functions that go on in the background as he searches for a way to bring about the *becoming*. He devotes scant attention to playing the role of Daisy, focusing instead on ways to get rid of everything that *is* Daisy.

He's barely present with Daisy's family at home. He walks straight past Amy in the school corridor and unknowingly settles in a different seat too, so he sits away from her. The hurt this causes Daisy's best friend goes unnoticed by Quark. And whereas Daisy's marks in tests and for homework are always at the very top of her year, Quark's are barely satisfactory. But then, why should he care? How could any sane person feign an interest in dead kings, simple sums and arcane rules of grammar?

The whole educational system seems fatally flawed to Quark. Why would anyone choose to be inside, listening to a boring grown-up wittering on about glaciers, people who lived a long time ago (and so are both dead *and* irrelevant), or tediously basic chemistry? It's a sunny day, Quark thinks, and even tiny Scuttleford is full of stimulation. In the buzz of emotions, he forgets he's supposed to be disconnecting from emotions and settling Daisy on course for oblivion. He can't help imagining what the nearby town of Braedon would be like! Or he could take a train and go to London — that would be a-mazing!

Unsurprisingly, this is the day that new Daisy makes a real impact in school ...

"You swore at Mr Ford!" says Mrs Griffin, sternly. And, don't forget, if Mrs Griffin *starts off* steely, she is *seriously* miffed! For her, stern is the equivalent of waving her arms around and screaming at you.

Quark sighs. "He was rude to me."

"Rude! Daisy, he was not rude. He asked you to sit down."

"He did not *ask*. He *told* me, actually. Rather severely."

"Your actions fully justified his severity. You were standing up on a desk in his classroom, shouting at Robert Jones."

"He was rude to me too." Quark casually examines Daisy's nails, pondering tones of varnish.

Mrs Griffin sighs and shakes her head as though this is the most upsetting thing she's ever heard. "It was a Maths lesson, Daisy. And you love Maths."

"S'borin'."

"I beg your pardon?" Mrs Griffin replies in astonishment.

"Said, s'borin'." Quark genuinely does not understand where this is coming from or where it's going, but he's open to exploring the sense of teenage angst and righteous (and totally unjustified) indignation that has fizzed up from somewhere inside him. It seems to be atypical Daisy behaviour and therefore another potential stride in the right direction for him. If not for Daisy.

There's a moment of silence as Mrs Griffin considers this. "Daisy, what do you mean it is 'boring'?" She is very careful to enunciate the word with perfect precision. "You are top in Maths. Top in your year. She shuffles some papers on the desk in front of her. "In fact, your grades now would top Year 11, let alone Year 10. You are an exceptional mathematician."

"Yeah, well, now I think s'borin'."

Mrs Griffin takes a deep breath as if trying to control a sense of the deepest frustration. "Daisy, I spend much of my time trying to rein in the behaviour of a small percentage of pupils in this school. Occasionally I am called on to act to help with another slightly larger group of pupils. All this is only possible because most pupils cause me no problems and another small group of pupils act like a shining beacon and have a positive impact on the behaviour and attitudes of those all around them. You, Daisy, are at the heart of that latter group. You're the youngest in your year, but the most mature. You are my shining beacon. You are someone I thought I'd never see in my office for anything other than positive reasons."

"Should make sure Maths isn't so borin' then." Quark sniffs and wipes Daisy's nose on the sleeve of Daisy's usually pristine blazer.

"You have always done well at Maths; in fact, in all of your subjects, but Maths, English and Science in particular. Why then is Mathematics suddenly 'boring'?"

"Too basic, innit?"

"Isn't it, Daisy. You know how to speak properly; there's no cause to sink into this ridiculously exaggerated, Estuary-speak, teenage pose, now is there? The fact remains that you stood up in class. On a desk. You shouted. You swore — at a teacher and a fellow pupil." The head-teacher takes a deep breath, trying to contain her frustration and disappointment. She sighs and tries a different tack. "Working out who you are is part of being a teenager, Daisy. It is part of growing up. But this — this ... attitude, this behaviour — it's not you. It's not the person you are."

Quark burps audibly. "Yeah, but Fordy is only a substitute for us and he just droned on and on. And we did no theoretical calculus at all! None!"

Mrs Griffin looks confused. "Calculus?" She takes a deeper breath. "That does not change the facts: your behaviour was not in any way acceptable. If you thought there was an injustice, you are mature enough to know how to go about resolving the issue."

"You are a bit removed from the battlefront, Mrs G. But it may surprise you to learn that there has been no discussion at all of Isaac Newton OR Gottfried Wilhelm Leibniz. Not in Maths. Nor in Science, where Mr Lucas refused to discuss the fact that humanity is an irrelevance: a mere speck in the immensity of space."

"Indeed?" Mrs Griffin looks so taken aback by this whole statement that she barely knows where to start. With Mrs G? Or the abrupt shift away from the subject under discussion? Or the disturbing nihilism encompassed in Daisy's view of humanity as an irrelevance? Or the abrupt switch from exaggerated teen-speak to a crystal-glass-like tone that could — almost — be mistaken for her own? Before she can decide where to leap in, Quark continues. He's *really* on a roll now.

He nods and leans forward to press his point. "Yah, not in one single lesson. I say, do you think you could have a confab with Mr Ford? I mean, I know he is a pretty awful teacher, but, gosh: it would be lovely to ruminate upon differential — or even integral calculus; that would be simply divine! One would be *so* grateful."

Whether Quark acts deliberately or subconsciously is unclear. However, his mode of speech has switched suddenly from angsty teenager to ... well, pretty la-de-dah, actually. His enunciation is suddenly clear, his elocution perfect, his use of language is strictly from the standard book of Queen's English. He doesn't sound stroppy anymore, or at all like Daisy; in fact, he sounds like an exaggerated, even *extravagant* version of Mrs Griffin herself — all "ay" for I, "laahh-v-ly" for lovely and "one" for I.

Mrs Griffin does not take kindly to this. There's no doubt now:

she's sure she's being mocked. And by Daisy Jacobs of all people! The very last person she thought she'd ever have to say this to: "Enough! You will have a half hour detention this evening!"

"But, I say Mrs G, that's frightfully — "

This time the Head definitely notes the Mrs G. "Detention for one hour, in fact. And I shall also talk to your parents, Ms Jacobs." Not Daisy anymore, no more 'Mrs nice-guy, we're all in this together, do me a favour and just behave.' Now she's cold, distant and businesslike. "You need to rethink this recent run of behaviour. It does not suit you and will do no good at all for your long-term educational and career prospects. I know we were all thinking about Oxbridge for you — "

"More school!? You must be joking! I'm coming to the conclusion that this school-lark is just a pointless waste of time."

Later, at home, Daisy's parents are almost as pleased as Mrs Griffin with how Daisy's day has gone. "You got a detention?!"

"Yes, mother."

"But you never get detention! What happened?" asked her father.

"I just set them straight on a few things. Pointed out the error of their ways."

Her mother is aghast. "But Daisy, I don't understand, you love school and you worship Mrs Griffin."

Daisy's dad nodded, "yes, she said you were rude about some teachers and not very polite to her either."

"Well, she asked for it."

Daisy's parents cry out, simultaneously. "That's not acceptable!" "What do you say, Daisy?"

"What do I say?"

They both lean forward and nod.

Quark sighs with depthless exaggeration. "Why don't you just naff off!" He stands and leaves the room, calling back over his shoulder, "and leave me alone!"

Chapter 17

THE STEALTH ROOM

I listened to this with a sense of stunned dismay. Even before his outburst, Quark seemed indifferent to the mood at the dinner table. On the few occasions when he looked up and focussed my eyes on them, I could read the expressions on the faces of my family. But Quark was doing that thing with my eyes where you let them drift slightly out of focus, so that everything you see is a bit blurry. I hope that's what he's doing anyway, otherwise I may be shutting down even more …

I feel increasingly helpless. With my benumbed senses, just thinking about how to escape from this is like trying to run in treacle! And I can't afford the data capacity in the little headspace I have left to try to out-think myself!

But it's clear from what I can dimly see that my family know something's wrong. I don't remember seeing Quark talk to my family much. And they seem to have given 'me' space to think things over. Out of the corner of my eye, I see Mum and Dad exchange glances while Quark keeps his head down as much as possible. He seems lost in contemplation too.

Circumstances change how we view even everyday things. This dining table is one of the key spaces in my life. The cosy heart of my home. It's where we sit, twice a day for breakfast and dinner, the four of us together, sharing our days, discussing events great and small. From Love Island, Doctor Who, Big Brother and Bake Off to the most serious issues of the day's news. We consider and debate, we laugh and take the mickey out of each other. Luke and I learn how to make a case and construct an argument, and we learn that our voice matters.

Subdued voices, muted but for the occasional, "pass the salt, please," show how much things have changed recently. The four of us — with 'me' very much the outsider — sit in oppressive silence and pretend nothing is happening. Dad pushes food around his plate without seeming to eat anything at all, Mum nibbles at a lettuce leaf like it's the key to enlightenment and Luke glances between 'me' and Mum and Dad, anxious about the poisonous atmosphere in his previously happy home. Quark, of course, eats as though food is about to go on ration and he needs to scoff it while he still can.

Then Mum and Dad make their tentative opening and all hell breaks loose. Quark doesn't want to talk. He's acting like the stereotypical, stroppy teen that I am not. However, seeing the stricken faces of my parents after Quark's hurled insults is enough to make me turn off the TV in my imaginary room, so I don't have to face this situation anymore.

Knowing that no one in the entire history of the universe has ever outrun Quark doesn't exactly ease the pressure I feel. And the idea that Quark might be lurking in a dark corner outside my room is seriously scary. Especially as, deep down I know the idea that my room is a safe haven is as imaginary as the room itself. But at least it does help keep the constant anxiety at bay.

So far, I've only peered round the edge of my door and haven't dared leave my room. Outside are what looks like clumps of day-old porridge and walls that are grey and dimly lit. I can also see those mysterious duct pipes that appear to serve no purpose other than only to add an air of grim menace to the setting. There's no decoration, apart from an occasional Bio Hazard warning sign.

Of course, I know none of this is real. My brain is still in my head, where it's always been and it looks just like yours does. But as I'm literally out of my mind at the moment, I'm happy to go along with the imaginary space I have created.

I've got a chair now, so I can sit and watch TV (when I can bear to – and on the few occasions I can get a clear signal). I've got a little table too and I've put a framed photo of Mum, Dad and Luke on it. It's not a real photo, but compared to 'imagineering' the TV, chair and table, downloading an image of them from my mind was a doddle! Weirdly, I'm still finding comfort from 'wearing' my school uniform in here.

How I hide the room from Quark is equally vague. The only thing I can compare it to is when the points change on a rail track and instead of heading one way, the train goes off in another direction; that's kind of what I've done. I've switched round a few neural connections, twisted a couple of synapses and hidden a room in plain sight. If you happen to be looking directly at the inside of my brain, that is. It's like my own stealth creation. The big superpowers build stealth bombers and fighter aircraft out of who knows what magic metal or plastic or polymer or whatever. I've built a stealth room out of a few million neurons.

I don't know how a normal brain works beyond the fact that certain bits are responsible for movement, vision, language and all the rest. I seem to have got my own special package deal — like you get from your mobile phone provider. Except, whereas they'll give you x-minutes of calls (never enough!), all you can eat texts and a set amount of data (also never enough!), I've got a certain amount of vision, some hearing, lots of memory, but absolutely no touch or taste (and none of what I've got is anything *like* enough). I can see a bit of what's happening and try to build details of a conversation from partially overheard chunks, but I can't feed myself chips, taste a cup of coffee, speak to my friends or hug Mum.

I'm seeing a bit of what's supposed to be *my* life and from that I'm trying to build the bigger picture, but I guess it's a bit like when a palaeontologist tries to come up with a complete picture of a Ginormous-Rex, with only the right little toe, the jawbone and a couple of ribs: there's a fair amount of imagination, poetic license and wishful thinking involved.

This is my way of telling you I'm laying all this out like it's gospel. And it is ... kind of. But I can't see everything, I can't hear everything and a lot of what's going on ... well, I can't make head nor tail of it. So I fill in the blanks and give you a version — and it's obviously a slanted version — of what's happening. But that's okay, isn't it? Because who are you going to trust? Me, or the one who'd turn you into a pile of dust before you could say, "ashes to ashes"?

Chapter 18

IF WE SHOULDN'T EAT AT NIGHT, WHY IS THERE A LIGHT IN THE FRIDGE?

At midnight, Quark is back downstairs, sitting cross-legged on the kitchen floor, illuminated by the light from the fridge which is open in front of him. He doesn't understand what happened today. He woke up feeling edgy and uneasy. Then he got to feel good, showering and getting ready for school. Then, almost immediately he felt bad again and was gruff with Daisy's parents over breakfast. He left home in a huff and then thrilled with excitement at the stimulation of the world around him. Yet by the time he reached school he felt overwhelmed and *over*stimulated by the seething mass of humanity in the corridors and so had ignored Daisy's friends. Initially intrigued and moved by his first lesson, the day soon turned sour again. And so it continued — life as a constant roller-coaster of emotional turmoil and upheaval. And why? Over what?

The balance of chemicals in her body shifted constantly, like quicksand. It had been a seemingly normal, ordinary day. Yet he'd found the constantly yo-yoing emotions utterly exhausting. What was it with these humans?

He'd spent the day desperately searching for a foothold in a world of chaos and confusion!

But now Quark has found the perfect cure: he sits on the floor, surrounded by jars, packets and containers — mustard (English and French — a used teaspoon in each), three different flavours of yogurt — all opened, pickles of all sorts, guacamole, hummus, chutneys, a deli's worth of cheeses, cream, Tupperware containers of left-overs from the last two suppers, even a packet of butter.

He's taken crisps, biscuits and dried fruit from the pantry and is washing his feast down with soya milk, fruit juice, Lucozade and a bottle of chocolate milkshake.

If this doesn't make him feel better, nothing will …

Chapter 19

SAFE HAVEN

I don't remember much about the first few days I spent locked in my head. I have vague images of some of it, but it's an incomplete recording — like trying to work out the detailed plot of over a thousand pages of Lord of the Rings by looking at three or four random lines. I mean, I know 'I' spent time with my family and with Amy; I know I've been to school, and that there was a Maths test I must have aced. But *I* didn't do those things, if you see what I mean. I have no real memory of them. The disconnect from reality is extreme.

Now, although I'm still locked in my head and am pretty much de-sensitised to the rest of my body, I know from the distant discomfort coming from the direction of my tummy that something's happening that I'm pleased Quark will have to deal with, rather than me. That might distract him enough for me to build a better picture of what's been happening.

I think this is day four or five of the invasion. To begin with, everything I saw was blurry: I saw light and dark and vague shapes, but couldn't make out enough detail to distinguish between one person and another. Sounds were unclear too. I could tell the difference between a school bell and a car horn, but couldn't make fine distinctions or, after that initial burst of semi-clarity, make out too much of whatever was being said. I think I had a meeting with Mrs Griffin in her office, so something out of the ordinary must have happened. Maybe I did *really* well in those tests!

Right now though, my head (or my bit of it) feels a little clearer. Coming into the mid-month surge of hormones always adds a layer of clarity to my thinking and a surge of energy to my body. This time, although my *body* is like a distant memory, every atom of my brain seems alert and alive. I feel supercharged. Ready for anything … almost.

That body of mine is flaked out on my bed and Quark is groaning for reasons probably not unconnected to whatever caused that stomach ache. I don't know what happened, but with Quark inactive, I seem to have more brainpower to work with, so I recognise Mum's footsteps approaching my door. There's a gentle knock.

"Daisy?" The door opens just a little. "Are you okay, sweetie?" There's concern in Mum's voice.

All she gets from Quark is a low moan.

"Can I get anything for you?"

Another moan.

"Well, if you want anything, just give me a shout and I'll come." This time there's a grunt.

Mum shuts the door and I hear her talking in low tones to Dad.

"I don't know what's got into her, I honestly don't. This stroppy attitude — it's so unlike her."

"No," Dad says, "but you know it's pretty standard teen behaviour."

"Not from Daisy. And the talking back! She never does that."

I talked back to them? I know that sometimes I dig my heels in and may just possibly be — in a certain light — a teeny bit stubborn; no, that's wrong, that's not how Dad talks about it: "strong-willed and determined" he says, never stubborn. But I don't talk back just for the sake of it, only ever to make a case or state my point.

"And to Mrs Griffin too." Mum continues.

I argued with my head teacher! What on earth —!

"I know, love," Dad agrees. "But I think it's just a phase. And her age. We thought we were getting away without the whole angsty-teen stuff, but maybe that's all it is."

"Maybe ..." Mum sounds doubtful. "It's a lot to take onboard though: swearing at a teacher, arguing with Mrs Griffin, failing a Maths test, getting detention and then being sent home."

What? What! WHAT?! I don't know where to begin with that! Which teacher did 'I' swear at? What did 'I' argue with Mrs Griffin about? Why did 'I' get my first-ever detention? And — I can hardly bear to write it — how did 'I' fail a Maths test!?

"I don't know what's happened to our lively, happy girl," Dad says, "but all we can do is keep watching her closely and let her know we're here for her when she's ready to speak about whatever is going on."

"Mmmm," Mum agrees. "We'll have to keep a close eye on her if last night's over-eating is anything to go by! It's like she's the stereotypical teenage nightmare all of a sudden!"

"You may be right, love, but she's paying for last night's episode — big time! That's not something she's likely to repeat anytime soon." I can hear the smile in my dad's voice.

"I still think there's something deeper going on." Mum's on the right track here, but even as a GP, I don't think this is a problem she'll be familiar with! I'll have to sort this out myself and with the disaster Quark is making of my life I need to get on with it. And this is the perfect opportunity — while Quark's in a weakened state and my mind is buzzing with energy.

In fact, I'm not sure if it's Quark's prostrate state or my own heightened awareness, but my senses — the few I have available to me — are hyper-aware this morning. I could hear Mum and Dad clearly and they were whispering on the other side of my bedroom door, which is closed and all the way on the other side of the room. In case this is a temporary thing, I need to get a move on.

What I need now is information. Quark can move my body and access my memories. There's a link. But does that link work two ways? I need to access his data and figure out how he works. I need to open communications on my terms. And I need to use it against him.

I'm going to take a brief trip out of my room. I know the further I stray, the greater the risk. But there's no choice: I have to see more of my brain and look for a weak link in Quark's defences.

I know all the bits of my brain communicate with each other — and the rest of my body — through millions of neurons. I'll explore some of these neural pathways and see if I can find a way of exerting more control over my body.

I hold the handle of my door and try to think myself brave, even though I'm petrified at the idea of leaving the so-called security of my room. I need to be more human to combat this alien. In fact, I need to be superhuman. And start messing with *his* mind!

Chapter 20

BECOMING
A scholarly analysis of its meaning, justification and role in the universe

It may surprise you to learn that Quark hasn't been entirely honest with Daisy. His name really *is* Quark; he *is* the smallest building block of matter known to man — an elementary particle. All of that's true. However, he is far from an ordinary example of the genus. He's a Dark Matter Quark: and a Quark with DMs has infinitely more kick than an ordinary Quark ...

There are billions upon countless billions of stars in the universe – the visible universe. But the part of the universe that we can see is only a tiny bit of what's actually there. Most of the rest is probably an invisible substance called dark matter. This substance dates from the time right after the birth of the universe and used to be made of tiny particles. Scientists believe it could be made of chunks ranging from the size of a tennis ball to the size of a comet or asteroid.

Quark used to be one of these small particles. And it was in those very early days that he got kind of glued to other particles and become dark matter. You might say he went over to the dark side ...

At the very beginning, soon after the Bing Bang, the temperature was over three trillion degrees centigrade. So he was staggeringly hot when first formed, but he's now cold – and cold-hearted. In theory, dark matter is not only invisible but also intangible. However, Quark likes to be tangible. He likes to make an impact.

Scientists and engineers have spent billions building a hugely complex experimental facility in Switzerland and part of what they're looking for is quarks. Imagine how surprised they'd be if they discovered that while they perform obscure experiments under a mountain in central Europe, a real, live Quark is tucked up in bed in a small town in England! It costs at least $1 billion a year to run CERN — and all they need do was spend £50 to buy a train ticket from Euston and then they could shake hands with a real Quark. Of course, they'd be instantly vaporised into their constituent molecules, but think of the honour!

These same scientists believe quarks are smaller than sub-atomic matter. What they don't know, and if Quark has his way never will, is that this particular Quark is also the most powerful. In his natural state, Quark is tiny, but he has a power totally out of proportion to his size. He's responsible for some of the largest explosions in the universe. If he were a criminal, rather than a mindless perpetrator of criminal acts, he'd be very difficult to detect (as scientists at CERN have proved) because he doesn't leave any evidence behind. It's hard to prove he exists at all — although try telling this to Daisy!

To her (and to us) there's a much bigger question than the one being asked at CERN: what *is* becoming? What is Quark trying to do to Daisy and every living soul of the planet? Well, *becoming* is what happens when Quark comes into contact with a chunk of ordinary matter — such as a young alien on a distant planet in the outer reaches of a solar system (one that, naturally, no longer exists). As long as Quark deems the contact pure or complete — judged by a set of arcane rules known only to him — that ordinary matter (the child) is converted into strange matter.

(There's obviously a lot more to it than this; reams and reams of gumf about how the nucleus in every cell in the child's body liberates the energy from the cell, in effect setting of a chain reaction which has been Quark's driving force since his inception, but has unfortunate side-effects for the child.)

Why this has not happened to Daisy is unclear. It could be something to do with cosmic rays, or the earth's magnetic field, or the interaction between positively and negatively charged ions, or strange things called, with startlingly economical use of language, strangelets. Or it could just be down to hormones; that, after all, is the get-out clause of a billion teenagers …

As far as Quark's concerned, we humans are molecules floating through the air, encased in skin. Apart from providing a thirsty entity with a well-deserved drink (we are all at least fifty percent water), he didn't think Earth would detain him for long.

How to get Quark's perspective on this? Let's imagine Daisy is the science reporter for a snazzy TV show; she has an array of lights behind her and cameras to each side of her. There's a sound-operator holding that long, furry mammal-like boom-mic just in front of Quark …

The director is in the booth and whispers into Daisy's earpiece, "we're galaxy-wide in 3, 2 and 1 — take it away." Daisy smiles at the camera that's behind Quark's right shoulder to get her reaction shots to the nuggets she will tease out of him during the interview. Or before he assimilates her into his collective, whichever comes sooner.

"Good evening, everyone and thank you for joining us on Armageddon TV. Tonight, in an exclusive special edition, we are honoured to be joined by Mr Quark — the … well, Mr Quark — how would you describe yourself?"

"Good evening, and thank you so much for inviting me onto your wonderful show. What is Quark? Well, put simply, Quark is everything. Quark is nothing. Quark is everywhere. Quark is nowhere. Quark is infinitely dense. Quark is the basis of every living thing in the universe."

Daisy nods, as if to convey that what Quark is saying makes absolute sense. "Well, one out of six is not bad …" Quark frowns, then regards us with an unsettlingly wolfish grin. For some reason, the image of a small, helpless girl walking through a dark forest wearing a red cape and carrying a basket of food pops into Daisy's head.

She shakes off this troubling picture and continues her questioning with impressive backbone and professionalism. "And what is it that brings you to our beautiful, isolated and entirely innocent planet, Mr Quark."

"Well, that's elementary, my dear — see what I did there? See, I'm a Quark and so ... elementary!"

"Mmmm." Daisy smiles and nods at his extraordinary wit and tries not to appear quite so much like a teeny-tiny bunny sitting in the middle of the road with powerful headlights bearing down on her ... powerful headlights attached to one of those vast road-train transportation trucks.

"Yes, you see I'm a singular singularity. An elementary particle. But, some might say, also the most powerful." He flicks his hand modestly as if to brush away an irritating and insignificant speck of dust — like humanity, for example. "I spend long eternities in an endlessly slow drift through the vast emptiness of space."

The director twiddles a dial in the control booth and in the background we hear the recording of an audience "ah-ing" in sympathy. Daisy nods with forced, and in the circumstances, prudent empathy into the camera over Quark's shoulder.

"And then," Quark continues as he acknowledges the compassion of the imaginary audience, "I come across a place that is just ... ripe for development."

"And that is becoming?"

Quark nods and sighs, taking on the look of a Bond villain, stroking a white cat, as he continues. "Becoming, yes. It is mind expanding. Mind-blowing, you might say." He grins a textbook-evil grin.

Daisy smiles again and steals just the briefest glance at the corner of the studio as she tries to calculate the distance to the nearest Emergency Exit and the time it would take her to get there. She regrets her decision to fight tooth and nail for this assignment when instead she could have been on a beach, or in a fancy restaurant or having all her teeth extracted without anaesthetic.

Quark sighs, "listen — a cloud of dust and gas forms your planet, and with just a few chemical reactions, it creates life that over just a few hundred million years becomes human beings. But everything comes from the original stars. All you are is a collection of atoms arranged in to a human-being pattern for a short span of time. When that time ends, you all *become*, and return to that star stuff. It's beautiful, really."

"So, you're here to supervise that process?"

"Not so much supervise … as carry it out."

"To destroy humanity."

"That's putting it a bit strong."

"Kill. Is that better?"

"Sorry?"

Daisy's found her feet now and is actually pretty wound up by this interview. For some reason, she feels that she has a stake; something not unadjacent to her imminent oblivion, perhaps. "You keep saying, *'become'*: you want Daisy Jacobs and so all of us to *'become'*. That isn't what you really mean though, is it? You want us all to die. You want to kill me and then all the rest of us."

"That's not true at all!"

"No?"

"Certainly not, you will not die, you will *become* —"

"Yeah, as I was saying: you want to kill us."

" — Become *more*, is what I would say. Become *greater*. From being just a girl, you'll— "

"Ah! So you're sexist *and* murderous: 'just a girl'! Thank you for that, Mr Quark. This interview is over." Daisy turns to face the camera.

"There you have it: we're small, we're insignificant, we're made of the ashes of long-dead stars, and some of us are 'just girls'. Is it so surprising that homicidal dark matter should want to terminate our existence?"

She speaks with fervent and heartfelt sincerity into the camera. "Look up into the night sky folks, and you'll see where we came from and where ... eventually, we'll all return. But not now. Our time is not now. Human beings are more than just bags of atoms. Our humanity is a wondrous gift and we will not go down to Mr Quark. We will not sink into a drifting anomaly in space. Right now I feel like a brilliant shooting star, and the most unpleasant surprise — and biggest frustration of Mr Quark's entire existence. Let's try to keep it that way, shall we? Let's fight for the right to live. Thank you and good night."

Chapter 21

ISOLATION WARD

"When will it be on?" Quark does his best to sound casual. "When will what be on where?" I match him for laid-back nonchalance.

"The interview. When will I be on television? I will encourage your family to watch me-you-us."

"It won't ever be on, Quark."

"Why not? I thought I was excellent and I am sure your planet-colleagues—"

"'Planet-colleagues?'" I scoff. "You mean fellow humans? Or just people?"

"Yes, them. I am sure they would feel reassured by my comforting words."

"About their impending doom, you mean."

"About their harmony with the universe. About the extraordinary wonder of being made of the same stuff as stars. I think it will thrill them to know every one of them can become a star."

I pause. "Unfortunately, you're partly right there. Many of them do want to be stars — without doing any work for it at all. But I think they imagine their names *in* lights, rather than their bodies *as* light. I don't think they'd be happy about the kind of star you're planning on turning them into."

"Well, when they watch me on television, I am sure it will reassure them."

"Sorry to disappoint you, but it's not gonna happen."

"The television programme is not yet scheduled?"

"It never existed."

"But I was on it. I was in the studio. I saw the lights, the cameras, the interviewer — actually, she looked quite like you."

"She *was* me. There was no interview. You were in my head — where you do *not* belong and are *not* welcome. And I was … dreaming."

"It did not happen? There was no interview? And I will not be broadcast all around the world on Armageddon Television? But it seemed so real!" Quark sounds petulant.

"Oh, I do hope so! I was dreaming a wonderful dream of your downfall and destruction. Best dream I have ever had. I hope it comes true very soon!"

"Why did you do that? What was the purpose of … deceiving me like that?" Quark asks huffily.

"I didn't deceive you; I had a dream. I'm planning your eviction. If I have my way, you'll soon be history!" This may not be something to brag to Mum and Dad about, it may not be something to shout from the rooftops, it's not something I can honestly say I'm particularly proud of, but it turns out I am a pretty darn good liar!

"You are just a child." Quark scoffs.

"I am not a child! I am very nearly fifteen!"

"Exactly: a child."

"I am a teenager. Almost an adult."

"You are basically a toddler with raging hormones."

"I am n—" I start. Then pause. If I'd had control of my body, I'd have done that frowning-thing and the side-to-side head movement people do when they consider the pros and cons of an argument. "Actually, I see your point. Kind of."

He considers for a moment. "Your thoughts are unusually vivid."

"How would you know? You've never taken the time or the trouble to get to know your victims."

"*Hosts*, Daisy. Hosts. They are not victims."

"Sorry, my mistake: hosts." I fill my inner voice with as much sarcasm as I can put into it. "Hosts … who all happen to die very soon after meeting you."

"You sound awfully bitter."

"Oh, really?! I simply can't imagine why that could be."

"Me neither."

My sarcasm is wasted on him. But Quark's right: I'm like a child facing the overwhelming force of destiny. Stuck in here by myself, how can I hope to stop it? I'm alone and I don't know how to exist in a world where I have no-one to help me. I don't want to be in that world; in this lonely world in my head. I shouldn't have to face such things alone. I'm too young. I know that at my age, I shouldn't want Mum and Dad, but I do. I want my brother and Amy. My God, I'd even settle for Icky! Yeah, to not be on my lonesome, I'd promise not to have mean thoughts about Ellie Watson, even though she's a total—

Reader, you have no idea what it's like being stuck inside one place for a long period of time. Imagine: locked down, in isolation! But now I want my family, and my class and my school and my village and my country — I want the entire world. ME: I want it! And Quark is not, absolutely NOT going to have them. The world will not *become*. Not on my watch!

Starting to fight back helps me to feel less isolated and just a little more in control. I know that if Quark hadn't landed in me, it would have been someone else. And, though I say so myself, I've made a pretty good job of holding him off until now. If he'd landed in the Prime Minister or Mrs Griffin or some random person in London or Cairo, would it all be over for them — or us all? — by now? No way of knowing. And irrelevant anyway, because it was me he landed in. It's me who has to deal with him. And if he gets through me, he'll be on a roll and it could well be over for all of us; for the entire human race.

But I did trick him. And I have stopped him … for the moment at least. Day to day survival is not good enough, though. I'd like the chance to get my GCSEs and A Levels. I want to get a degree in science from a good university. I want an interesting job. I want to make a fool of myself with Connor or some other worthy boy. I want to make mistakes and have the chance to learn from them, rather than have myself (and all of humanity) die from them. I want to look back and reflect (from the distance of many, many years) on what's happened to me in the last week and to tell others about it. Although I think that's more likely to get me confined to a small room with padded walls than any form of official recognition. Who in their right mind would believe this story?!

But Quark believed the TV programme was real. And that's something to remember: he has control of my body and he's running most of my mind. But he doesn't really understand how our minds work. He doesn't think like a human. He's a primordial beast. A moveable black hole. The universe's vacuum cleaner!

Quark's right about something else though: it's true that our brain is incredibly powerful and if we put our minds to work, we can learn new things. We can play tricks.

I think shock and fear may have masked some of what, despite Quark's unwelcome presence, I can still do. It's like my brain, the little I have of it (yes, yes — hilarious), was babbling away after my Quark-seizure with the whole 'an alien's taken over my brain' thing and I couldn't focus. I need to get that focus back. Stop Quark, get my brain back, and then we can all get on with wars, global warming and Love Island.

The fear, the loneliness and the isolation are all good things. Because all are painful. And if I'm in pain, I'm alive. And being alive is a very good thing!

What happened to me after my brain-napping was like one of the panic attacks that grip me. Except, instead of frozen limbs, clouded thoughts, rabbit in the headlights helplessness, I desperately sought to figure out why I had NO control of my limbs — or my senses. There was nothing I could calm down with focussed breathing, so I *shut* down. And my previous experience and that instinctive, almost reflex action, may have been enough to stop him finishing me (and all of us) instantaneously. Imagine that: there's a good side to having a case of the panics! This is a skill they should teach in Ethics in school, because it almost certainly saved my life! It was like a computer re-set. I just stopped thinking altogether.

Under even the most basic laws of physics, what's happening to me *can't* be happening. It's impossible. I know enough to know this. I also know that this *is* happening to me. So I have to rely on myself and the law of the jungle, rather than the fixed laws of science to get out of it. Just imagine if (when!) I get through this; my science thesis at university will be the stuff of absolute legend!

But for the moment I am trying to ignore the fact that it's just me who can save the eight billion people who live on our planet. And I *must* do this before my grade average drops too low ...

Have you ever felt like you're not living up to your potential? That you're not the best you can be? Because of family, friends, work and school, our phones and other technology, sports and other hobbies, our time and attention are always split. It's like doing loads of work for a test, but watching TV or going out with friends the night before. Then your test marks aren't quite what you wanted — say a catastrophic 90% — and you feel deflated. As though you could have done more. So next time you vow to do more work, go that extra mile. Use the extra brain power that's just lying around, doing nothing.

It's not true though. It's a fallacy that we use 10% of our brains. We use it *all*, and we use it all the time. Our brain is always active — even when we're sleeping. (I can definitely vouch for that! These days I do most of my best thinking when Quark is sleeping rather than walking around, living my life!) But our brain is adaptable. I watched one of those TV documentaries a while ago — a real one this time. I think it was the very wonderful Alice Roberts talking about neuroplasticity. She talked about how incredibly adaptable the brain is, how it's constantly changing in response to learning, experience ... or adversity. And if Quark doesn't amount to adversity, I don't know what does!

And I already know I'm capable of this — how else could I have tricked him with the TV interview? And how else would I have created my room, my lair, my *castle*; every English girl's home is their castle, the drawbridge of mine just happens be in my head. I now need to strengthen my fortress and to send out patrols to build up a bigger picture of how to drive this invader out of my territory!

Chapter 22

SLIPPERY

Quark can now officially confirm that eating a lot of food doesn't solve emotional problems! He's seen people do this on television, but it's a lie: eating lots of creamy, salty or fatty food (or in his case, all three) is not a panacea for life's vicissitudes. A little midnight feast had seemed the solution to a day of the greatest confusion and temperamental turmoil.

But he rapidly learnt that Daisy's body was not capable of successfully digesting potato crisps, left-over lasagne, mustard, yoghurt, chocolate milk and—

Actually, that's where the list of food and drink ingested should end. The body Quark inhabits still does not feel as though it is operating at optimum efficiency. And, to be frank, both ends of the body's waste disposal system have had quite a sufficient workout.

He had already made Daisy's mother aware — in no uncertain terms! — that keeping such a wide range of unsuitable food and beverages within reach of an irresponsible teenager is inadvisable.

And he's still angry at Daisy for the dream which led him to believe he was on the verge not just of conquering her, but also of worldwide fame. And he's not entirely convinced the dream was the accident she claimed it to be. He'd found it strangely satisfying to trash her reputation at school with her precious Maths test and foolish head teacher. Although in retrospect, he felt something akin to … guilt? This was an unfathomable reaction for an entity set on destroying every living thing on the planet. Regardless, her response was petty!

However, his way of recovering from the upset of his lack of fame and his day of sensory overload was not Quark's finest hour.

Yesterday had not been pleasant. He'd tried to discuss things with Daisy's father and brother, but it seemed that too much information was unwelcome. Quark doesn't understand this as clearly one of the few things Daisy's body is very good at is expelling — but no, he remembers: do not go into detail about such things. In any case, the eating solution failed during the night and the talking solution failed during the day.

This leaves him to try to sort things out by himself. But actually, that's not true, is it? He doesn't understand what talking to the hand is, but he knows he can talk to the mirror. He does so now. After all, a problem shared is a problem halved. He's sure Daisy will be more than happy to help him ...

"Daisy? You in there? Silly question I know: you very clearly *are* in there!" He essays a grin. "After all, where else would you be?" He pauses, a self-satisfied smirk on Daisy's face. "Please come out, Daisy. We really need to talk."

"What do you want?" comes the huffy response.

"Ah, finally! Where have you been, dear?"

"Wouldn't you like to know? And don't call me dear. I am not now, and nor will I ever be your dear."

"Well, you are touchy, aren't you?"

"I can't imagine why that should be, can you? Unless you also have a vicious alien monster camping out inside you."

"Your opinion is irrelevant in the face of the overwhelming force of nature."

"Nature? There's nothing *natural* about you. You are preposterous. You cannot exist. You are a figment of someone's warped imagination."

"And yet I am here in your head. No one would believe you if you told them. You cannot call the police or the fire brigade or the army. You cannot go running to mummy. There is no one who can help you. The cavalry will not charge over the hill to rescue you."

"Get out of my head!" Daisy yells, in as loud an imaginary, stampy-foot voice as she can summon from the virtual nothingness in which she currently resides.

"Well, strictly speaking I have all of you, not just your head."

"Ha! But you don't, do you? You don't have *all* of me! You don't have the bit I'm in now."

"Only a matter of time though, Daisy. You can't stay in there forever, now can you? Your life is disordered at the moment. In fact, as I have discovered, mankind's entire existence is based on an entirely flawed system of chaos. This cannot last. Order must emerge. You have to come out, eventually."

"Why? Why do I? Us teenagers spend most of our time in dark rooms. And I tell you: order is not gonna emerge from what you call chaos. That's not how being a teen works. All that results from chaos is *more* chaos. And I have no incentive to come out. You're doing the eating. And the over-eating. You're doing pretty much everything in fact. I'm just doing the stuck in a dark room thing…"

"True."

"A room you can't get into."

"Also true … for now. But I will get in. Eventually I will break down your foolish, imaginary door and I'll —"

"If it's so foolish, so lacking in reality, why can't you huff and puff and blow my door down?"

"I — I — I don't know." This conversation is not going how Quark expected. Daisy is not straightforward. In fact, she is slippery and dishonest with him.

"Now, Daisy, let's not argue. We can be honest and open with each other. You can say what you want, you know. But please don't lie. If you lie to me, you are literally lying to yourself."

Chapter 23

WHAT'S YOUR SUPERPOWER?

I am flabbergasted; literally lost for words. "Honest!? We're being honest with each other?"

"Yes, Daisy, of course," my own cheating, lying voice says in a tone so full of cool reason it could only fool a complete simpleton. "You know yourself that honesty is the best policy." It's obvious that Quark's trying to make a sucker out of me, but two can play at this game. So, while I rarely tell outright lies, I can easily tell less than the absolute truth — and maybe, just maybe find another way to trick him.

"Look, Daisy, we got off on the wrong foot," Quark continues in my suddenly all-too weaselly voice that bugs me *so* much. Was I always such a conniving, goody-goody? No — don't answer that. "It's fair to say that things got heated," he says. "A bit out of hand. We lost our sense of perspective. It's not surprising our nerves are frayed. I understand I upset you; it is natural you are concerned."

"Concerned! Believe me, I am way more than concerned. What you're doing is wrong!"

"I understand. After all, I am made of the same stuff that you are, Daisy."

"Well, I know that!"

"You do?"

"Yes. To be precise, you're made of the exact stuff: you *are* me." I continue with increasing anger and frustration. "Because you nicked my body. You took me over. And then you tried to push me out; forever!"

"That was a misunderstanding."

"You didn't mean to clamber inside my head?"

94

"Well … "

"If that's the case why didn't you get out of me as soon as you realised the error of your ways?"

"Well — "

"In fact, why don't you get out of me right now?!"

"It's complicated."

"It's not complicated at all. Just go. Depart. Leave. Skedaddle. There's a whole universe out there for you to explore."

"I know, I have been there. And you can too!"

"Look, I'm fed up of being talked down to by grown ups. And I'm certainly not gonna be taken for a fool by myself! You think I'm stupid? This is *my* body and *my* mind we're talking about. There's nothing complicated about this! Just get out of me!"

As I listen to him speak, I wonder at Quark's quietly correct tone and overly precise choice of language and phraseology. It isn't how I speak. Do my family, friends and teachers really think *this* is me? But how could they think otherwise? Logically, they're not suddenly going to go, "that doesn't sound like Daisy, I reckon she's been kidnapped by an alien body-snatcher; let's help her — quick!"

I reluctantly admit it's my voice. But behind it is a simulation of my personality. A fake. And as I hear my voice speaking again, a feeling of vertiginous uncertainty washes over me: I can't connect to the thoughts and feelings behind it, to the true part of myself that could put a stop to —

"You know that Sherlock Holmes saying?" says Quark.

"Huh?" I'm drawn rapidly from my wandering thoughts and thrown by the sudden non sequitur.

"'Once you eliminate the impossible, whatever remains, no matter how improbable, must be the truth.'"

"Okaaaay."

"Then, it follows that …"

"Sorry? What follows?"

He lets out an exaggerated sigh. "I am here. I am Quark. I am real."

I don't understand where he's going with this, so I give up and go for my own conversational gear change. "How do you know about Sherlock Holmes?"

"Duh! I am in your head, girlfriend!"

"Yuck! Don't get all 'with it' with me, Quark, because, believe me, I have never met anyone more *without it* in my life!"

"I think I may be insulted." My face does indeed look all huffy.

"It's like Dad-dancing: it's excruciatingly embarrassing, you know?"

"Okay, now I am definitely insulted." My arms are crossed and there's a definite pout on my lips.

It still so weird: looking at my own face in the mirror and seeing those eyes — my eyes, I have to keep reminding myself — staring coldly back at me. Quark may learn the basics of being human, but he can't yet mask his true feelings … fortunately. While there's a lightness to his words, and he seems superficially friendly, scratch the surface and there's cold steel in the tone of my voice as he speaks. And there's no hiding the icy chill of my eyes — now definitely more steely-grey than green.

His hostility scares me. It's partly the simple fact that I see me there in the mirror being so two-faced, forbidding and lacking in emotion. I tend wear my heart on my sleeve. I'm not much of a shouter, but I love a good cry and can be a bit over enthusiastic and passionate about people and stuff I care about. (Not that you'd have noticed …) Whereas, this creature in the mirror is joyless and cold-blooded.

I quash the familiar rising panic and swallow back my fear. "You were about to explain your general Quark-ness to me, I think. So — I'm listening," I say with as much of a tone of supreme self-confidence and indifference as I can instil without being able to say the words. "I'm listening with great interest. How can you explain this?"

"I do not think you have realised how lucky you are."

I say nothing. I try very hard to think nothing; to clear my mind entirely; to keep that clarity of thought I know is essential. All around me, people I know — some of whom I love — are going about their lives. My parents go to work, my brother to primary school. For them life continues to be as dull and normal as it ever was in Scuttleford. But normal is subjective. Reality is an illusion. Life is far from normal — even for those who think it is. Life as I knew it — and as they know it — is over. The difference is that they just don't realise it yet.

"All around you are people you know and care about."

That's weird! Has he heard what I was thinking?

"They are all made of the same fundamental matter as you. But you are more than that. You are truly star-stuff now, Daisy. How amazing is that?" He pauses, no doubt expecting me to see the error of my ways. He gets nothing but continuing silence and so continues. "You are extraordinary now. Unique! And yet this is just the beginning of your potential."

"I know!"

"You do? You realise what you can become?" Quark thinks he's made a breakthrough.

"Yes. I have an extraordinary super-power."

"You do, Daisy, you do."

"I can be anything I want to be. There are no limits, imposed by you or anyone else. I can be a doctor like my Mum. An engineer like Dad. I can be a scientist or a brilliant teacher like Mrs Griffin. I can become Prime Minister — and definitely make a better job of it than the one we have now, because I'd help develop a huge planetary shield to stop us being invaded by monstrous, molecule-munching space entities! *I'm a girl*, what's your superpower?"

In the mirror, my shoulders rise and fall as Quark exhales. He ignores my question and his reply is far calmer and more reasonable than mine would have been in the circumstances. "You disappoint me, Daisy." He cooly flicks my hair away from my face as he reaches round to fix it into a ponytail. He does in fact sound sad about the situation.

I hate listening to and seeing myself like this. It's my voice, but the words aren't mine. The real Daisy, the true Daisy is locked inside, while this imposter speaks with my voice! I'm used to my body, the way it moves, the way my face and body react to what I think and feel, to what happens to me. I can sense the way it quirks now when Quark speaks — it's a Quark quirk! I can hear the sheer lack of 'Daisy-ness' as he speaks. It's horrible being disconnected from myself like this!

I know myself, so it's frustrating that no-one else knows I've gone away, as it were. Maybe in my life until now I've been too quiet, too contained and worried about what other people think. Partly that's to keep the panics at bay. Also, I faff about being the youngest in my year and my consequent lack of physical development. And I'm maybe a teeny bit over-concerned about my marks and being the best I can be, academically. But surely what Quark says and how he acts as me is strange? But does everyone just think I'm acting weird (or, weird-er in the case of the Satellites, as they saw me as pretty freaky to begin with)?

I've heard my parents talking and I know it divides them. Dad thinks I'm over-compensating for the panics; Mum's considering intervention: she thinks the bang on my head may have done physical damage and wants me to have an MRI. (I wonder if an imaginary lock on a fictitious door in a hypothetical room would show up on an MRI? And if it did, whether the technician would immediately see it for what it was. "Ah — PSRS: Phantom Stealth Room Syndrome! Take this pill and sit in the corner; you'll be right as rain in no time.") But at the moment Mum and Dad are playing the waiting game and just seeing which way it goes.

But I'm not normal. Not me. Not Daisy. I try to focus, but the 'who' of me is distant and out of reach. I'm too far away from myself to make sense of it all. Usually there's a warm glint in theerd eyes that Quark now looks through so coldly. I'm sure my intelligence is still there. And I seem as strong willed as ever. But I can absolutely guarantee that he looks at the world with less warmth and sees it as being a whole lot less fun than I do, even if he's less panicky about mundane stuff and more certain in his psychopathy!

I tear my gaze away from my own face. I can sense the flush of my cheeks and feel the pounding beat of my heart. Quark's getting frustrated; in fact, really, seriously angry.

"If you are not coming out, then what has happened until now is trivial compared to what will happen."

"What do you mean?" Feelings, like electricity pulse through me. I sense the anger, the rage within him — within *me*. It scares me. It's not something I'm used to; not something I feel comfortable with.

"I will start with your reputation. You will no longer be top-girl, you will fail tests, miss homework deadlines —"

"But you can't do that! That's not who I am, that's not what I do!"

"You seem to forget, Daisy Jacobs, *you* are no longer you. You have ceased to be."

"I can't just give in!" It sounds petty, ridiculous even, but I am top — at *everything*. I'm the youngest, the littlest; I always have been. I'm competitive. And being good at stuff matters to me. It's what calms me. "Why do you to trash my reputation and trample me into the dirt?"

"This *will* happen, Daisy. It is inevitable. You can accept that this is fated for you and go out at the top. Or you can, as you say, see your reputation left in tatters, your relationship with your family and your friends tarnished — and still end up the same way."

It's so hard, seeing myself like this. With Quark manipulating all the parts of me he's in control of. And he's closing in on *all* of me. But I can't give in! He's the one who must fail. I *will* be Daisy again!

Chapter 24

CONSORTING WITH THE ENEMY

"What are you doing, Daisy?"

Quark jumped, as surprised by the sudden interruption as Mrs Griffin had been to see Daisy with her nose pressed to the glass of the school entrance when the head teacher arrived to open the school at 8am. Mrs Griffin had complemented Daisy on her determination to "get her nose back to the grindstone" (whatever that meant) and allowed Daisy into the library to use a school computer to 'finish her homework'.

Now, confused by the jittery reaction of Daisy's metamorphosing body to the sudden interruption, and trying to remain calm despite the body's wildly beating heart, Quark turned to see Ellie Watson leaning over Daisy's shoulder, peering at the computer monitor.

"What's that then?"

"Good morning, Eleanor, I am on the internet."

"I can see that. What are you looking at?"

"I am researching teenagers."

"But we *are* teenagers."

"You are, but I am not."

Ellie Watson goggled at Daisy in confusion.

"I mean, of course I am a teenager too," Quark essayed a laugh which he could not quite bring off and probably appeared awkward. Or maybe just weird. "It is just hard sometimes, is it not? And there are some things about being a teenager I do not quite understand. I mean —" Quark stumbled over the words, unsure how to explain what he needed to find out, but keen to use the knowledge of an expert — a real live teenager (and a girl!) —

rather than a dumb computer interface.

"Oh, I see!" Ellie's face brightened, and she nudged Daisy's shoulder, "doing a little 'research' are you?"

"Yes, that's what I said."

"You're confused about how some things work ..." Ellie nodded at the monitor.

"That is correct."

"Well, if there's anything you need to know, I'm sure I can help you. I'm a woman of the world, if you know what I mean." She nudged Daisy's shoulder again. "Know what I mean?"

It dawned on Quark what Ellie was talking about. "No, that wasn't what I meant. You are talking of sexual intercourse?" he said loudly. "Have you done that?" he asked, suddenly interested in a new line of human knowledge.

There were only a handful of students in the library at this hour, but all of them, plus Mrs Thomas, the librarian, stopped what they were doing. At that moment, a pin dropping would have sounded like the lunchtime gong at a hotel. A very large hotel. Everyone stared, open-mouthed, at Ellie, who flushed wildly. "No, of course I haven't!" She waved her hands in front of herself, patting the air in the universally recognised sign for "FOR GOODNESS' SAKE BE QUIET!" Unfortunately, though Quark had visited large portions of the universe, he'd clearly skipped the bits that would have told him what this gesture meant.

"You are not an expert at sex then?" He continued in a voice that would easily reach the back of the stalls at most large theatres.

"Well, I mean —" Pink bloomed on Ellie's cheeks and she looked far from her usual brash and confident self.

Quark frowned. "Why is this so embarrassing? You don't use the internet for answers about sex, do you? Surely it would be easier to ask your parents or a teacher?" He glanced around, seeing that Mr Ford had just entered the library, "Mr Ford, for example. I'm sure he could help you with sex." Mr Ford gaped at them like a drowning goldfish, then suddenly seemed to remember he had to be somewhere else at this precise moment and performed an about turn that would have melted the heart of the sternest regimental sergeant-major. He left the library at twice the speed he'd just entered it.

This gave Ellie a moment to compose herself. "But you were doing the same just now. Looking up information on sex and how the body works."

"That was nothing to do with—"

"And then you shout stuff out across the room. Accusing me of being a tramp or something."

"I never said you were sleeping rough! Although, I wondered if you were sleeping <u>arou</u>—"

"Stop!" Ellie shouted, no longer caring about the disturbance they were creating. She picked up her bag and looked back over her shoulder as she turned to leave. "That's it, Daisy Jacobs, I was wondering if you needed someone to talk to as you've been in so much trouble recently, but you're turning into an even bigger crackpot than you were before." She turned on her heels, marched to the door and left the library.

Quark blinked at the students who'd watched Ellie's exit with rapt attention and who now turned to look at Daisy as if wondering what further entertainment this library visit would bring them. He realised this had been a missed opportunity. Ellie — or Amy — was *exactly* the kind of person to talk to about what was going on with Daisy's body at the moment.

He played back the conversation in his head. He could 'see' everything that had happened to him so far on earth by accessing his personal Netflix-like memory bank — one of those useful extra senses that us backward humans have never mastered. Reviewing his interaction with Ellie, he realised where he had gone wrong — and how he could get her back on his side. He'd wait for her to calm down and then ask her advice again. Once she understood, Quark knew Ellie would be more than happy to help in the development of 'new Daisy' …

Chapter 25

WHAT!

"Y ou're friends with who?!"
"Eleanor Watson. A delightful child. You have her wrong — she is much misunderstood. And 'I' am not her friend, *you* are. She really likes new Daisy."

I'd heard the goss about their over-loud conversation. And, far from ending their would-be friendship, the scandal's boosted Ellie's reputation and she's now even more popular with Scutttleford's girls — and boys. So 'I' now have a new buddy!

"Icky is not misunderstood. I understand her all too well. She's a trouble-maker and a bully."

"She is a nice girl. Kind. Thoughtful."

"Wait! There must be some misunderstanding. I thought we were talking about Icky Ellie Watson."

"How can you call Eleanor a bully and then refer to her as Icky? Does that not strike you as double standards?"

"She's mean to people and when I tried to stop her, she was mean to me too."

"It is an act, Daisy."

"Well, it's a highly impressive act. I was certainly convinced that she was a full on b-word."

"B-word? There are many words that begin with 'b' — for example, bougainvillaea, bounder, buzzard —"

"Quark, I don't need a rundown of every word that begins with 'b'! And that wasn't what I meant. Icky is *not* a buzzard!"

"Well, why not say what she is?"

"I try not to cast aspersions on other girls. But Ellie loves to gossip and the slightest hint of trouble can easily become a fully-fledged scandal by the time she finishes with it. She wallows in the chance to be vindictive the way a hippo wallows in mud. Except, worst luck, she's far from hippo-like in every other conceivable way."

"I did notice that. She is tall — taller than you. Is that why you are jealous?"

"Me — jealous?! It's not difficult to be taller than I am and I'm not at all worried about being petite. Sure, she's long-legged, rangy — all sharp features and shiny skin. She's catwalk-model-slender, except for —"

"Yes?"

"Well, you'll have noticed Ellie's … well developed."

"In what way?"

"Quark, you're so dense sometimes!" I pass on, not wanting to explain further to him the ins and outs of the female form. "I agree that Ellie is just ridiculously perfect — apart from her attitude, of course. And her personality. I mean, she's got that whole model-girl look going on — as if she channels the latest 'in' designer, even when she's wearing a school uniform. But then, looks aren't everything, are they? I mean, if it wasn't for her overall Icky-ness, I'd kind of like her."

"And yet you do not …"

"No …" My own thoughts confuse me. What is it? I mean, we have different friends, different interests, and a totally different way of going about things. She seems so confident. And I know she's funny, and sometimes says things in class that make her sound almost intelligent — but then it's like she makes a joke or pulls a face to hide the fact. But when had the not-quite-hitting-it-off with Ellie begun?

"You should let her in."

"In? You want to put her in my head too!"

"No, I mean be her friend."

"Let Icky be my friend?!"

"No more Icky, Daisy. Ellie is a good person; she is just afraid of you. In awe of you."

If I could have spluttered, I would have done. "Of me?!" Where on earth does he get this idea? I've never heard anything so ridiculous! "She bullies me, how can she be afraid of me?"

"Because you are funnier than she is. Cleverer — the cleverest girl in the school, she said. Plus, you are more popular."

I shake my inward head again. "No, you've got that wrong. She's *way* more popular. She's super confident, gorgeous and she can be funny; sometimes what she says is a bit cruel, but it's often hilarious," I admit with some reluctance.

"Tell her."

"What?"

"Tell her she is funny. Tell her she is pretty. Tell her you admire her." Quark pauses. "You are jealous of her, as she is of you. Talk to her; do not hide your light under a bushel."

I mentally frowned, "okay, no bushels, got you." Oh, to be a normal Year 10 girl again. I'd give anything to just sit at the table in the very heart of my family or to spend just five minutes with Amy. Hell, I'd even hug Icky Ellie … well, no — maybe I wouldn't give *anything*.

I don't think that will be possible anyway, because it seems Ellie goes nowhere without her Satellites circling around her. That creates a distance that's difficult to bridge —

"Maybe. And it gives her an audience she can work without reference to you."

Then suddenly, out-weirding all the unearthly things that have happened in the last few days, I hear footsteps! Not on the floor of my bedroom. But *inside* my head! I race as fast as my imaginary legs can carry me over to the door of my room. Thankfully, it's still locked.

But the familiar fear bubbles up inside me, dousing the small flame of hope that I'd allowed to flicker. The footsteps stop outside and there's a sudden rattling at the door. Quark has found my room

"Huh?" I've been so caught up in the closest approximation to a genuine conversation I've had in, what — over a week? — that I was suckered by Quark's veneer of chumminess. I allowed myself to have unguarded thoughts for the first time since that first meeting in the mirror. He read me then and I just allowed him to do it again. Well, no more! Now he knows where my room is, I have to be extra vigilant. I can't control when these encounters take place; I can't stop him from facing me in the mirror or just talking to me in quiet moments as and when he pleases. But I can be ready for him; and I can shut down my thoughts to block his access.

"Good try, Quark. That was close, but no cigar, I'm afraid. For now, you're welcome to Ellie Watson — whether or not she's Icky. I'll sort that relationship out when you're gone."

I must be on my guard and ready for him becoming tricksy — and more human. And I need to remember that if Quark's losing some of his alien-ness and becoming a bit more human, then maybe I can use that to *my* advantage.

Chapter 26

MOPE, MOAN, GRUMP & FROWN

Nope, this isn't the name of a long-established firm of lawyers. It's a summary of Quark's state of mind after almost two weeks spent on a task that would normally take seconds.

He can't believe it!

Just think what he could have done in that time: laid waste to continents; wiped out entire civilisations; decimated whole planets!

That's been the history of Quark. Although in normal circumstances (if anything is normal about Quark) he's a strong contender for the title of the smallest thing in the universe, as you'll already appreciate, he is anything but inadequate — especially in his own mind. After all, he's the singularity usually found at the centre of a black hole.

I won't insult you by going all science-y about this, as you obviously know that black holes form when matter condenses into such a small space that gravity takes over, and forces the matter to be squished into a single point of infinite density.

That's what the laws of physics say, at least. Although, admittedly, the current laws don't have a great deal to say about singularities that do their squishing away from the black hole motherlode. In fact, general relativity and quantum mechanics are strangely silent on the whole subject of squishing. Which is surprising, I'm sure you'll agree. After all, loud explosions, mass destruction and scenes of people screaming and waving their arms uselessly whilst trying and failing to avoid their imminent extinction are the very backbone of some of Hollywood's most esteemed output. Just think what such things would add to science lessons!

Scientists think they'll gain a greater understanding of black holes when they come up with one great, over-arching theory of relativity, quantum mechanics, quantum gravity, and probably the ultimate preparation method for the perfect cup of tea.

Until then, Quark's personal history of havoc and annihilation will guide us. His track record makes Attila the Hun seem like Attila the Huh? Here's just a tiny sample of his Greatest Hits (excuse the pun) ...

The Strathairns? You *should* have heard of them by now; and if it hadn't been for Quark, you undoubtedly would. However, way back when bits of rock and offcuts of the Moon were just beginning to coalesce into what would eventually become the Earth, Quark happened across them. That was a dark (though admittedly brief) day for the Strahairns.

They had been a gloriously rich and technologically advanced race that, over countless millennia, had spread their wise, open-hearted enlightenment across whole parsecs of their particular galaxy. Quark exterminated them — and snuffed out their whole, cuddly notion of planet-dom, eradicating the attainments of one of the universe's most sophisticated cultures in rather less than an Earth afternoon. Just as for teenage boys everywhere, for Quark the moment had been sweet, but over all too quickly to provide lasting satisfaction ...

At the opposite end of the spectrum to the Strathairns, the Gnarg had been a warrior race with a fearsome reputation that held an entire galaxy in their thrall. There had been twenty-six billion of them with more vast fleets of the fastest, most armed-to-the-teeth space-cruisers than even the geekiest gamer could ever imagine. Their ships had scary laser cannons in places where most planet's spaceships didn't even have places.

And how long did the mighty battle between Quark and the Gnarg last? Barely longer than a decent full English breakfast.

The Whaplish, Exele, Vicia, Zantede, Deflexa, Glydia … all of these and literally countless other small isolated planets, complex solar systems, federations of star clusters and random space ships that Quark had happened upon were liquidated (in some cases liquidised); simply reduced to rubble and wiped from the universe. Most of them in a time span somewhere between the blink of an eye and the length of a football match (without the extra time, let alone penalties).

And in fourteen whole days, what had Quark achieved on Earth?

A C2 detention, a note home to Daisy's parents, a severely upset stomach and the beginnings of the trashing of Daisy's status as a goody-goody.

He'd thought he was finally getting somewhere with the Ellie conversation. Distracting Daisy, with news of her sudden and unexpected contact with Eleanor Watson, allowed Quark to conduct a sneaky attack. At first, Daisy failed to notice Quark insinuating himself deeper into her subconscious. He almost made it! His hand was reaching for the handle on her imaginary door when Daisy saw through his ruse and made sure he was still well and truly shut out.

But maybe his own burgeoning humanity was what would lead him to outwit Daisy Jacobs and enable *all* of humanity to join the glorious history of *becoming*.

He'd continue to use the most basic human traits: deceit, double-dealing, trickery — and gossip. It wasn't the glorious, technicolour victory he'd envisaged, and after vanquishing the mighty Gnarg, it seemed somewhat petty to focus on how he could further ruin the reputation of a single human girl. But as Quark had learned in History only the previous day, even the most infamous tyrants began their evil empires with small victories.

And soon, it would not be just Daisy Jacobs' reputation that would go down in the annals; the whole human race would be *history*!

Chapter 27

BREAKFAST OF CHAMPIONS

The smell of toast wakes me. Toast and Dad's morning pot of coffee.

I realise this is something new in my current existence: it's definitely the aroma of breakfast that wakes me. It wasn't a real sleep, obviously, more like an extended loss of focus. Then I remember where I am — still. But there's at least a hint of something I thought had gone forever. Everything else is unchanged: although I've just woken up, *my body* is already here; already sitting at the table.

This has happened a lot. I guess impending doom really tires me out! I'm dressed, ready for school and having breakfast, yet I have no memory of and took no part in getting out of bed, showering, dressing, or coming downstairs. But there's my bowl of cornflakes on the table, Mum and Dad to either side, radio mumbling with traffic news, and my brother in full Lego Star Wars mode opposite me — all of this morning blabber competing for my attention. Although Quark is absolutely silent, my home is loud, hectic, chaotic — a full sensory overload. And I 'woke' because I smelt toast and coffee.

Now, what would I give for a *taste* of that toast and strawberry jam. I mean, I know my body will be having it soon — Mum just put a plate in front of me — but I won't actually taste it; I won't get to savour the melty-butteriness of the toast or the tangy, tart sweetness of the jam. So, no jam for real-Daisy. Add that to the (long) list of the things that are just *so* not fair! Because I have no access to my sense of taste, which is weird because I can most definitely smell it. And that makes it worse. I can see it, I can smell

110

it, and, dimly at least, I can feel it being eaten, but, although I know just how good it tastes, I can't actually taste it now.

But I couldn't do this yesterday; I could smell nothing then. What did I have for dinner? Did I tell you? Could have been … pasta, maybe? Nope, can't remember. And I definitely can't remember having toast yesterday morning. So this is an ability I didn't have yesterday.

Does it mean I'm coming back to myself? I certainly hope it doesn't mean I'm becoming more Quark and less Daisy! I sense no more of him than before. He got as far as my door yesterday and he's still in control, obviously, but no more than he was yesterday and maybe — just maybe — a little less.

Thinking about it, even the sleeping is weird because, technically, I'm not awake in the first place. But I guess Quark has to sleep, so at night when my body shuts down and everything's still and quiet, I just drift away into the dark unknown. Although I think he *is* asleep and I need a bit of downtime too, this is when I need to be most alert. I *must* be careful; I need far less sleep now, so I get what I need when he's asleep. Not just because of the danger to *me*, but also because, once I've napped, that's when I can be the biggest threat to *him*.

If I'm not careful, whole days and nights drift by. I try to get a grip on the days Quark lives on my behalf, but sometimes I get only images — and they are seriously disturbing. I know I seem distant to Mum and Dad; that I'm not as close as usual to Amy and I'm somehow closer to Ellie and the Satellites — to the probable horror of Amy! And I'm pretty sure while Quark's trying to kill me, he's not killing my schoolwork in the way I usually do!

I'm constantly thrown off balance. I'm not seeing, and often am barely even aware of everything that's going on. It's like watching the reflection of someone else's life in an old and warped mirror, or trying to watch a 3-D film on one of those ancient TVs that entire streets of people supposedly sat round to watch the Queen's Coronation on. But I want to live myself, not be an observer of this pale imitation! I don't want to see what happens in class, I want to be the one who answers the questions. I don't want to hear what Amy says. I want to gossip with her about our lives. I don't want to see one of Mum's fantastic meals on the table in front of me, I want to taste it — and to talk to Mum, Dad, and even Luke, while we eat!

"Penny for your thoughts," Mum says, breaking what must have been, for our family, quite a long silence. Normally all of us are talking at once, chatting about the day to come, what we saw on TV last night, what's just been on the news or in the paper — in fact, about anything and everything. We're normally a chatty, gossipy family, always debating stuff, none of us ever seeming to be short of something to say.

Not today, though. So — a penny? I'd give *way* more. In fact, I'd give everything I have, including my second-hand MacBook and Justin Bieber download collection (just joking!) to know what's on my mind! To know what Quark's thinking right now; what he's planning. Who knows, maybe it's nothing. He's certainly not in a hurry to answer Mum.

An Englishwoman's home is her castle, that's what I thought. And here I am in my home, *my castle*, where I should be most secure. Where I should be safe from the panics. But there's no comfort in these familiar surroundings. Instead, the atmosphere is tense and edgy in this warped version of reality. So even when Mum pulls my body into our usual early morning hug, even in the warmest and safest place in the entire world, I feel trapped, insecure, uncertain, afraid.

Outside of me, Quark continues to live my life and continues to act in a way I never would. I can't help thinking what he's doing now sounds a lot like a deeeeep, moooooody and oh, so teenagery silence.

"Stop acting like a teenager, Daisy!" Dad thinks so too.

"I am a teenager!" he replies. Luke laughs and covers his mouth when Dad gives him a mock-stern look.

"Yes, but you don't usually act like one. You've been playing up to the stereotype recently. It's not like you and it doesn't suit you." Dad certainly has his stern, poker-face on this morning.

Inside I'm screaming: THAT'S BECAUSE I'M NOT ME!

"You okay?" Mum asks, her forehead crinkling into a frown as my parents take on the good cop/bad cop routine that I'm experienced enough to recognise immediately. It's funny to see it from the outside. What's not so amusing is the anxiety that's behind my eyes too, back where I'm still stuck. How am 'I' going to get out of this?

"Yes, I am just hunky-dory, thank you for asking." Quark is even starting to get the flippant tone. It's like he is the one who is *becoming*, but not as he'd have hoped. For all the world, it sounds like he's *becoming* a teenager!

But it's like I'm living in my own shadow: since when did I say stuff like 'hunky-dory'? Except, of course, it's obvious when that happened.

"Daisy, this is so unlike you." Mum's unease is showing. "Honestly, I don't know what's come over you lately."

I guess, from their point of view, I'm just acting teenagery. Higher up the scale than they're used to from me — hence the hesitant mention of family therapy I overheard last night — but maybe not extreme enough for serious concern ... yet.

My hard-earned goody-goody reputation is being slowly trashed, but Quark hasn't blown his cover. Is that a good thing? Or would it be best for me if I really stood out from the crowd?

I can hear Mum and Dad, but I can't *really* see them. My TV is a bit fuzzy. I'd like to think that's due to Quark's interference or because I need an upgrade. But I think it's due to my weepiness. I can cry, even on the inside! I'm growing up and I know I'm not supposed to need Mum and Dad now, but I really miss them. You know what it's like: when you're practically fifteen, whether you're a boy or a girl, you try to be big, strong and independent, but sometimes just knowing Mum and Dad (or your own particular significant grown-up) is there makes a massive difference. Right now I miss their common sense that I used to pretend to ignore, but would really, deep-down listen to. And I want the comfort that actually being *with* them brings me.

The bit of me I still inhabit works easily and well, but it's only a *tiny* part of my true self. I want *all* of me. But at the moment, Quark has most of what makes me Daisy Jacobs. He's everywhere in me, not just in my head, but in my veins too — and throughout my body. Like a disease running through my blood. A head cold. A virus. A potentially deadly infection. My own personal pandemic! Ridiculous that the thought hadn't occurred to me until now. Because two can play at that game. Maybe what's been happening to him in this last, what?— day or so? — maybe that's me: my humanity coming out in him. Corrupting him like he's corrupting me. He's infected me; so why can't I have the same effect on him? Why can't I give *him* a virus?

I've been in despair about my impending death, but as this idea radiates through my tiny little mind, I feel a faint glow of optimism kindle within me.

Chapter 28

BIRDS, BEES AND SUBSTANCE ABUSE

How is Quark feeling? Furious — again! — that's how. It comes from 'Daisy' not doing as she's told.

"Come on, Daisy," Dad cajoles, "your turn to help me with breakfast."

"No! I do not want to. I am reading in this news magazine about a female singer, seen out in public with a female sport's star. It is quite interesting and the suggestion is they both might be gay — like Amy Porter."

"You don't usually read magazines like that," said Daisy's Mum. "It's all a bit prurient, isn't it — delving into people's lives like that? What does it matter who does what with whom? And who's really interested, anyway?"

Quark's fury subsides, momentarily. This subject is even more interesting than impotent rage. "I think human sexual relations are fascinating."

Luke laughs. "Sex!" he said in that 'oooooohhh' way that ten-year-olds have. His parents — and Quark — give him a look and a sad shake of the head.

"That's as maybe," said Mr Jacobs, "but if you're not going to help me in the kitchen, you ought to finish your homework."

"That is unjust! This is just so typical of a patriarchal society. You are picking on me to do so-called female work, whilst the young male person," Quark points at Luke who regards Daisy as if she were speaking a foreign language, "is just sitting there on his ar—"

"Daisy!" Daisy's dad took a deep breath. "I don't even know where to begin with that nonsense. Let's see: I'm cooking and I'm a man. Next, that 'male person', your brother, Luke — remember? — a) has just finished tidying, and b) is not just sitting there on his ... bottom, he is actually doing *his* homework."

Daisy's parents are increasingly worried about her, because — outwardly at least — nothing has changed. She's their girl. There's less sparkle in her eyes and more slump in her shoulders, but ignore her utterly abhorrent behaviour and she's the same Daisy. Being parents, they're having a hard time discounting so called bad behaviour, though.

Daisy's mum stepped in, forestalling any argument and taking over the role as peacemaker. Daisy's parents frequently tag-team in this way. "Why not at least lay the table, Daisy, then you can finish the rest of your homework before you go to school."

"That is *so* not fair! I have a hard day at school to come and want to sit and enjoy my social commentary magazine."

Her parents overlap. "Social commentary!" (Dad.) "How long has *Glam* been social commentary?" (Mum.)

"Why are you suddenly so argumentative?" asked her mum.

"I'm not arguing, mother, I am simply explaining why I am right."

"'Mother'!" Daisy's mum spluttered, "since when did you call me that?"

"Since now. There is too much informality around here. I think it must be something to do with unruly hormones."

Too surprised to comment at all, Daisy's mum and dad just stared at their daughter in open-mouthed amazement.

A little while later, after they'd eaten the breakfast that Daisy refused to help her father prepare, her parents silently considered that while science might explain why so many teenagers exhibit uncontrollable mood swings and inexplicable temper tantrums, it doesn't make everyday communication with individual teenagers any easier. They know from very recent experience of 'peak Daisy', as her dad had taken to calling his favourite girl-child's current behaviour, that Daisy did not seem to greatly appreciate displays of anger, worry or even warmth from them. On the contrary, all of a sudden, any overt emotion freaks her out.

As to her irrational decision-making, little did they know it had barely started and what was to come would freak *them* out …

"What shall we do at the weekend, Daisy?" asked Daisy's mum.

"I would like to try animal flesh, mother."

"What?!"

"I mean … meat. A cow's bottom."

"Cow's —? You mean rump steak?" She said over Luke's sniggers.

"Indeed mother, that is exactly what I mean."

"But Daisy, you're a vegetarian."

"I am?" Quark paused in momentary confusion. "Of course I am!" he said, recovering (for him) quite swiftly. "I simply want to … to expand my repertoire. Wanna try new things, new experiences." Daisy's voice seemed to stumble over the "wanna," as though this too was something she wanted to try out.

"Really?"

While the universe is only 13.8 billion years old, it doesn't act in the random way of a child, or handle the maelstrom that is the world of the human teenager. Though young, the universe is structured and logical. This explains why Quark, who, of course, is as old as the universe, struggles to cope with the chaotic contents of Daisy's head — let alone what's going on in her body. The universe is not emotional. And Quark is in the very early days of learning how to make decisions. At the moment there's not so much of the weighing up of pros and cons; he's more of the school of random, scatter gun, say the first thing that comes into your head approach.

"I think I may be gay as well."

There was an explosion of cornflakes as Luke went into paroxysms of coughing. Mrs Jacobs, her GP training allowing her to remain utterly unperturbed, calmly patted her son's back, while cooly regarding her daughter.

"Is this some more social commentary on human sexual relations?" asked Daisy's father, who received an A-Grade scowl in return.

Daisy's mum poured oil on troubled waters once more and continued to talk as if Daisy's non sequitur was the most obvious conversational gear change she'd ever heard. "Really? So you're coming out as a carnivore and gay? And all before — " she checked her watch — "0755?"

Quark wondered how humans could trust emotions. Emotions have no basis in logic; they barely even have any basis in reality. In fact, humanity tries to bend reality to fit their version of the way their emotions tell them it should be. After all, why trust logic, mathematical precision and rigorous scientific theory, when you can base key life decisions on the alignment of the stars or what the chemical balance of your hormones tells you is for the best? Even though tomorrow they might tell you something completely different. Quark, for example, has no real clue as to why, when he was feeling so perky when he got up, now felt as though he was on the verge of an explosion.

"Why have you suddenly decided to be gay?" Daisy's mum asked.

"Oh you know. I thought I'd just give it a try." Actually, Quark had no idea why he threw the last two conversational grenades into the breakfast mixer.

"'Give it a try'? Based on what? You can't just randomly decide to give it a try, Daisy. That's not logical."

"Why not?" And why, Quark thought, would a supposedly clever human adult, who not only must have at one stage in her life gone through adolescence, but who also makes a living in medicine, think that logic would have any impact whatsoever on the decision-making capability of a teenager?

"Sexuality is not just something you pull on and off like a party dress or a pair of trousers."

"Oh …"

"Darling, if you're telling us you are gay, that's fine. We love you. It doesn't matter what you are or what you do, we love you."

"Right. That is good." Quark shifted in his seat, hoping that this love talk would not lead to more hugging. Physical contact made him *so* uncomfortable!

"But don't feel pressured into it. You don't have to be anything or anyone you don't want to be. You don't have to be anything or anyone but you." Daisy's mum paused and considered, exchanging meaningful looks with Mr Jacobs on the other side of the table. With these two, a look, a few mouth twitches, some head tilts and a nod could constitute an entire conversation.

"We know you are fourteen, sweetheart — nearly fifteen," Daisy's dad added swiftly, knowing how sensitive she was on the matter — "and that you need to be allowed to make your own mistak— decisions, but we wouldn't be doing our job if we didn't try to help you. To advise you."

Her mum nodded. "This isn't like you, my love. We're just worried that's all. We expect a few bumps through the teenage years, but recently it's like a stranger's moved in with us. You're like a completely different person."

Mr Jacobs continued. "You're acting ... well, a little out of character ..."

"Really?"

"Is there something you want to tell us?"

"You mean apart from wanting to be a carnivore?"

It's Mrs Jacobs turn. She smiled, "yes and trying out being gay. Is anything wrong — at school, for example?"

Quark frowned. "I do not think so." He is a girl. He is a teenager. But he thinks he's missing a few connections along the way and so may be failing at simply being human.

"Well, your father and I will, of course, support you in any lifestyle choices you may make, Daisy. But you're not yourself, and these decisions seem quite sudden and arbitraryss."

"You do not trust me? You think I am a teenage girl and I will not act in my own best interests?"

"No, Daisy, that's not what we're saying at all. But the detentions, the answering back — at school and at home — failing tests, the obstreperous attitude and now this; it almost seems as though you're randomly picking things to try out or experiment with. We're worried you might be using — that you might have tried —" Mrs Jacobs paused, as if wondering whether to go further. "We're just worried about you, sweetheart."

"You think I have tried some sort of pharmaceutical, is that it?"

"No!" Mrs Jacobs claimed, her eyes seeking those of her husband, who silently nodded and mouthed, "go on ..." She sighed and did so. "You haven't ... have you?"

Both parents stared anxiously at the being they still assumed was their daughter as the silence lengthened and become uncomfortable.

"How little you know me," Daisy said, finally.

Both parents gasped in relief. "Well, in any case, I think it's a bit early in the day for life-changing decisions," Mrs Jacobs said with a tight smile as she set off upstairs to get ready for work.

Chapter 29

TEENAGE DIRTBAG

Inside, I'm already curling up in shame, wanting to hide away from the conversation with Mum and Dad. I just want to "la, la, la" over the top of it and pretend it's not happening, but I'm scared this is just the start; I bet there's loads worse to come.

And I can't stop it.

I am so *not* gay! I mean, honestly who cares — Mum and Dad don't and would love me whether or not I was. But the fact is, I'm not. Amy's my best friend, she's gay. I hadn't mentioned this before Quark outed her to you, because why should I and why would I? What does it matter? It's not relevant at all. She is wonderful, I love her dearly, she's gay, I'm not. So what? It's no big deal. She's my bestie and that's that. I don't want, as Quark said, to 'try the experience', thank you very much!

And I don't want a steak either!

Quark has now finished *my* breakfast and is preparing to leave for school.

Mum comes back downstairs dressed and ready to go to the surgery for the start of her morning practice. She's wearing the dress she bought last time we shopped together. It's short-sleeved, asymmetrically cut, knee-length in soft blue linen. It's also … well, close fitting. She'd said it was great for her job as a GP — "business like, but comfortable and very stylish". I'd not been quite so sure, thinking that though she looked great, the dress emphasised her curves maybe a little too much for work.

She hesitates as she reaches the bottom of the stairs, and as soon as I see her again — through Quark-controlled eyes — I realise that, if anything, I feel almost worse now. The world is utterly tantalising. I'm sure I can see more clearly, but I still can't touch or fully sense anything that's happening around me. But this is Mum. I *so* want to talk to her myself — *as myself*. I want to tell her what's going on and have her make the bad stuff go away — like she used to when my problems were manageable and not planet-sized. More than anything, I wish she'd just hug me so I could feel her arms around me, pulling me in to the all-encompassing embrace that takes *everything* else away.

But it's not to be, because I can't take part in my own reality. I'm a mere observer, a powerless passenger forced to remain an outsider as my life ebbs away. I know that outside the window the blackbirds are squabbling like — well, like stroppy teenagers. I know that the orange juice on the table before me is sweet and tangy. I can see the flowers Mum's brought in from the garden and placed in the Moorcroft vase in the centre of the kitchen island, and I can vaguely appreciate a dim version of their brilliant colour, but I can't revel in their early summer scent.

I want to tell her this. But she just adds to the torment: she gives me a brilliant smile as her eyes meet 'mine', holds her arms out wide and gives me a twirl, "what do you think, Daisy?"

Quark looks up, tuts, shakes his head, sighs dramatically and says, "did anybody lie to you and say it looks good?"

Uh, oh — awkward! There are three audible intakes of breath. Mum bursts into tears. Even Luke looks stunned, and he wouldn't know fashion if it rose up and stamped all over his Lego.

"Daisy, how could you?!" Dad asks, shocked to near apoplexy. There's a pained expression in his eyes, and his cheeks are red with a fury I have never seen. "I can't believe you —" He shakes his head, looks at me, and then turns and walks over to embrace mum. "Apologise to your mother, Daisy Jacobs," he says.

"Using my full name — now that has *got* to be bad news!" Quark says with a sarcastic smirk.

"That's it! Leave now, go to school. We'll talk about this later."

"Why? What have I done wrong? It really does not suit her, does it? I mean, the words 'mutton' and 'lamb' spring to mind."

"DAISY! ENOUGH! GO! RIGHT NOW!" Dad's positively screaming at me, his words like nails hammered into my heart. But he's not talking to *me* at all, is he?

I hear myself give a heavy, exaggerated sigh. As if it's all too much. As if my brain can't cope with even the tiniest extra smidgen of angst Dad is imposing on *me*. As if I might explode with the sheer unfairness of it all. And I must, reluctantly, admit I'm in two minds (no irony intended) about this. Firstly, this is *not* at all how I behave: I am reasonable and usually thoughtful and considerate of other people's point of view. And would in no way diss Mum's dress, even if Quark is — sort of — right about the cut not really suiting her gorgeous curvy figure. I'd tried to find a subtle way to tell her so in the department store where she bought it, and either Quark's picked up a hint of this from somewhere in my brain, or he's being stereotypically teen — and atypically me — because there's no way I would hurt her feelings like he's just done. For all I know, he could have taken lessons in advanced brat-dom from Ellie Watson!

But secondly, there's just a teeny bit of me (only a fraction of the me that is still me) that thinks he's starting to get the hang of this teenage thing. Clearly he went *way* too far and came over like an utter, dragged up cow, but right until that moment … good skills, Quark. He may not be becoming more 'me', but he's getting the whole Teenage Dirtbag thing down to a T!

I mean, come on, you know what we're like — we're unpredictable. We keep the grown-ups on their toes. We need to keep their minds active, thinking of ways to surprise them, shock them, and (my personal favourite) embarrass them. I love Mum and Dad with all my heart, but gently winding them up is one of life's great pleasures. Until Quark arrived on the scene, I never pushed it too far, and I have to say, becoming a lesbian carnivore is a tad too far for me, but up to then he was getting the gist of it.

Going through the whole hormonal roller-coaster thing is a nightmare. So sharing your problems with people who love you is natural. They're so much older than us that I reckon they'd just ossify if we weren't around to keep them young.

If they don't both keel over from heart-attacks in the next few minutes, the shock of this morning's little episode may have added years to their lives. Their hearts are probably racing as though they've been jogging instead of eating jam and toast!

My normally unflappable mum is clearly upset. She looks pinched and tired and nothing like her usual staunch and resolute self, but then who is nowadays ...

More than that, though, she looks almost haggard with worry. Looking at your mum and seeing her tired or upset is one thing; seeing outright fear is quite something else. This is *Mum*; she's practically Wonder Woman! She's really strong, so it's extra frightening to see *her* look scared! There's no way in the world she can guess what's happening to me — because that is literally out of this world. But I know she realises it's something serious. I wish she could help, but I know with absolute certainty she can't. Frankly, the fact that she'll be there for me if and when I get out of this is comfort enough right now.

Chapter 30

ME, MYSELF & I

"You were very rude to Mum, Quark," said the voice in Daisy's head.

Quark sighed. The girl will not shut up with her incessant nagging!

They're in the bathroom again, looking into the mirror. Quark ignored Daisy as he swished her hair from her eyes, tilting her head this way and that and pouting at the reflection. He still doesn't respond.

"You hurt her feelings," Daisy continued.

Quark said nothing.

"Okay, I get that, in some warped way, trashing my reputation is a strategy; one way of — as you see it — achieving your evil aim. It won't work; it makes me sad, but it also makes me determined to fight you harder. And I see why you think it could be an effective strategy with a person who some might see as ... a goody-goody, maybe a bit of a rule-follower."

This time there's a slight grunt from Quark.

"But insulting my Mum is way, way below the belt, Quark. There have to be rules in this and that comment was both hurtful and wrong."

Quark thought Daisy was making a reasonable point, but can in no way admit this, because ... because why? Because it would be too straightforward. It would be to admit guilt; an error. A fault in his stars, to quote a book that's being discussed in English lessons at school. And he doesn't think accepting a reasonable argument is what a teenager would do. So he grunted again.

"Quark, have you nothing to say in your defence?"

"Gwalgf", he said, and spat out toothpaste. "I am brushing *your* teeth, Daisy. Trying to take care of *your* body."

"Oh, sorry, thank you."

There's silence as Quark rinsed the toothpaste away and dried Daisy's hands.

Quark ..."

"Yes?"

"Why?"

"Why what?"

"Why are you brushing my teeth?"

"Because we had pasta and garlic bread for dinner."

"I know — fettuccini is my favourite, and I didn't even get to taste it! Was it good?"

"It was nutritious."

"Nutritious! *Alfredo* and garlic bread have nothing to do with nutrition! It's carb-overload. It's comfort on a plate. It's the very definition of happy-tummy food."

"Well, I ate the food and my — your — stomach is now full."

"Mum's cooking is wasted on you! Like Dad's curry over the weekend — and his veggie chilli too; I bet you've had that recently with the guacamole he makes — was that good?"

"I have no recollection. It is all food. Sustenance. Fuel."

"Fuel! Aaaaaagh! You're a philistine, Quark."

Quark simply shrugged and raised Daisy's eyebrows in a particularly irritating 'yeah, whatever' kind of way.

"Anyway, why did you brush my teeth?"

"I told you, I ate —"

"But that's not a real reason."

"What do you mean?"

"You're here to kill me."

"Daisy, we have talked about this. I am not here to —"

"Yeah, yeah — yada, yada, yada." Like a game of tag, it's Daisy's turn to be the teen in the conversation. "Make me *become*, execute me and my family, friends — everyone. Whatever you want to call it, that's what it amounts to. Your use of the word *become* is like the ultimate cover story. Just a way of trying to mask your true intentions."

Quark placed Daisy's hands on the edge of the sink, squared her shoulders and stared intently into the mirror. Daisy's face is a mask of strained sincerity.

"You are young, brave and —" he added, ruefully, "much stronger than your puny body would lend anyone to believe. Your questioning and your pushing at boundaries is interesting. If frustrating. You show promise, especially considering that you are at such an early stage of your evolution."

Daisy clearly sensed an opportunity. "Our world may be a little speck, lost in the enormity of space; it may seem insignificant to you, floating out there alone in all that inky blackness, but to me, to *us*, it's home. And it's *full* of life. Life that deserves the chance to grow and mature, to explore and to live. To be *more*. We don't deserve to be cast into endless cosmic darkness."

"How many times have we talked about this now? I am not here to kill you. Yes, the conscious Daisy will go, but the essence of you — the molecules, the building blocks that make you will still be here. And —"

"Stop!"

"What?"

"You said it: 'the essence of me'. Well, my *essence* is right here — I'd tap my head now if you'd give me my body back — right here in my head. That's me. That's where I am. My brain is who I am. My personality, my hopes, my fears, my dreams, my spirit, my … soul. If I'm not conscious, I'm not here, I'm dead and gone. And that's too soon. Having my constituent bits being 'part of the universe' is all well and good, but my molecules can't go to Paris, discover a cure for cancer, write a book, fall in love — or even go for a walk in the park or eat Veggie Dippers."

Quark leaps on this. "Your molecules should not *want* to eat fast food! Don't you think meals should be about more than imbibing as many calories as you can."

"Oh, well excuse me, Raymond Blanc! I just meant —" Daisy halts, her thought process interrupted. "Wait … Quark, was that a joke? Did you just make a joke?"

"I don't know, did I?"

"I think you did, you just — wait … you just said 'don't' too! That's a contraction."

"What?"

"An abbreviation."

"So?"

"People do it all the time. It's easy (see!), it's natural — it's … human."

"I repeat: so?"

"You've never done that before. I do it — that is, *Daisy* does it — all the time. And I think that's one reason why some people — those who know me best, like Mum, Dad and Amy — think there's something wrong with me."

"Because I don't use contractions?"

"Yeah. It makes you sound stiff and stilted."

"And that is not a good thing? I thought you were a goody-goody?"

He hears the tinkle of Daisy's laughter in his head. "It might be a good thing for me if you don't, but maybe not for you. And yes, I … may have a slight tendency for being honest and law-abiding and following the rules, but everyone uses contractions in day-to-day conversation. It's informal. Chatty. Friendly."

"So … you are helping me?"

"Quark, remember: 'you're', not 'you are'. And, yes … I am."

"Why? Because doing what you are now will help me be a better Daisy. Help me keep you at bay, locked inside."

There's no response from Daisy.

"So why would you consider doing this?"

More silence from Daisy.

"Ah, you are regretting helping me, aren't you!? You think you have made a mistake. A tactical error. Your silence has come too late. I can use this against you now, can I not? I mean, can't I?! See! I am learning, I am becoming more Daisy now. More human."

Daisy has nothing to say about this.

"It embarrasses you, this slip up. Does it not? I mean doesn't it?"

Yet more silence.

"Aaaagh!" Quark finds it *so* irritating when she just absents herself in the middle of a conversation. "Adolescents are infuriating!" There's a flash of something in Daisy's eyes — surprise, pain, anguish even. But it's gone before Quark is even fully aware of it. And Daisy's face was blank once more; her mouth firmly set.

But just for a moment, he'd thought about something else too. Something that made him feel distinctly uncomfortable. Something connected to brushing her teeth. To taking care of this human.

"Well, you are tenacious, I will give you that; and meddling too." He stared sullenly at the mirror. "And you think you are clever, but *I* think this was unwise of you — an error. And I'm sorry you cannot admit you have made a major mistake. I am sorry you do not see that this will lead to humanity's destruction and the downfall of your carefully laid plans. You might think you were being cunning, but I do not think so. This is a little step, but it is a step on the way to helping you to see more of who I really am. How I fit in. How I can be 'more' as Daisy Jacobs than mere molecules."

Quark's learning about contractions, about how real people speak. And, slowly, he's starting to experience what it is to be human. But he has not yet learnt the meaning of irony.

Chapter 31

WHAT A PIECE OF WORK IS MAN

"It is hard to know what is in and what is out," Quark says.
"What do you mean?" I've let him stew overnight so the
thoughts I left him with could percolate for a while. Now, as
'we' get ready for school, it looks like we're also ready for the next
lesson in How to be a Human.

"Well — when I said that bad thing to your mother, I did not
mean it. I was not aware I was even thinking it. I mean, what do I
know about fashion? I can tell you about the abundant energy in
space — for example most of the space between planets, stars and
moons is cold and dark, but space is full of electromagnetic energy.
Every star —"

"Okay, Quark, I get it, you can —"

"— produces energy and planets and moons reflect the energy
back."

"Yes, Quark, I see —"

"The planets also release energy from —"

"OKAY!"

"What? Oh, yes, what was I saying? That's right — I know about
space, but I do not know the first thing about human clothes or
correct behaviour. It was never necessary before."

"Well, it is now."

"Okaaay!" he says with an exaggeration that made me smile.
"And I am learning. Anyway," he continues, "the image of those
words, that phrase, passed through my head and the words
apparently came out."

"Oh yes, I can confirm: they definitely came out!"

I see myself nod in the mirror as Quark ruefully agrees with me.

"Apologise to her."

"But I did not mean it."

"You still need to apologise."

"Even though —"

"If you hurt someone's feelings and get the chance to say you're sorry, take that chance. In fact, sometimes you should apologise for things you don't do at all."

"But why?"

"To make the other person feel better."

"But if you're not in the wrong …?"

"Then they'll feel better and you'll feel righteous. And in the greater scheme of things, it doesn't matter; it's like an investment in your future. The relationship with the person you're talking to will be better, and so you'll both benefit. You'll both be happier."

"You know, Daisy, you sometimes make me feel guilty. As though I've done something wrong."

"I can't imagine how you could possibly feel that," I say with some asperity. "And I certainly hope you don't expect me to apologise to *you*!"

Quark puffs out my cheeks, "being human is difficult," he says.

It is, I thought to myself, it sure is!

"'What a piece of work is man, how noble in reason, how infinite in faculty,'" says Quark.

"Wait, what is that? Is that … is that Shakespeare?"

"Mmm."

"You're quoting Shakespeare at me? Where did you pick that up?"

"From you."

"But I don't know that! I've never heard it; I don't even know what play it's from."

"Well, you have heard it, because it's in there." He taps the side of my head. "I picked it up inside your brain. From a dark corner, admittedly. So you heard it sometime. And then forgot you heard it. It is Hamlet, by the way."

Doesn't that take the biscuit? I'm getting English lessons from an alien entity! Seeing things from the outside, like an observer of my own life, is really strange. But just when you think you've maxed out in the weirdness stakes, things get wackier! It's as though my life is a film and there are people that I can't see with mics and cameras, recording me; like I'm the star of a save-the-world blockbuster. Actually, no, scratch that — I'm not the star, am I? We've established that I'm barely an extra in my own life!

But seeing the relationships with those I love most being destroyed by Quark's uncaring clunkiness, makes me think that maybe I should do more, not less, to help him acclimatise. In the long term, it could work to my advantage.

You know how it is: we're young, and we can do *anything*, right? On our best, non-panicky days, we actually believe we're gonna grow up and change the world. But although I may well be subject to the delusional optimism of a teenager, I have to believe that. Except, I don't have time to grow up to do it. I must do it *now*.

"Quark, you need to work harder with my family and friends if you're spending time as me."

"Why?"

"The way you are acting — it's wrong. It's not what I do. Not who I am."

"*Were*. Who you *were*. You used to be good at English, so do not get your tenses confused."

Okay, apparently the lesson goes on!

"Plus, you were too good, anyway," Quark continues.

"How could I be *too* good?!"

"Parents expect their children to lie to them. To answer them back. If you don't, you'll be disappointing them; not living up to their expectations. And you'll be letting the side down."

"What side?"

"The teenage side."

"Oh, so you're suddenly an expert in human adolescence, are you?!"

"Well, the whole broody spaceman thing isn't working," he says with an entirely unbecoming grin. "So I'm learning; and I am planning a lecture that I will presenting to you soon."

"Wow, remind me to be elsewhere for that!"

"Elsewhere? Like where else are you going to be?"

"See, this is the mean behaviour I've just been talking about! I'm sure even cruel kidnappers don't rub their victim's nose in their lack of freedom."

"Daisy, I want to do this nicely. I want this to be a pleasant, two-way thing. If it is entirely voluntary on your behalf, it is so much better ... it is more harmonious. You have much to gain from it."

"From what? My English lessons?"

"No, Daisy. Don't be obtuse. I do not need lessons in how to be human, in how to be you. I am learning from experience."

"But you're upsetting people as you do."

"I'm a teenager! Do you think I care about that?"

"Okay, another lesson. What you've just said is strictly clichéd. Teenagers *do* care; we care very much what people say."

"Well, in this case you need not worry about what 'you' say and what anyone thinks about it."

"Why?"

"Because you won't be around long enough for it to matter."

"Oh, that tired old story again," I sigh.

"If you will not volunteer, it will force me to come in and get you."

I laugh uproariously at this. (Inside and only to myself, obviously.) "You can't."

"What?"

"You can't do that. You can't 'get me'."

"Oh, but I can, Daisy."

"No, you can't. Because if you could, you'd have already done it."

"Oh, come on, Daisy, don't be like this."

"How often is it like this, Quark?"

"Like what?"

"How often do your victims fight to stay —"

"You are not my victim."

"It's a matter of perspective, Quark. And from my perspective, you're the predator and I'm the prey."

"You disappoint me with your endless negativity, Daisy."

"I know, I saw the video on YouTube: 'Always Look on the Bright Side of Life', yes? So, I should smile and be positive about dying. Like the band continuing to play as the Titanic sank."

Quark shakes my head, sadly.

"So, answer me: how often is it like this? How many of your victims fight back?"

Quark's silent.

"Has anyone or anything ever truly fought back? Defied you?"

"Briefly. But they failed. As will you."

"Quark ... "

"Daisy?"

"I will not fail. I will not give in. I will never, ever give in."

"Eventually you will die."

"You going to hang around for — what? — seventy years? Eighty, maybe?"

"If necessary. But it won't come to that."

"No?"

"I can force you."

"I thought we decided you'd never be able to get in."

"I mean I could ... "

"What ... make me commit suicide?"

He says nothing.

"Nope. You couldn't do that!"

"Why? I could. I am in control of your body. I can make your body do that."

In a way Quark's right: I'm so tired and scared, I'm entirely alone, and facing the biggest crisis of my life; the biggest crisis of anyone's life — anyone, anywhere, in the entire history of the world. And the easiest thing to do, far and away the easiest option, is to give in; unlock my door and shout out: "come and get me!"

Even though it sounds easy, it's hard not to be afraid — to simply fear dying. To be bricking it about the whole process, from the dying itself — how it would happen and how painful it would be — through to simply not being here anymore. But it's also terrifying to fight back and *not* give in. Because I AM alone. I'm in the dark with no one to advise or help me. And, let's not forget, with an alien thing creeping around INSIDE me, wanting to do away with me!

But, although it's the scarier option, it's the one I'm taking. I'd like to think I'm doing it for altruistic reasons — doing it for you and for all of mankind. I like the whole Hollywood idea of fighting for the greater good. And, of course, I am. But all the hype is way in the background. It's a by-product. Because if mankind gets continue onwards and experience the full glory of global warming, Russian hacking and a North Korean firestorm, it'll be because I get to grow up, have 2.2 children and a house in suburbia. Because I succeed. Because I win. Because I *live*.

And, when it comes down to it, that's what I want: to live. "I'm sure you can throw my body off a cliff or under a bus, but I don't think that's the way you work."

"You'd be surprised."

"No, Quark, I wouldn't. You say you're learning about humanity and you're learning about me. Well, I'm learning about you, too. And that isn't how you operate. There's a lot about this *becoming* thing that I don't understand, but I'm sure there's always some fast, probably instant assimilation — like you're a Borg from Star Trek. When that doesn't happen, then the giving in, the surrender, the bit where your victim gets to choose — I think that's really important to how it works. There's something about the energy transfer at the point of … impact or spawning or whatever that can wreck the process. I know I'm not using the right terminology and I'm not sure of the specifics, but I'm sure I've got the gist of it. You need that purity. Somehow, that's dead important for you." I pause a beat. "'Scuse the pun."

Quark's silent again. But my face in the mirror clouds with a resentment that leads me to think I'm right.

"I don't think killing me in that way would give you the pure energy you need. It wouldn't be suicide, but murder. And I don't think you can *become* from that. You are undoubtedly the biggest mass-taker-of-life there ever was or ever will be, but in some weird, warped way, outright murder doesn't work for you."

More silence. A whole lot of silence.

"Hello? Hellllooooo? Quark? Oh, Quarky?"

"What?"

"Thought you'd gone to sleep on me."

"No."

"That all you've got to say?"

"Yes."

"You can't throw me off a cliff?"

Reluctantly, "no."

"I have to give in or you've got to hunt me down in my own brain … or you've got to wait for eighty years."

Even more reluctantly, "yes."

"Not going to happen. And meanwhile, no matter what you think about how long I'll be here, please be kind to the people I love."

Silence from Quark. Poker face in the mirror.

"Nothing more to say?"

"Yes."

"What?"

"Do not call me Quarky."

Chapter 32

BESTIE

N ext day, Quark found it even harder to concentrate on the inanities of school. During last period Geography, he ignored oxbow lakes and came up with a plan. He decided to *be* Daisy, rather than merely inhabiting her. But he'd be *his* Daisy, not the boring, scaredy-cat one. He's a modern teenager, after all — not a bland, sanctimonious one who gets sniffy about the correct sharing of power in a relationship.

After school he approached Amy just as she reached the gates. "Why have you been avoiding me all day, Amy Porter?"

"As if you don't know."

Quark frowned at this non-direct answer. "I would not have asked you the question if I already knew the answer. That would make no sense."

"It's you who's shutting me out." Amy's reply was staccato.

"You are my friend, and I have no desire to shut you out. Please explain." Quark was puzzled. Amy's eyes said one thing, but her words said something else. Wait: how could eyes speak? And how on earth did the concept of speaking eyes even occur to him? Was new Daisy emerging already?

"Huh? You don't know?"

As Quark's expression remained confused, Amy continued. "What's going on, Dais? You're like a sleepwalker at the moment, just going through the motions at school. And I hardly see you out of school. You spend more time with Icky and that whole Satellite-crew than with me."

"That is not a pleasing way to talk of our school friends, Amy. Their names are Ellie and Claire and —"

"And it seems you'd rather be with them, than with me," Amy interjected. She sighed and took a deep breath. "And … also I'm now learning new things, *important* things about you from other people, rather than directly from you." Often the girls walked home together, arm in arm, but it's been a while since that happened. Now Amy reached out to touch Daisy's arm. "Including from my own mother, Daisy."

"Really?" Quark flinched away from the contact, bringing a flush of anguish to Amy's cheeks.

Amy bit her lip, and a frown knitted her brow as she fought to hold in her distress. "Yeah. Your mum told my mum you're not vegetarian anymore."

"I'm hardly a carnivore. I simply want to try flesh — meat, I mean. Bacon, you know. Bacon is what us vegetarians miss most. Tasty, crispy bacon — yes?"

"Maybe someone who likes bacon would miss eating it. But you've always hated it."

"I have?" For a moment Quark was puzzled. "I have! You are —" Quark paused, "*you're* right there, my friend, Amy Porter. But maybe I want to see if I still hate it. Or not. Maybe I like it now!" He smiled and patted Daisy's tummy, "mmmm … bacon."

Amy shook her head. New Daisy wasn't going down well at the moment. "Mum said something else too."

"Yes — about cow's bot— steak, I mean?"

Amy didn't answer immediately, but bowed her head, regarding Daisy from under her brows questioningly, her eyes, a sharp discerning blue, now brimful with misgiving. Her hand toyed at a strand of hair that had come loose from her braid. "No. She said that *you said* … you were gay."

"Well —"

Amy flushed as she continued to stare resolutely at Daisy. "You told your mum, who told my mum, who told me," she finished, sounding crestfallen.

"Yes?"

138

"What is this crap, Dais?!" Amy broke out abruptly, the expression of melancholy deepening on her face.

"Well —"

"Is this some kinda joke?"

"Is it funny to be gay? Ah! Two meanings, yes? Old gay — to be happy, cheerful; new gay — to be bodily familiar with the same sex. I get it! I get the joke, Amy Porter. You are a funny girl. It is no wonder that I like you. We are so alike with our funny-ness."

Amy looked at Daisy as if at a stranger. As if Daisy had become another person entirely. "Daisy, what the —" She took a breath. "Listen, I know we disagreed last week." She paused again, sighed and shook her head. "And at the weekend."

Quark nodded.

"Because you and Icky —"

"Ellie is a nice girl —"

"Yeah, whatever, the bully has turned over a new leaf; she's now a born-again member of the human race. But, Daisy, if coming out as gay or trying to be gay is your way of trying to get close to me again, you don't need to, okay?"

"Okay …?"

"It's flattering you want to be like me, but — Daisy …?"

"Yes, that is me."

Amy gave Daisy a weary smile, "you are so *not* gay!"

Chapter 33

THE ULTIMATE MAKEOVER

A my's face softens, and she smiles at me, making me realise all over again why I love this girl. I mean as a friend — not — Look, she's right, I am *so* not gay. And I don't know what Quark's playing at.

"What are you playing at?!" I yell at him later in the privacy of our (aaaggh! that makes me so angry!) bedroom. We find that sitting at my dressing table, looking at the mirror is the best place for these conversations. It's still bonkers; looking and talking at/to yourself, but it is marginally less crazy than just lying on my bed talking to myself, or doing so while walking around the room — because our conversations often lead to arguments. And then to shouting. And then we get very strange looks from Mum, Dad and Luke. Singing off-key to YouTube hits is one thing; shouting at and insulting yourself is far harder to explain away! We'd both rather avoid those explanations.

I just wish Quark could talk in my head, like I can — 'think talk' — so that these conversations could be silent. Actually, scratch that: I most definitely do NOT wish he was in my head talking silently to me at all hours of the day and night. I get no space anyway, but at least I have my room — my *locked* room. I get *some* respite from him!

"What do you mean?" he asks.

"What's with being a carnivore?"

"You will not let me *become*, so I want to see what it is like to absorb animal flesh another way."

"Do you enjoy eating flesh? I mean meat."

"I do not know."

"But you've done it millions — billions — of times."

"Not like that. Becoming is not eating."

"So, what's it like?"

"It is … not the same."

"Wow, Quark, I'm not sure if I can cope with that much detail."

"It is hard to describe."

"Clearly. So, break it down: what does one *becoming* feel like?"

"Each is different. No one *becoming* is the same, but all are …"

"Yes?"

"Fast."

"That's it? That's the level of scientific detail that billions of years has brought you to?" I gather my thoughts and continue. "But, if I *become*, I'm gone. Daisy Jacobs is just … no more, yes?"

"It is not dying, not death. It is renewal."

"Like reincarnation?"

"That may be where that idea came from. A being that *becomes*," Quark shakes Daisy's head in wonder and sighs blissfully, "it is like the ultimate make-over! You are re-imagined. Made anew. You become new and you also become forever."

"You almost make it sound like an attractive proposition. I'm pleased you didn't get to make this pitch on a real TV show. I know lots of people who'd like the ultimate make-over!"

"And they would be right! Afterwards you are you, but you are everywhere. You are endless."

I (inwardly) shake my head. "But if I *became*, I'd no longer actually be *me*."

"You'll not be Daisy Jacobs, no. You will be *more*! You will be someone else."

"No, not some*one*, some*thing*."

"That's right," Quark acknowledges. "But the essence, the elements of you will continue to exist. Like an eternal echo — down through the ages, on and on."

"Forever?" Concern builds within me, like a dark cloud on the distant horizon. This all sounds too neat, too simple … too

141

attractive. It's like Quark's hypnotising me, lulling me into accepting the impossible.

"Until the end of time," he whispers breathlessly.

I need to break out of this, to change the seductive mood and escape the hippy-trippy tone that's making mass extinction sound like an attractive proposition!

"Well, I'll take it under advisement, Quark, because when it comes down to it, I'll still bite the big one."

"Like if I eat cow's bottom; that cow is not likely to be walking in the field the next day."

Despite myself, and sensing exactly the opportunity I want, I laugh. "That's funny!"

"I made a joke?"

"Well … nearly. And it's steak, Quark. If, heaven forbid, you get to eat it, it's called rump steak, not cow's bottom. But do try not to pollute my body with meat."

"It is important to try new experiences, yes? To become more human?"

"Why would you want to be *more* human? I thought you wanted to get rid of all humans."

"I think maybe I get to be more human and so you become less Daisy and then you just … *become*."

"So you're tricking me?"

"Absolutely! And you are falling for it!"

"That's right, I am. Hook, line and sinker."

"That is why I think we are now gay too."

"You think being gay makes you more human?"

"No … well, maybe. I do not know. Just … you love Amy, yes. So this is a good way to get close to your friend."

"Wait — you want me to — with Amy — and — WHAT?! What are you thinking?!"

"She is your best friend, yes?"

"Yes, but —"

"So, it is good to be close to your best friend. And also, who knows how long I may be here."

"You thinking of leaving?"

"No, but if I do ... I want to try many things before I leave."

"Quark I am only fourteen-years-old. I am way, way, way too young. I will NOT have sex with Amy."

"How about Conn—"

"I will not have sex with Connor either! I forbid you to make my body have sex with anybody at all! Is that clear? Just so *you* can see what it's like! I am too young. I am nothing like ready for that."

"You are a mature girl."

"Quark: it's a no. No. No. NO! I am too young. And also — I am not gay. I love Amy, but not like that; I do not ... fancy her."

"There is a difference, yes?"

"Yes!"

"So you do 'fancy' Connor?"

"I don't know. I like him. He's a nice boy. I'd like to get to know him more."

"Why do you like him?"

"He's nice ..." I sigh, "that's not a good answer ..."

"Maybe feelings and emotions are as hard to explain as *becoming*. Maybe *becoming* is the same as love?!"

"No Quark, when you fall in love you do not disintegrate into your constituent parts and vanish into the ether. Being in love has precisely nothing to do with *becoming*. And I don't 'love' Connor. I like him; he's funny and clever. He's kind. He is tall and has a lovely smile and warm eyes."

"His eyes are warm?!"

"The *look* in his eyes is warm."

"Ah, yes. When he looks at you there is more warmth."

"I don't know ..."

"I do know. I see this. I see ... heat."

"*Heat*!?"

"Yes, in his eyes when he looks at you. And his eyes get bigger. Also, there is colour — heat — in his cheeks."

"How do his eyes get bigger?"

"The pupils of his eyes, when he looks at you."

"They do?"

"Yes. You do not see this?"

"No …"

"I do. When I look, I see this. I think this is something like your X-Ray vision in bad science fiction. I see it like a heat map. I will try to let you see like this sometime."

"You will? Thank you."

"You are welcome. But Amy — you love her but do not look at her in the same way. So she is nice, but she is not warm and kind?"

"It's different. There's no … tension with Amy."

"Tension? Connor makes you tense? Afraid? Scared?"

"No. A different type of tension. It's sort of …" I whisper, "sexual tension."

"Sexual! Ah, so you do 'fancy' Connor!"

"No. Yes. Well — I don't know. But I might. I could."

"But not Amy?"

"No, I love Amy. But she's no threat."

"So Connor threatens you? And this is attractive?"

I sigh. How did this happen? How did I get into this? I'm a girl who's barely even kissed a boy, who has precisely zero actual (as it were) hands-on experience and I'm trying to explain human sexuality to a billions-of-years-old space entity. I mean, honestly — you couldn't make this up!

"Let's try this again. I am a girl —"

"Yes, we are a girl."

"Be quiet, Quark. This is awkward and embarrassing and confusing even to me."

"Why are you confused?"

"Because my hormones are racing; especially now — it seems like I'm changing every day."

"I know!" His tone is emphatic.

"Shhhh! Let me try to think." I speak gruffly, not looking at the mirror. As if not looking at him will make him not see me, and so make this situation easier.

"I do love her. I enjoy being with her more than anyone else outside of my family. I talk to her about everything. That's why she'll be so upset that I'm not talking to her about what's happening now."

Chapter 34

FLYING SLUGS!

At the end of the day, Amy and Daisy walked home from school together, with Amy clearly trying hard to get back her accustomed closeness with her best friend.

"When you think about it, what were the chances you'd enter the lion's den and live to tell the tale?" Amy linked arms with Daisy, whose body didn't relax into hers as it usually did.

As always, Quark was unsettled by physical contact. He simply couldn't, as it were, get to grips with it. The space in and around Daisy's body was *his*. He wished others would respect this and keep away. Or become. At the moment, either would be fine! "The lion's den?" he said, gritting his teeth in an effort to avoid cringing away from Amy.

"Yeah — the circle of despair that is the Satellites."

Quark said nothing; so far he hadn't understood a word Amy had said. This girl was most confusing; he doesn't really understand why Daisy was so fond of someone who couldn't string more than a few words together without descending into a fug of supposedly shared obscurity. And why was she constantly trying to hug and touch him? It was most disconcerting — especially when Daisy said their relationship was not at all 'like that'.

"Anyway, you shouldn't have done it, Dais."

"Done what?"

"Spoken to Connor. Love is a dangerous thing."

"Ah, yes — I was talking about that with Da— I mean, I was thinking about this subject only this morning."

"Oh, and did you reach any conclusions?"

"No, only that love and desire and sex and romance and being gay — these are tricky things."

Amy forced a laugh. "And you make it even trickier when you say you'll experiment with being gay just to please your bestie! You really do know better, Daisy: you can't manufacture emotions like that."

Quark was sure Daisy's long time best friend would notice how he held himself away from her. He was trying to balance authenticity against the extent to which physical closeness made him want to puke. His notion of gender experimentation had hurt Amy in a way that he didn't understand. Surely his wanting to be like her should make Amy happy? They were supposed to be practically joined at the hip, according to Daisy.

Yet now Amy released Daisy's arm, clearly hoping to relax her friend and bring about a return of that closeness. "Anyway, you've not been the same since you tried to talk to Connor. I think you screwed up there. Cosmically," she added with a shrewdness that momentarily threw Quark.

He stifled a gasp with a cough. "What?!"

"It's like you're not yourself. You're gloomy."

"Really?"

"Yeah — you've lost your sparkle."

"Sparkle? Right — I will endeavour to rectify that situation. Could you possibly tell me how I might sparkle once more, Miss Porter."

"Jeez, Daisy! No need for sarcasm; I was only trying to help." Amy took a step away from Daisy, frowning as if trying to figure out a reason for her friend's mystifying behaviour.

"Yes, indeed. And your assistance is most appreciated." Quark still couldn't get a grip on this conversation. Amy's feelings were too raw for him to cope with. He cleared his throat and nodded, grasping for logic in a sea of intense emotion. "Listening to, and learning from, one's peers is a fundamental component of the human condition, is it not?"

"Huh? What the— Listen, Daisy, are you sure you're feeling okay? That bang on the head and the fainting … you really haven't been the same since."

"I am quite alright, Miss Porter, but your concern is most appreciated." Quark's face kept its rigid expression.

"Oh, it's stern Daisy, is it?" Now Amy's face was serious too. "Where's the warmth, wit and animation? Where did my friend go? What did you do with her?" She poked Daisy playfully in the tummy. Quark flinched as if he'd been shot.

A look of panic scudded across his features before he regained control and essayed a smile. "I am here." He waved at Amy from a distance of about a metre. "Hello, Amy Porter, my friend, I have gone nowhere." He let out an unnatural and unsettling giggle. "Unlike Elvis, I have not left the building, so your talk makes no sense." Without him realising, Quark's guard was slipping again … and his use of language with it.

"My talk?"

"Your statement. Your comment. I am Daisy; who else could I be?"

"You're not looking well, Dais. Honestly. I'm worried about you."

"I feel fine. Practically optimum!" Quark retreated further into his version of normal.

"You don't *look* fine. And you haven't since that bang on your head. You're *not* yourself at all! There are bags under your eyes. And your eyes have lost that ocean green shine. Where's your wit? Where's my Daisy?!" Amy continued to stare intently at her friend's face.

"What? I am thinking. Contemplating. Life is serious, my friend Amy."

"Again — 'my friend Amy'. Who talks like this? Are you auditioning for the role of a Russian spy?" She looked around in mock exaggeration. "Is this a YouTube prank?"

"I do not understand what you mean."

"Oh, flying slugs, Daisy!"

Quark looked up into the air in absolute confusion. "What?"

Amy stopped walking so suddenly that Quark had moved on several steps before he realised Amy was no longer alongside him.

"You don't get that?"

Quark still looked confused. "Slugs?" He looked up into the sky again. "Slugs do not fly, Amy. In this you are mistaken."

"Wait — you really *don't* get it, do you?"

"It is just simple science, Amy — slugs crawl, they do not fly."

Amy's face was impassive. "Artichokes!" she shouted so suddenly that Quark jumped.

Quark was flustered, unsure where Daisy's friend's conversational gambit was heading. The girl was crazy! But, for Daisy's sake, and for the slim chance that the blind alley down which Amy's conversation was heading might lead him to a greater understanding of humanity, he played along, rather than run home as quickly as he could.

He nodded seriously. "Yes, Amy — artichoke. A vegetable. Very nutritious, but can have unfortunately windy side-effect on the digestive system. And also not relevant to our slug discussion."

"It's our way of swearing, Daisy."

"Swearing?"

"Our three-stage swearing — 'Melons!' for mildly upsetting. 'Artichokes!' for something worse. And, if something is really serious or disturbing, 'Flying slugs!'"

Quark shook his head in utter bafflement. "These are not swear words, Amy. A good example of a swear word is fu—"

"Stop!" said Amy, holding up her hand, palm towards Daisy. "We do not use actual swear words." Her voice has taken on a playful, exaggeratedly ladylike tone. "We decided in Year 7 that we are ladies, and that swearing is *un*-ladylike. That's when we created these swear words and you *know* that."

There was a long pause as she continued to stare into Daisy's eyes. "Or rather, Daisy knows that," she finally said. "*My* Daisy knows that. We invented this way of swearing together."

Quark jumped as if poked by a cattle prod. "Ah, yes indeed. I remember! We like a good swear — FLYING SLUGS! Ha! A good swear, yes, Amy?"

Amy remained unimpressed. "What's happened to you, Dais?" Her generous lips thinned as her mouth set firm. "What's happened to you and why won't you tell me about it? Who have you become?" Her tone was harsh.

"I am Daisy Jacobs —"

"No, you're not. Not *my* Daisy Jacobs. She's nothing like this. Babe, you're —"

" — of 9 Castle Walk, Scuttleford."

"Nope. I don't know what's happened, but you're not my Daisy. My warm, funny, brilliant friend."

"We —"

"Daisy! Listen to me, what happened? What have you done to the girl I love?"

"Me? I—"

"Where is my Daisy?!"

"Amy Porter, please do not shout. You are causing a scene. And scenes are not good, this is one thing I *do* know."

"Daisy —?"

Even Quark could read Amy's fear and distress now. But he remembered her earlier comment: he couldn't manufacture emotions to solve this. He caught her open-mouthed gaze, but although his eyes saw the flood of tears begin, his part of Daisy's brain failed to register them. He left as fast as Daisy's legs could carry him.

Chapter 35

THE EPICENTRE OF ABSOLUTELY NOWHERE AT ALL

"Quark?"
"Yes?"
"What's the purpose of your life?"
There's silence while Quark considers my question. "To exist," he says finally.

"That's it — just exist?"

"Yes. I drift through everlasting emptiness — that is if moving faster than the speed of light can be called drifting and deep space can be called empty."

"So, your life is just existing in emptiness? Wow, that must be *so* inspiring! No wonder you want to get right back to it."

He ignores the dig. "Well, there is a lot of nothing." Weirdly, in the mirror I see the corners of my mouth quirk upward into a small smile at this. "And there is a lot of what you would call solitude. Or isolation. Or … loneliness." The smile vanishes, replaced by a frown of concentration. "An aeon in terms of my overall existence is not a long time. Aeon is Greek, and it means an age in everyday language, but in scientific terms, an aeon is a billion years. And —"

"Boring!" I interrupt before he can get into full flow. "You're lecturing again, Quark. How do you cope with all that … nothing? I couldn't do it — I enjoy company too much. An afternoon by myself is okay. A day or two, not so good. But being alone for a billion years?!"

"Well, you can see a lot if you have a billion years to spare. At the speed of light, you are travelling at about 300,000km a second. So, in Earth terms you can travel a fair distance."

I'm not convinced. "If you travel that far, where would you be?

What exciting things would you see? None! Because you'll have arrived at the epicentre of absolutely nowhere at all."

"It would be wrong to say nothing," Quark continues, pointedly, "because you would still see the twinkling of distant stars — without pollution or atmospheric interference. But, yes, they would still be very, very distant. There would be a great view of your Moon, but even that would still be over 80,000 kilometres away. That's in just one second, though. In a mere eight minutes you would reach the Sun, less than 150 million kilometres away!"

"I hate to detract from your lecture, Quark, but that's eight minutes out of a billion years! And you'd *still* be alone," I scoff. "In fact, even more alone than you were eight minutes earlier. And you'd be a lot further away from the nearest McDonald's!"

Quark frowns, and my lips firm in disapproval at the interruption. "From there you could look into the darkness beyond and maybe head for your nearest neighbour … ?"

I sigh, "Proxima Centauri".

He nods. "At the maximum speed humanity can currently capable travel you would get there in 81,000 years. But you travel at light speed, so you would make it in just over four years."

"So a long way in just four years. And over that distance you'd see an awful lot of very little."

"Well, almost no dust or debris — it is not called the void for nothing!"

"Is that what passes for a joke on your planet?" I answer, tartly.

Quark stares at me balefully. "The average density of much of this space is about a single atom of hydrogen per cubic metre. So there is stuff. There is a bit of plasma here and there. A tiny amount of dust, some cosmic rays, some background radiation."

"Wow! Well worth travelling 4.2 light years for! It's hardly a trip to the fair, a beach, or a rock concert, is it?"

"I suppose it is not even a Thursday afternoon of double Mathematics."

I giggle. "Now, that *was* pretty funny," I admit.

"I agree," Quark continues, in full flow now, "it is, in every practical sense, a void. An unimaginable amount of nothing at all."

"And you wonder why I want memories. Why I want to live my life and not just exist!"

"You live life in 3D all the time. It is full of colour, vivid high-definition, 24/7. Daisy, you do not know how lucky you are. How lucky you have been. Talking about my average day, my average year — or century — I realise now that my existence has been shapeless and ill-defined. But now, in this body, I am aware of everything going on around me. My senses are on high alert." He frowns, "sometimes it's too much."

The frown deepens, furrowing my brow. Then he shivers and continues as if nothing has happened. "And just recently, in the last day or so, things have become even clearer. I am seeing the world in a whole different way. My senses tell me that the chemical balance in your body has changed and colours appear brighter, birdsong sweeter. The meal your father cooked last night — gnocchi and garlic mushrooms ... I could taste it, really taste the garlic and the tartness of the dressing on the salad. It was ... delicious. So good that I felt as though my head would explode."

"Hey! That's *my* head you're talking about!"

"And my eyes leaked when I watched television after dinner."

"Leaked?"

"A strange experience. There was a drama on about a baby elephant that was about to die, but its mother and aunts cared for it and, Daisy — it survived!"

"That wasn't a drama. That was a David Attenborough wildlife documentary. It was real."

"It was certainly a dramatic story!"

"And it made you cry?"

"Cry, yes! That was it; I was sad, so my eyes leaked. Then I was happy, and they leaked again. Strange to cry when sad *and* when happy. A most curious feeling, but it was an *experience*. I *felt* it. That was just one moment — not an aeon! — just one single moment.

And I felt as though I was living. As though I was alive." He speaks with real warmth and feeling.

"But it is *my* life you are still living! Mine!" I'm furious with his unfeeling attitude — reeling off experiences that should be mine. "You're living a stand-in life in *my* body. Like an understudy in a play when the audience have paid to see the star — the lead actor — playing the role.

"The way you've been talking recently ... it seemed like you were being friendly. Like you were getting to know me. And I've been helping you too. Trying to let you see the good things about being human. About being truly alive."

"I see that, Daisy. And I am very thankful to you for your help."

"But I thought, if you saw what my life was like, then you would let *me* live it."

"I can also see how you might have thought that. However, what I have learned from being you and what I have learned *from* you, will help me be a better Daisy Jacobs."

"What about my *becoming*?"

My body leant forward, closer to the mirror, and an eyebrow quirked. "Are you going to give in? To surrender to me?"

"No, I'm not."

"Then we have reached an impasse. In chess, this would be a stalemate. For the moment, you are correct — I cannot dig you out of your redoubt. So I will simply wait you out."

"What does that mean?"

"I would prefer to get this over quickly, to enter the stage of *becoming* tonight — right now. But this life, this living, this learning about your world, I find it fascinating. I may stick around."

"For how long?"

"Not long."

"And then you'll leave and let me live my life?"

"Well, *I* will live your life for you. I will experience your life, and then when it is time, the boost of energy should be enough for the next *becoming*."

"Exactly how long do you plan on staying?"

"Well, I got the idea from something you said the other day, when I gave you the English lessons. It's hard to say how long your life will be, you *are* only fourteen after all. But I think I can get at least seventy years of experiences from you."

"You'll live my entire life and then use me to take over the world, anyway?"

Talk about the lingering effects of catastrophic near-death experience! I wonder whether to just give in and let Quark finish me off now. That'll end the constant fear, the continual questioning of my existence and the frustration of the simple question of '*why me*'.

In the mirror my lips curve into a cold smile and my head nods at another little victory. He's pulled the rug from under me — again. He's busted me back down once more, blowing away my illusion of progress. So here I still am, hiding in my lonely room, and once more I sense the pulse of life within me fade as I choke back the fear and desolation that could easily overwhelm me. The light I've been clawing my way towards grows ever dimmer.

"Quark, you are a bas—"

"Remember, Daisy, we are a lady!" Quark interrupts. In the mirror, my eyes have lost any hint of the green that usually gives them warmth. They stare back at a vulnerable girl who's looking at a life-sentence, locked in the gloomy darkness of her own head. My usually generous mouth thins into a grim smile as Quark's glance slices into me with invasive intensity.

"Don't forget the swears we created with our friend, Amy Porter. I think you would say, 'flying slugs, Quark, you are an artichoke!' I am sure, under the circumstances, the use of two of our really bad swears is fully justified." And Quark smirks. He has the cheek to actually smirk!

Chapter 36

WHY ME?

"Why me?" Daisy asked.

"Sorry?!" Quark jumped in surprise. He'd been practising applying make-up, hardly aware of looking into the mirror and so of Daisy looking out at him.

"Was that an apology?!"

"What! No, it most certainly was not." Quark pursed Daisy's lips and turned her head to see what effect *Sun-Kissed* blusher and *Foxy Red* lipstick had on his appearance. He dabbed away the extra blusher Daisy's interruption caused him to apply. He's toying with bending one of Daisy's ridiculously austere rules by wearing make-up to school. "What do I have to apologise for, anyway?"

"I just can't imagine," replied Daisy with a hint of sarcasm that passed Quark by. Frankly she'd have to batter him over the head with derision for him to notice, so absorbed was he in his cosmetic routine.

"What do you mean?" Quark's trying to work out the correct degree of 'discretion' required to make a sufficient impact on the school authorities. He decided that, on the whole, there was subtle … and then there was *Foxy Red*!

"I mean that I could've walked across the playground a few minutes — maybe even a few moments — earlier or later, or waited until the next day, or decided I didn't want to talk to Connor and just left him in the clutches of eager-Ellie."

"So?" Quark's barely paying attention to her; instead he's now selecting eye-shadow. Kohl for moodiness or turquoise to highlight the depthless grey-green of Daisy's — no *his* — eyes?

"With a single change to one of the factors that led me to be in that precise place at that precise time, I might have been saved from all this grief!"

Silence from Quark who now had one kohl eye and one turquoise and was flipping Daisy's head from side-to-side to work out which suited his colouring and which would make the impact he desired.

"Quark?"

"Mmmmm?" Kohl gave a certain moody-oomph, but turquoise made him appear … mysterious?

"Am I the chosen one?"

Still nothing from Quark.

"I mean, if it hadn't been me, it would have been someone else. But would that be a good thing? Though I do say so myself, I have made a pretty good job of holding you at bay until now. If you'd landed in some random person in London or Amsterdam, Cairo or Kolkata, or even in one of the other kids in the playground, then who knows?"

Quark had just realised that such a thing as nail varnish existed; a whole new part of his body to decorate! Now — *Wanton Red* or *Flaming Coral* … which was more him?

"Surely if you'd picked Mr Ford, it would be all over for him — and for the whole planet by now. He'd have rolled over and surrendered like a flailing beetle. But maybe Mrs Griffin would have kicked your butt and saved us all!"

"Huh?"

"Quark, have you been listening to me at all?"

"What? Of course I have!"

"Then why do I suddenly look like a sun-burnt panda then?"

"I think I look rather fetching, actually."

Daisy looked deep into her own eyes, trying — and failing — to see the demon there. She looked for the darkness, the brooding nemesis that hung over her — that had stalked *within* her. She failed to see him. Could be hiding behind the kohl and turquoise eye-liner, of course!

"And how did you do what you did to me so quickly? Get so deeply into me, into my head and into who I *am*? You took me over in an instant."

Quark rested Daisy's hands on the sink for a moment as he thought about this — and pondered his appearance in the mirror. "Why you? When I approach a planet, I receive a kind of signal, a notification if you like from the surface that reaches out to me. It indicates intense neural activity, detectable from the moment I enter the atmosphere. It is the intensity of that being's signal that powers the subject's own *becoming*."

"I matched your criteria?"

Quark nodded, focusing on his reply, but still taking time to admire the different tones of *dazzling* red he'd painted Daisy's fingernails. "The level of synaptic energy radiating from you was higher than I have ever encountered before. I think it is possible, from what I have learnt since, that you were emitting the greatest emotional intensity. It wasn't physical strength I sought; it was the force of the electricity given out by your brainwaves." He paused and frowned. "I had not realised that equated to moral strength, courage and determination too. I chose you and you alone. But if I had known better, I would have selected someone else."

"Really?"

"Yes, but I do not think Mr Ford would have made a good subject."

Daisy laughed. "Why?"

"He has insufficient moral fortitude; he would make a poor *becoming*."

Quark wondered whether to get Daisy's ears pierced so he could add further decoration to the body that is now his. "Daisy?"

"Yes?"

"What was it like for you?"

"My near *becoming*?"

Quark nodded.

"A blankness and confusion that cascaded through me. Like

dominos collapsing down upon each other within by mind, forcing me deeper and deeper within myself."

Daisy's lips pursed as Quark absorbed this. "It sounds … hard."

Daisy didn't reply.

"Daisy Jacobs, I do not appreciate how you have temporarily prevented your planet's first *becoming*." He paused. "But I commend your courage and bravery."

"My moral fortitude, huh."

In the mirror Daisy's lips formed a tight smile. "Yes."

The smile loosened a fraction, "and Daisy … "

"Yes?"

"I admire the way our molecules have coalesced. You are a remarkable accumulation of atoms."

It was impossible, as he himself made neither sound nor movement, but Quark could have sworn that he actually felt Daisy's sudden intake of breath.

"Why, Quark," she said, "I think that's the nicest thing anyone has ever said to me."

Chapter 37

NO

The Earth is our home: steady, solid, dependable, and taken completely for granted. That's obvious, isn't it? It's just there, beneath our feet and all around us. Except right now, I can't even feel the earth beneath my feet. It's like my life's over. But there's a major problem with that; not only would the world not get to enjoy my presence and my myriad achievements over the next seventy or eighty years ... the world would miss *your* accomplishments too. Since, if *my* life ends, *yours* will too.

Because that's all Quark needs: the boost of power, the *oomph* from me to generate the impetus he wants to get to you and everyone you've ever known and so on and so on until there's nothing left on earth but floating atoms and space dust.

You'd understand, though — yes? If I gave in, I mean. I'm just so tired. Tired of being alone. Tired of being in the dark. I've already held Quark back for longer than anyone in history. Quite an epitaph, I'm sure you'll agree. Of course, it's still an elegy that would end with — "but still failed ... and died".

And that's the big issue here: I can give up. I can surrender; I can just ... go to sleep, I guess, and wake up dead. But I can't make that decision on your behalf. I hold your fate in my hands; in my little locked room. And so — for your sake as much as mine — I'll fight on. I'll exert all the powers of my tiny mind. I won't give in.

Quark's been around for the entire history of the universe, yet what he's seen of actual life is less than the blink of an eye! He's had so many opportunities to live. But that's not the way he works. He *becomes* quickly and moves on. Sitting around for eighty years is not the way he operates; it may be a moment to him, but I don't think he has it in him to just sit inside my head and wreck my life for all that time. If he does, we'll really drive each other bonkers!

We're in my bedroom, at the dressing table mirror. Quark's smile has disappeared like it's outlived its usefulness. On my face, the smile is replaced by a steely glare. "You need to be logical about this," he insists.

"You forget, I am a mere human; I can't always be logical. And by the way, it's unlikely I'm going to faint away under the pressure of that glare. I mean, first I don't think I could possibly squeeze what's left of me into a smaller space. And second ..." I pause and take what would be a raking breath, had I lungs of my own to use, "I know my face too well, and I practised scarier looks in the mirror long before you were a blip over the horizon."

"My, you *are* a clever girl."

"Don't patronise me." I give him my meanest inward scowl, which naturally has zero impact. "Anyway," I continue, "sometimes the mind's a bit wayward. We aren't always logical. And sometimes the mind's not even in control."

"How can that be?" He's baffled.

"When the heart rules the head."

"The heart? Your heart pumps blood around your body, it does not decide what you do."

"Yeah, well mine sometimes does. And right now it's telling me to hold out. To be strong. To fight my corner. My heart's telling me I'll win."

"Well, I do not understand how it can tell you anything at all. And if it does, then your heart — which, incidentally, *I* control — is clearly as misguided as the rest of you. You are being illogical ... even for a human."

"You only think that because you're cold-hearted."

"Cold?"

'Yes, and I am warm-hearted."

In the mirror, I see him hold out my arms and look down at my body. "I am in your warm bedroom and for some reason, I seem to be wearing a fleecy onesie that looks like a teddy bear, Daisy. I feel utterly ridiculous, but I do not feel cold."

"Well, I rest my case. You don't even know why you are wearing one of the most desirable items of clothing I own. You are cold *and* hard."

My head shakes from side to side, as Quark, who seems baffled by my argument and saddened by my attitude, reverts to his usual point of attack. "You will stop this nonsense, this prevarication, and surrender right this minute!"

"Do you know who Rosa Parks was?"

"What? No, I do not and what is more I —"

"Rosa Parks was a great and fantastically brave woman. She changed the world."

Quark sighs, forced for the moment to accept my diversion. "And how did she do that?"

"With a single word."

I can see my eyebrow do that quirky thing in the mirror. Despite himself, Quark's curious. "What word?"

"No."

"You will not tell me?"

"The word was 'no'. Look it up. It's important; and it will tell you all you need to know about the capacity of a single individual to do something amazing. About the power and bravery of one person, an incredibly vulnerable woman — or girl — to refuse to give in to the inevitable. To face down seemingly impossible odds and win."

"These odds are overwhelming, Daisy Jacobs."

"I disagree. To quote Rosa Parks' inspiration — 'I will not be trampled over by the iron feet of your oppression'. Overwhelming or not, my answer is the same as Rosa's: 'no'"!

Chapter 38

WHERE THE WILD THINGS ARE

"Become, move on, become. That is ... life." Quark pauses in the middle of Daisy's bedroom, and strikes a dramatic pose. "Doesn't sound like it to me. It sounds like existence," Daisy says.

"Excuse me," says Quark huffily, "I was thinking. This is not a conversation for you to join in."

"So why can I hear you? See those little squiggles in the sentences up there? They're quotation marks. You're even present tense now. And you spoke those words out loud, not in *my* head, which you should leave — right now!"

"In the words of Rosa Parks: 'no'!" Quark smirks. But it's wasted on Daisy because he's not looking into the mirror at the moment, just walking about Daisy's room and occasionally lying on her bed. He's talking to himself. And he's talking out loud, because he still gets muddled over the difference between this thinking and talking lark.

It's been a tiring day at school, with much food for thought, so he's in a contemplative mood. Should he need to talk to Daisy — or harangue her — he'll do it later. Now he's thinking about the meaning of life.

(I'm not certain, but I suspect this next bit might be a bit ... well, dull. By now you know what Quark's like — all equations and logic. And I've got the feeling he's going to go all philosophical on us. If you're sticking with it, I'll make sure Daisy wakes you up before the next interesting part; if we're lucky, she may even save us altogether.)

Life and existence are synonymous for Quark. Is 'life' actually necessary at all, he wonders? Does anyone or anything really need to do more than exist? From his position now, inside a living, breathing human, it appears what he's done in the past has been to just go through the motions.

He can't resist going all dramatic and Shakespearian again. "In retrospect, the brief flashes of what passed for life now look like just being alive rather than *living* a life."

"You're right — that's just what you've being doing." Daisy's voice once more interrupts Quark's contemplations.

"There you go again! This is my bit," huffs Quark. "This is my chance to put my case. To make people understand the reality of being Quark … just a teensy, tiny single point of matter." He speaks in as insignificant a voice as his colossal ego will allow.

"That's as maybe, but you keep spouting this gumf out loud," Daisy says. "I think you'd secretly like to know what life really is, rather than tell people about misbehaving objects that complicate the laws of physics."

"Right then, oh, wise oracle, I guess you think you are the one who can explain the meaning of my existence … of my *life*." Quark feels Daisy's — his! — body swell with annoyance. He's an impossibly ancient, infinitely wild … thing from the very heart of the universe. He's lived countless lives; well, okay, not exactly *lived* — he's very, very briefly existed billions of times in a wide range of creatures, forms and beings. Yet this pipsqueak human feels able to teach *him* about life! "I can barely restrain my frustration," he says.

"Well, you're doing a good job of voicing it, but I think you're beginning to lose control. You need to learn more about the world around you and about yourself. Being truly alive is about growth — at any age. About being more than you think you can be."

Quark laughs. "That is so far from reality! You are looking for meaning when there *is* no meaning. You question the justice of what is happening to you with that typical teenage 'it is not fair' attitude." Quark's mockingly exaggerated teen voice is pretty good — apart from his inability to use contractions. "There *is* no fair and unfair. There is no meaning or message or explanation. There is just existence. And lack of it. So, Ms Oracle, it turns out that I am here to teach *you* the meaning of your soon-to-be lack of life. Ha!"

He pauses dramatically, expecting something cutting from Daisy.

He's now at the dressing table mirror to better continue his lecture and avoid more parental interventions over Daisy's 'shouting at herself'. But Daisy is unforthcoming. He can sense her simply staring out at him.

Finally, she breaks the silence. "You should really give a stagey laugh at this point. Deep from the belly, you know. Like some kind of Evil Bad Santa — 'ha, ha ha' and then kind of rub your hands together with glee at placing me in such a perilous predicament."

"Daisy, I am trying for serious here. Trying for apocalyptic menace. I'm trying to scare the bejesus out of you and all you can do is mock me."

"Oh, sorry, sorry! Okay, straight face." Daisy makes a sound that, if she were in control of her body, would be a deep, steadying breath. "Right, I'm now taking your terrifyingly intense menace absolutely seriously …"

"Good, because you will not find laughing in the face of adversity in any survival manual, you know," Quark says with a hard edge quite unlike Daisy's usual dulcet tone. "It is not a suggestion of what to do when confronted with your imminent oblivion."

"It's a coping method."

"Well, that is facing by not facing."

"Yes, sort of facing with a squint."

"That makes no logical sense."

"I know, sorry. That's my pesky humanity again, screwing with the universe instead of just lying down in abject surrender. And it's extraordinary that you make *such* sense; you being a singularity that goes around the universe ending the life of every living creature that's struggled to haul itself out of the primordial swamp and into precarious existence. After all, it's *such* an important job you do."

"It is not a *job*."

"Oh, sorry! Did I accidentally undermine the fundamental purpose of your existence? Awfully sorry about that, old boy. But ultimately, you're talking about death and destruction. Don't hang a fancy label on it. You're just a cosmic vacuum cleaner, that's your job."

"What?!" Quark sputters.

"Just a scaled-up Hoover."

"How very dare you! I am hurt."

"Oh. Dear. What. A. Shame. Never. Mind."

After the near bantering tone of the past few minutes, a heavy silence hangs between them.

Finally, Daisy speaks again with weighty anguish. "I know you think I'm little more than a child, but there's so much I want to do. So much I *will* do." She pauses and then her voice rings out, louder in his head than it has so far been, "today I am stronger than I was yesterday. I feel it, and I know you do too. I *am* getting stronger."

Quark sighs inwardly, keeping the truth of this to himself. He feels sure that *he* is stronger than before; a little less in control, maybe, and he does truly feel the power of Daisy's redoubtable spirit. She still refuses to bow down, refuses to give in. And her life-force remains resolute.

Her voice continues to echo from the room in her head she still occupies. "Tomorrow I will learn something new. I will grow. I will be more than I am today. And this will continue until I am dead. And until I am dead, I am alive!"

Chapter 39

A SPADE

"Listen, Daisy, when I came here, I had no intention of causing you any trouble at all. I really hate to be the bearer of bad news —"

I interrupt him, "oh, no you don't. You just love it. You picture yourself in a big black hood, carrying a scythe. You're the Grim Reaper made real. And you just *love* it!"

Quark shakes his head sadly. "Not at all, this gives me no pleasure."

I make a "pfffft" noise.

I know I've made a fuss about my age — and being proud of it; being a teenager and not a child, but as a teenager by definition I'm not fully formed and so I admit — reluctantly, obviously — I'm not always equipped to make the best decisions (although being an adult doesn't guarantee infallibility on that count — see recent political decisions around the world for proof of that), or to cope in the most stressful situations ... such as having the entire future of the world on my shoulders.

I guess this means we spend most of our time in the 'now', rather than wasting energy thinking about what might happen in the future. The innocence of this is just great: it means we can enjoy ourselves in a way that our parents can't truly share, because their existence is clouded by responsibility, duty and the harsh realities of everyday life — like tax, food shopping and saying "no" to their children at least eighty-seven times a day.

But at the moment, the future (or lack of it) looms as a rather large obstacle on my horizon, and it appears the innocence of childhood (as it was such a tantalisingly short time ago) is gone forever. My (*our!*) future is what matters and I reckon you're with me on this. So that's the prize I focus on.

Sitting at my dresser, Quark pouts into the mirror, pushing my lower lip out in an exaggerated grumpy face. "Why the long face?" he says. "There is no need to get upset about it. No need to be down in the dumps. This is exciting! And entirely impersonal. I attach no feelings." Has my own voice ever sounded so obsequious? I sound like the slimy Uriah Heep from Dickens' *David Copperfield*, all cloyingly insincere.

"No feelings?"

"None at all," Quark confirms, still wheedling.

"So you don't care about me — at all?"

"Sorry?"

"You've lived within me, you have virtually *been* me for, what? — almost three weeks now."

"Yes …" He's not sure where I'm going with this. To be frank, neither am I, but I hope there'll be an opportunity for something more than meaningless point scoring on the horizon. "You've got at least a vague impression of what it is to be a teenage girl. A human being. To be *alive*. To exist in a corporeal state … even though you haven't really taken advantage of it," I add, *sotto voce*.

"Yes?" He really doesn't get it!

"And this has been, what — a waste of your time? You've gained nothing from the experience?"

"Well … "

"Because if you don't want to live my life, I have news for you: I DO! I *love* my life. I'm clinging on with everything I have."

"Yes, I do see that! And that is precisely what we need to settle. Once and for all."

Look — I've had issues with bullying, I've lived through my panics, and once I even scored only twice the required pass mark in a Maths test! But I know that compared to many, my life has been plain-sailing. And even in stressful times, I've never feared living before. Right now though, deep inside my tiny broken body,

I'm too scared of dying to think much about actual living!

"I am freeing you from worry," Quark pronounces.

"Huh? For a moment I'm too stunned to speak. It's like he's been listening in to my thoughts again. "So, what … I'm free? Just like that? You're setting me free?"

"Yes indeed. I am liberating you. Undoing the shackles that bind you to this lonely, isolated planet." Quark sounds almost breathless, so touched is he at his own philanthropy.

"But not really free? This is just another way of 'doing me a favour' by eliminating me, yes?"

"Your life here is not preordained. You are on Earth by the merest accident."

I sigh. "That's why some people believe in something greater than themselves — God or whatever. And I agree: our presence is wonderful. Fantastic. Totally mind-blowing."

"Yet your existence is precarious and you are making a bit of a mess of it."

"Well, I'm not: I recycle, I shower instead having a bath, I'm vegetarian — unless planet-munching space monsters force bacon down my gullet! I do the best I can."

"I am sure you do, Daisy," Quark says, with a condescending smile and in a tone that is only ninety-five percent patronising. He may as well add, "there, there" and pat my head, except he'd look pretty silly sitting there, patting his own head! "And this is where I can help you."

"Experts and scientists all over the world are looking for solutions. Everyone knows this, Quark. We need to find a balance between humanity and all the creatures that share our home, and I think — I hope — we will. But it's *our* mess to sort out."

"Then there is global warming. Deforestation. Nuclear weapons. Loss of habitats. Population growth." He makes that hands wide movement, which, combined with the pursing of my lips, clearly means he rests his case.

Except he doesn't, because no case goes under-egged with

Quark. "You have no divine right to exist. And your run of luck will end at some stage. Humanity has all these grand plans, yet when it comes down to it, what are you?"

My turn to sigh. "A girl. A teenager; a human being —"

"No," he interrupts, "I mean, fundamentally, what are the building blocks of your world? Your physical world, I mean."

"Well, if you're going to get all fundamentalist on me —"

But he simply talks over me again. Having the actual voice in our going concern, he does this whenever he chooses! Another of the many irritating things about my body-snatching space critter!

"You are a collection of cells and that is all you are. You have no more right to exist than an amoeba or a Gnexian rumblewoad."

"Maybe," I hedge (if you have any idea how I can answer and preferably disprove Quark's statement, answers on a postcard, please), "but my cells coalesce in a very special way. I can think, I can have an influence on my planet's future." Or at least I *used* to be able to think and I very much *hope* I'll be around long enough to be an influence. Actually, come to think of it, if I'm not around, there won't *be* a future!

"Humans do not always act in the best interest of the planet."

I inwardly glare. "Well, that's hardly my fault, is it? You can't take all of human history out on me. Besides, we're changing and taking better care of our world now. We *are* sentient; we have consciousness. We have a conscience. We can change; you've lived as one of us, surely you know by now that we are *way* more than just random cells.

"And also — there's no way you can say you're eliminating our entire global population just to save the planet from humanity and return it to the safe-keeping of amoeba and ocean-dwelling protozoa! Don't pretend you're doing us — or the amoeba — a favour. Because you're not. Let's make that clear. It's time to tell it like it is: you are a psychopath. You are the oldest and least wise so-called being in the universe. Don't leave our planet in the care of single-celled organisms!"

There's a pause. If we could have done, Quark and I would have either tried to out-stare each other or paced around the room trying to calm down and reduce the tone of our bickering. As it is, he just stares blankly back at my face in the mirror.

I try another tack. "Listen, Quark, can I ask you a question?"

"Go ahead, oh, wise and *sentient* being," he says deliberately and with some asperity. Clearly, I'm not playing fair. I'm not rolling over and playing dead. I'm not making goo-goo eyes at his perspicacity. He is, once more, showing his true colours. He tries a hard stare, but I think he's as tired of this as I am, and the glare lacks intensity and any real sense of menace. I think — hope — I'm wearing him down.

I imagine straightening my shoulders and pursing my lips as I simply ignore his sniping. "Be honest: in all the beings you've taken over — and slaughtered — have you ever felt so truly alive?"

"Well —"

"Or is it different this time? The experience, the feelings, the emotions, the … passion of humanity. Does it feel different?"

He shivers and tries to cover his discomfort by adjusting his position on the chair in front of my dressing table.

"Come on, Quark, you're part of me, or I'm part of you — whatever: we're practically related, so you can level with me. Break the habit of a lifetime and be honest." Is that sniping too? Or is it out and out bitchy?!

"Beings have fought to live. Fought for their pitiful existence." In the mirror, my eyes show a brief trace of regret, although whether at the loss of so many lives or their lack of fight, I can't be sure. "But this degree of feeling, of emotion is … somewhat unsettling and disturbing," he concludes, and my eyes look away from the mirror as if he can't look *me* in the eye.

This is interesting! My emotions, my teenage angst makes him uncomfortable. That's definitely something to file away for further reference.

"'Pitiful' you call me?"

"Yes," he says.

"It sounds like you're trying to distance yourself from your actions. From your responsibilities."

"I don't see it that way," he says, defensively.

"Well, *quel surprise* as my French teacher would say! Why am I not surprised! I think you've been missing out, Quark."

"Oh, yes, you puny little teenage human, and I guess you are just the being to tell a multi-billion-year-old entity exactly how they have been missing out?"

I think someone's rattled his cage! "Funnily enough, I think I am. I'm just on the verge of life —"

"Verge of death, more like," he mutters. "You *were* on the verge of life. But even *had* you lived, that life would have been a matter of a trivial few of your years."

"Again with the 'trivial' — belittling and trying to demean what you can't control; what you can't put in a neat box."

"I think I have you rather neatly boxed in."

"On the contrary, it's me who's done the boxing-in, and you who got locked out. But we're talking of your eternal lack of life, of —"

"Lack of what? Humanity? Hah! I am not human and I have no desire to be."

"No? I guess not. Not full time, anyway. Don't have the guts for it."

"What?! Are you suggesting I should move in permanently and learn to enjoy living as a teenage 'girl'? Become a young 'woman'. Get a 'job'. Live a 'life'?" He actually says those words as if they're in inverted commas, as if they're unclean, outlandish and unpleasant. Yes, including 'girl' and 'woman' — this is the kind of entity I'm dealing with here! Yes, he'd top Unipol's Most Wanted list (if such an organisation existed); he's the universe's ultimate psychopath, but that's not all — he's misogynistic too!

"Don't worry," Mr Misanthrope continues, "once I find a way into a being's consciousness, or central nervous system, or brain,

172

then I can take over. Take control."

"And then?"

"Then I —"

"Yes, come on — say it."

"I shut it down."

"You shut down the brain?"

"Yes."

"So, finally you've said it."

"What?"

"Brain death. That's the definition of the end of life. That's you killing them. An ugly word, yes? Murder. That's another ugly word. But that's you finally calling a spade a spade."

"A spade? What is the spade for?"

"It's just a phrase, an idiom. But in your case, if you stuck around long enough, I guess you could use your metaphorical spade to bury them."

Quark is silent.

"This is what you do. What you have always done."

"Yes."

"Why?"

"Why what?"

"Why shut them down at all? Why not live a little?"

"I have experienced brief glimpses of life." He pauses and, in the mirror, I see my eyes cloud and once more look away from my own reflection, instead staring down at my hands, tightly grasped in my lap. "But very few to be honest." He sounds downhearted.

"Out of the billions of lifeforms you've taken over and ... absorbed, you've never experienced anything. You've never seen a sunset through their eyes? Or caught the scent of a flower in bloom? Tasted a fine meal? Seen the look of love in the eyes of a parent, child or lover?"

"I have felt the lives of so many."

"Have you? Have you *really*? Or have you just snuffed them out, like a candle. Have you truly felt what it's like to be alive? D'you

173

know what it's to be alive at all? Or do you only know what it is to *take* life?"

"It never occurred to me before," he whispers.

"In however many billion years it never occurred to you to stop the killing?"

"There was never time —"

"Quark, you've had nothing *but* time!"

"No. No-one ever fought back before. Not for long enough for me to get any sense of who or what they were. Always just fragments of memories, flooding past over a swirling torrent of abstract, jumbled rapids."

I say nothing.

After a moment, he continues. "I saw flashes. Just glimpses of the beings they were. But I did not see how they went about their life. I did not know what they thought. And when I got that very brief insight, what I mainly saw was —"

"What?"

"Fear. Terror. Panic. Sorrow."

Do I push the knife now? Somewhere deep inside … well actually, in the circumstances, right in here where I currently reside, I feel a stab of pity for Quark, for his lack of … what? Maybe just the tiniest degree of empathy that would have allowed him to cease and desist with this absurd genocide millions of years before the Earth even existed. But I can't let this go. There's a glimmer of hope for me here, I'm sure.

"You're old, Quark, but you're not wise. You don't see life for what it is. You don't appreciate its significance. Its many possibilities."

All the while I'm talking, I'm thinking — I will make it through this. I must keep him talking, make him think, make him see what he's doing. In my ever-shrinking space, I think … I'm fine. I'm fine. I'm fine. And, if I say it enough, it might even end up being true. Yeah?

Chapter 40

DAISY SOUP

It rarely takes Quark more than one or two *becomings* for the momentum become so rapid that the end is effectively instantaneous. Blink and you'd miss a street, a city, a country, a *continent*, vanish into something rather less than dust before you opened your eyes again. Of course, in the time it took to complete the simple reflex of an eye blink, you too would be something less than dust ... and you'd have missed the downfall of your entire civilisation!

(There's probably a lesson here for us, but if we pause long enough to contemplate it, we may miss the end of our own planet and that would be a shame. Imagine standing at the Pearly Gates — should they exist — and overhearing the conversation: "Did you see that? It was amazing!" And having to admit that you were blinking at the most significant moment in the entire history of the planet ...)

The pace Quark operates at is such that no being has ever had a genuine effect on him. None has changed him. In billions of years, not one creature has impacted on him at all.

And then Quark met Daisy Jacobs ...

And this creature, this human being, this girl-child stopped him in his tracks. He knows the end is inevitable: she and all of humanity will become a glorious mass of space dust. But the impact she's made upon him remains.

And Quark thinks he may have changed. He —

"What would happen if I didn't believe in you?" Daisy interrupts his contemplation.

"What do you mean?" This time, Quark's actually grateful for the interruption; he's not given to self-reflection and the discomforting feelings it brings. Quark was unsettled right from the 'thinking' and 'feeling' in the very first contact with this young woman. She'd set him uncomfortably on the back foot. How this could happen when he controls over 99% of her body is beyond him. How can she fight him from a tiny bit of her brain, which she claims is a locked room (but is actually just a collection of ganglia and neurons)? She's squeezed all she truly is as a person, at the most basic level, into that space. She's kept her personality — and her attitude! And somehow stored it in that minuscule space. It's baffling!

Yet her room is just a square centimetre or so in the middle of her brain that she's convinced herself is some kind of fortified castle! And in convincing herself she's persuaded the rest of her brain — the majority, in fact — and all controlled by Quark himself, that the room exists. That it's *real*. The very notion is beyond preposterous, yet she's done it. She's made a room and a highly effective lock, out of literally nothing except her imagination; and she's kept him out of it for three weeks. Maybe there's something in this 'girl power' she goes on about!

And she's not just sneaky and tricksy, but she also talks. And talks. She's trying to talk him into submission! She's talking again now. Debating. Arguing the toss. Refusing to accept her fate. And always reaching out. Reaching further. Seeking to be more.

"Well, it's a heck of a leap to accept that a singularity even exists in the first place. Let alone one that hoovers up innocent teenage girls. How can you expect anyone to visualise such a thing? No one will get a eureka moment and say 'aha! Now it all makes sense: life is meaningless and I'll get gobbled up by Quarky.'"

"I told you what I think about being called Quarky".

"And I've told you what I think of psychopathic mass-murdering space entities, and that hasn't got me too far yet, has it?

Anyway, how many layers of reality would people have to break through to reach the conclusion that you do actually exist?"

Quark sighs. "Listen, Daisy, you have been lucky to have your moment in the sun. Now your luck has run out. Look up into the night sky and you will see the ashes of long-dead stars. And that is what you will be. You humans are merely a collection of atoms that briefly coalesce into an ordered pattern. And then break down."

"You are *such* a ray of sunshine! And anyway, I'm not ready for oblivion yet."

"There is nothing inevitable about your presence in the universe."

"I know! And that's what makes my very existence even more astonishing and miraculous!"

"Sadly, your future will be somewhat different to what you may have imagined." A look skitters across Daisy's features — a kind of distant cousin, three times removed, of sympathy. He tries his best, but empathy is a concept entirely — well, alien — to him. Billions of years as a psychopathic mass-murdering space entity tends to erode the finer points of the 'do unto others' parable ...

"I do think about it, strangely enough. Personally, I imagine growing up and falling in love and having children and a great job and — you know, a *life*. There's a lot of bleak stuff about nuclear weapons and global warming that humanity has to work out. But we'll find a way. And it's kinda comforting that in the distant future, whenever what the human race has evolved into, faces their inevitable end, our planet will go on, nurturing new life. Whether that's some super-evolved lizard or insect or whatever. Of course, that's *after* I stop you guzzling up every*one* and every*thing*."

Quark shifts, as if discomfited. Daisy's eyes glance down at her inter-twined hands again. "I am here for everything sentient, yes."

"You'll leave behind a barren rock. That is just sad, Quark."

177

Daisy's head comes up again and there's a fire in her eyes as her voice puts Quark's thoughts to passionate, evangelical voice. "Sad? It is far from sad. It is beautiful. It is clean, neat … perfect!"

"You enjoy this, don't you?"

"Enjoy?" Quark's confusion is genuine.

"Yeah, all this bad guy menace. All this murder and mayhem."

"It is not a case of 'enjoy', it is —"

"It's what? Go on: enlighten me. Tell me my death has meaning. Tell me that interplanetary destruction serves a higher purpose."

"No, it doesn't. The end is inevitable."

"But the clue is in the name."

"What name?"

"End. Death comes at the end."

"And the end is sometimes earlier than you expect."

"Agreed: illness or accident, I know."

"I am humanity's accident. An accident waiting to happen. So, don't get too comfortable in there. I can take you apart," Quark says.

"What?"

"Molecule by molecule, atom by atom. From the inside out. Break you right down to your constituent elements."

"Maybe … "

"Definitely!"

"I'm not sure that you can. But I'm certain you won't."

"I could too!"

There's a brief hiatus before Quark gives in and breaks the silence. "So why will I not do that?"

"Because you'd have to transform to do so and from what I've learnt from you (our exchanges *have* been two ways, and we've both maybe given up too much information), that would mean Earth would be safe."

"Not necessarily."

"Yes, absolutely. I know that you need the energy from the first *becoming* to move on to the second, and then it's cumulative, one to two, two to four, four to eight, etc. It gets easier with each incarnation. But that first is crucial. And if you take me apart, you'll get no boost, and that, my little singularity, will be the end of you on this planet. So go somewhere else and see if you can get a jump-start from some other innocent little creature!"

"But then you will be no more. You will be in bits."

"I guess that's right, but what a way to go. I'll be Daisy Soup, saving the world, one crouton at a time! Maybe not quite the rallying cry of a superhero, but it'll do nicely for my epitaph!"

Chapter 41

A FRIEND IN NEED

"Why are you so glum?" asks Quark the next day as we leave the house.

I so wish I could put my hands on my hips and glare at him with the disdain he so richly deserves. "Oh, I don't know, maybe because I am *still* held hostage by a homicidal alien."

"Daisy, you will soon experience all the myriad wonders of the universe. You should be optimistic. You should be happy. Joyous!"

"Yeah, whatever."

Sure, be happy about my rapacious captor and how he's trampling all over my life on the way to wiping me out of existence. And not only that, but making my best friend cry! I'd seen Amy's face crumple as Quark turned away and left her, so why hadn't he? Maybe he saw it, but where he came from — physically *and* emotionally — such feelings 'did not compute'.

I have a tight group of friends in school. We see each other all the time during the week and at least a few of us are together most weekends — just going to the cinema or hanging out in the shopping centre, at the park or in each other's houses.

But when we're not with the others, Amy and I are either together or messaging or FaceTiming. And we really do talk about everything. I'm pretty open. Mum and Dad will confirm that I'm never short of an opinion! But Amy knows everything about me, or at least she did. She can't possibly have the first notion of what's happening to me now, but she knows me like I know myself, and for sure she knows something's seriously wrong.

Quark's spent little time with her recently and there's no way he can talk to her like I can, or with anything like the same intimacy and warmth. I miss her so much and it's clear she feels the same. She's trying so hard to keep our closeness, despite the constant cold shoulder she's getting from Quark.

But, bless her, she keeps on giving 'me' another chance. She's trying again with the person she believes to be her best friend as we walk to school. I love that she hasn't given up on me, but PQ (Post Quark) Daisy obviously grates on her.

"Hey, coo-ee, Little Miss Personality," Amy says with a rare show of petulance.

"I beg your pardon?" Quark's deep in thought — although I have no clue what he's thinking. With any luck, he's pondering what we talked about last night. But it's more likely he's plotting more ways to bring about my downfall.

"I'm sure you're not listening to what I've been saying." (He wasn't, I know that for sure.)

"You are correct, I was not," (told you!) "but I am sure it was inconsequential," Quark answers, blunderfully.

"What! Was that a joke?" Amy's trying her best to see the funny side of Quark's behaviour. "Didn't sound like it … and it's unlikely because you've been so stiff lately."

"In what way?"

"In a not at all relaxed, easy-going, wise-cracking, fun-to-be with, Daisy kind of way. What's with the personality transplant? What's got into you?" And there, finally and without actually realising it, someone outside of me has nailed it. If Amy only realised, I thought, she'd push this point. Push until she finds out … what? But that's the problem: there's nothing *to* find out. Nothing that will make sense to anyone *with* any sense.

"I was talking, Daisy, as you'd know, *if* you'd been listening, about Ellie. She's got the problem of the beautiful girl," Amy says.

Oh, that I should have such a problem! Quark must have put on some sort of wary, frowny expression, probably not understanding where Amy's going with this.

"Don't pull that face, Daisy. I was wrong about her too, I admit it, but since you've been 'gone'," she puts the word in inverted commas and gives me a pointed look, "I've talked more to her. She's not sure if the sycophants who hang around her like her for herself, or just want to be in the orbit of a gorgeous, popular girl. And she's taking a hit for what's happened to you too."

Quark ignores the last statement. "You think she is pretty? Is that important?" But: hang on, Quark's actually joining in! By his standards, this is practically a conversation!

"You find it easy to be top of the class, and you're funny too, Dais — although admittedly not so much fun just recently, when you've been weird and distant and altogether a bit of a jerk. But it's not so easy for Ellie, so don't be so hard on her. She's not as bright as you or as funny as you — and there's not much she can do about that. But she tries as hard as she can to at least be as pretty as you."

I'm stunned; Amy's biased of course, but she's just said Ellie's beautiful. I thought she talked about all this sort of stuff with me, but now she says Ellie wants to be as pretty as me!

Suddenly I feel like a heel; like a truly mean person, thinking back over the times I've been with Ellie. Yes, she's been horrible, but it's clear that over the past couple of weeks Amy's come round to Ellie and now feels sorry for her. And I trust her opinion. Even Quark (in the guise of me) is talking to Ellie — and getting on with her. Although Quark getting on with her is not much a recommendation, admittedly!

It's also upsetting to hear my best friend be so complimentary to me after 'I' have treated her so badly. She's still trying hard to keep our relationship going. It's as though she knows that, deep down, I'm hurting. If only I could give her a sign that she's bang on: all is very much *not* well. I wish I could send up a distress signal!

The conversation has carried on and I've missed what Amy's said.

"— what Jamie, Simon and Chris did in school yesterday. Honestly, boys are a different species, aren't they," she says.

"Are they really?!" Quark answers. "That explains a lot!"

Amy guffaws, "now that's the sense of irony I've missed recently!"

What! The irony of this statement is not lost on me: 'different species' is exactly right, but while Amy thinks I'm suddenly more myself, she's the one *talking* to the different species!

Chapter 42

THE HUMAN TEENAGER
An alien on earth

Quark lay awake in Daisy's bed, thinking about the conversation they'd had before she drifted off to sleep deep in that room inside her head. Living inside her body, and like a squatter in her mind, Quark had seen deep inside himself too. He'd even experienced his own humanity!

Being used to unmitigated success, it's tough to come to terms with human frailty and weakness.

"Your molecules are not so strong, after all," Daisy teased.

He'd shaken her head, then tapped the side of it. "The emotional turmoil, the chaos inside a human head —"

"A *teenage* human head!"

And, as he'd discovered was so often the case, she'd hit the nail on the head: what was happening within her — within *him* now — was an emotional version of the chaos at the heart of the universe after the Big Bang!

Quark's observing humankind, but he's studying himself too.

As the human body changes with puberty, he notes, so too does the brain. There's a lot of re-wiring going on, with links and connections reforming and reshaping in a way that hasn't happened since the person was a toddler. Some think of teenagers as angry, self-conscious, callous or selfish. This isn't personal ... well, not always. But it explains why the smallest disagreement can assume the epic proportions of an intercontinental ballistic war!

The confusion within Daisy drives him to distraction, but also diverts from his main aim (to dismantle every atom of her being). So when he focuses on returning to the lair where she's hidden herself away, he finds the route constantly changing, like the points on that railway track she teased him with.

Quark recognises the pressures and daily traumas of teenage life from personal experience. And he knows life isn't always easy for adult humans. But apart from Daisy's parents, the only adults he's had dealings with are the teachers at school. And they have to endure the major issues of teenage life every single day, without the perks of actually *living* the teenage life!

But in his, admittedly limited, experience of life during his thirteen-odd billion-year existence, nothing's come close to the stress of living for nearly three weeks as Daisy. He landed when everything is changing for her and so she (now *he*) plunges daily into intense physical and emotional situations.

He knows she took her schoolwork more seriously than he has. Fear of failure is intense within her, and he knows she and her parents set high standards for behaviour and achievement. Her parents take pride in her high marks; or rather they'd previously done so. In the last few weeks, their standards had dropped along with his. Not getting a detention; doing any homework at all; getting any sort of a pass mark in a test — these are the aims of New Daisy!

Quark doesn't do sleepless nights, or angst and worry about homework and test results. He believes it isn't the end of the world if he fails a test or two on Daisy's behalf. Actually, he doesn't so much believe this as *know* it, with absolute certainty, because what he also knows is that a C grade is irrelevant in the greater scheme of things. If he gets even the slightest sniff of a chance, *he* is the end of the world, not a measly test result!

So he's ignoring the pressure Daisy's parents and teachers are putting on 'her' to return to her former levels of achievement. What he's having a harder time with is the pressure her mutinous body, with its oddly fluctuating hormone levels, is placing upon him.

He feels fully justified in being angry at Daisy for slowing down the inevitable destruction of her planet. But he's sometimes angry without having such a rational reason; in fact, with no idea of what he's raging against at all. At other times, he's ashamed to feel tearful — for example over the dratted elephant documentary created by the seemingly saintly Mr Attenborough; this man was knighted for creating television programmes that made a girl cry!

Quark knows mood swings are a biological part of growing up. The emotional rollercoaster ride, the spots, the hair growing in strange places — all of this is 'natural' and 'normal'! Logically, he knows this. But personally, it feels as though he has set down in the eye of a tornado. Logic is books and theory; reality is quite a different matter!

It's okay for Daisy in her castle, hidden by neural pathways that shift and change like the stairways at Hogwarts; she's oblivious to all this while he suffers every indignity her body can throw at him. Plus, he's protecting her with a shield of oblivious indifference from the cruelty of bullying and the burden of peer pressure.

He doesn't care what other people say about her wearing the wrong shoes or one of her mum's old dresses — and actually, the dress hadn't been so old, and Daisy's mum hadn't been best pleased about that either! But it was all water off a duck's back to Quark. He took the flak. And was Daisy grateful? Need you even ask …

The thoughts Quark's had access to have given him a real — but slanted — insight into humanity. His time as a walking, talking human have been female-biased, teen-biased, a bit geek-biased, and very Daisy-biased. But he's sure his perspective is the very definition of what it is to be human. However, it's not just inaccurate, but it's also incomplete because he doesn't even have the full picture of Daisy. Much is obscure, incomplete or baffling because of a lack of context. He's encountered nothing like a human, let alone anyone like Daisy in his entire previous existence.

Quark can't access all the knowledge, experience, memories and thoughts stored within Daisy's brain. Some are in her secure area and she controls them. And she firmly shuts him out!

He's lived as a human for almost three weeks — or at least as a teenage girl, and that's a close enough approximation. He's had experiences, talked to people, worked at relationships, watched television, read books. He's practically an expert!

But Daisy is on a different wavelength. She doesn't have the same life goals; her goal at the moment is just to *have* a life! But Quark isn't sure Daisy was a proper teenager anyway. She'd been altogether too stuffy and panicky about things. She'd forgotten what it felt like to just get out there and *live*.

Teenagers take risks, they try out new things that might not be the best decisions ever made in the history of the universe. Quark knows quite a lot about the history of the universe, having been around for most of it. He's sure, with that knowledge behind him, he'll make much better decisions. And, being of a scientific bent, he sets about proving that theory.

He'll win: Daisy Jacobs *will* become. It's inevitable. Meanwhile, why should Quark live in the style of the previous goody-goody occupant of this body? Why waste the opportunity of a lifetime? She'd stressed about not experiencing life. Quark decides to *really* live the teenage dream. No longer restrained, nice, sober and Daisy-like. He's been teen-lite. That will change — from now on he'll be the quintessential teen. The teen they'll write textbooks about — at least the teen they *would* have written about at some future date, had that future date not become irrelevant by the lack of a future!

Chapter 43

ADRIFT ON A BLUSHING SEA OF SELF-DOUBT

E ven being locked in, I can't help overhearing the gossip about why 'I' am acting (even more) weird, and why I'm not continuing my 'pursuit' of Connor. Personally, I can't understand why everyone's worked up about it; I'd only wanted to ask him a simple yes or no question.

"You are right, Daisy. We like him and we should find out what he feels about us. We have lost track of your desire to get to know him better in all this confusion."

"Us?!" I zone in on that one word.

"Yes, us. Me and you: us — Daisy Jacobs."

You know those situations when you wish you'd never opened your mouth? When you say something so dumb it's like you didn't engage your brain at all? Well, in my case I didn't even have to open my mouth to take that disastrous step! I never got to ask the question all those chapters ago! But I had no idea I'd actually thought it out in the open now — where Quark can hear me, I mean. Apparently, I did; and he's immediately all over it!

"Hang on, you're still getting confused," I tell him. "*Me* Daisy Jacobs, *you* Quark."

"Yes, but I am here now and so I can ask him."

"Here, where? He, who? What?! No!" We're leaving school after a long day of me screaming answers — all loud and out in the open in my speaking space — only for Quark to ignore them and say nothing, or say something stupid to get a reaction (which, surprise, surprise, he did), or just stare out of the window into space. To where he's free to return anytime at all!

"We are here, on the spot. I will ask him — right now."

"Quark — no!"

"Daisy, I will only say what you were going to before I interrupted you. There he is: over by the gates. If we hurry, we can catch him."

"Yes, but —"

"Except, I will do it much better." My body is now pushing through the crowd of laughing, chattering kids who are full of the near combustible energy that comes after release from being penned into classrooms all day.

"What? No! You don't understand!"

"Ah, but I *do* understand." He breaks off and calls ahead, "Connor!" His internal monologue returns to me, "you forget, I'm inside your head, Daisy."

"Believe me, I *never* forget that!"

"I know what you think. What you *really* think," he says.

"What I think and what I say are two different things. The way you spoke to Mum last week, the way you spoke to Amy and upset her, the rude way you treated Mr Ford today in Maths — all were wrong."

"But that was me, not you. Now I'll be you. Only better!"

I don't like the sound of this at all! Post-Quark-Daisy has so far had a few detentions, totally messed up my grades, all but cost me my best friend, over-eaten, attempted to come out, eaten meat, insulted Mum … and who knows what else. But PQD is positively not going to mess with my so-called love life! "You must filter what you say, what *I* say, Quark. You can't go around speaking your mind to a boy." But what can I do to stop him? That's the question. I have zero control over the mess Quark's making of my life.

"It is so much easier if you speak your mind. Especially with my help! Then everyone will know where they stand."

"Quark, no don't —"

"Connor! Can I walk with you?" Too late; now I *can't* stop him. PQD squeezes my body between Connor and one of his football

189

buddies and — oh, god no! — takes his arm. To everyone else it looks as though Daisy Jacobs has just run across the playground calling Connor's name and then linked arms with him. His buddy, Steve, gets the message and slopes rapidly away with raised eyebrows and a knowing smirk. And I bet, I just bet that PQD is gurning a smile up into Connor's face right now. Connor looks surprised and flustered enough for that to be the case.

"Hi Daisy, long time no speak." He dimples that smile at me and I admit, if I had a tummy of my own right now, there's no doubt it would flutter like crazy!

"You are correct, Connor," says PQD, leaning my body closer into Connor's, "and I thought we should remedy that right now by having a proper talk." Quark looks deeply into Connor's vibrant blue eyes and my view of him blurs and clears rapidly several times within a few seconds as if ... oh, so cringey! — I'm batting my eyes at Connor!

A flush appears on Connor's chiselled cheeks, but he speaks normally, as if girls throwing themselves into his arms is an everyday occurrence. "We used to chat all the time, but you've been a bit ... strange? No, maybe a little distant recently."

"I am very sorry if you think that is the case, Connor," PQD simpers.

"Yeah, you've been acting differently, Daisy. Not yourself. I'm worried about you."

He's worried? He *thinks* about me? Now this *is* interesting. This is something to explore delicately; to *finesse*.

"Well, believe me, Connor, it is not personal — to you, I mean. I do not mean to appear distant to you. But ... well, we are all going through a lot of changes at the moment." Quark presses my body closer to Connor once more. Just for a moment I got carried away and forgot that PDQ does not do finesse. For Quark, subtle comes wrapped around a sledgehammer!

"You know, Connor, with what is happening to me now, it is like all the bits of my body are in the wrong place or are the wrong size. I would like some bits to be different ... you know: prettier. And other bits to be, well ... bigger."

Connor's eyes widen and he swallows visibly. But, bless him, he tries to carry on as if this totally random conversation is the most natural development from our previously amicable but distant relationship. "Daisy, we're adolescents. We'd all like some bits to be a bit ... bigger." His blush deepens, but still he continues. "But we're all still growing and we have lots of time."

Quark is steaming right ahead now. He's on a roll. For him, this is a new pinnacle in conversational hyper-drive. "Actually, I think my whole body is just ... kind of wrong. I would like a new model. In fact, I'll take Icky's body: those hips and boo —"

I fling open the door to my safe room without a care for my own — and so your (sorry!) safety — and I positively scream in my loudest think-speak: "Do NOT have me say 'boobs' out loud to Connor, Quark! Just don't ever! I won't survive it — I'm not that easy-going kind of girl!"

Quark's so wrapped up in the moment, that he misses this open goal, this opportunity to get me and end it once and for all. He continues without skipping a beat, " — curves are in just the right place and just the right proportion."

"Icky?" Connor looks confused.

"Yeah — Icky Ellie."

Connor guffaws. "That's so perfect!"

Quark shrugs. "So, yeah: her bod, but I wanna keep my brain — with the added confidence and self-assurance that comes with great boo— a great body, of course." He is totally off on one now. He's abbreviating words again, just like a real person. Well, *almost*.

"You don't need Ellie's boo—" Connor stops himself abruptly.

"Quark!" I interject, "you've got Connor at it now!"

" —body." Connor continues, his recovery almost as seamless as Quark's "You're great just as you are: brains *and* body ... "

"Yes, but Ellie —"

"Ellie nothing!"

What?!! 'Ellie nothing'! What does that mean?

This time, Quark's listening to me. "Connor, what do you mean, 'Ellie nothing'?" I'm still out in the open! I slink back behind my door, relieved that Quark hasn't noticed what I did and pleased I can watch on my TV from a position of security once more. As I shut my door, I hiss at him, "Quark, don't put everything I think into words! Remember: there *is* such a thing as a filter!" I'm stunned at how seamless my link with Quark sometimes is and, I confess, I'm on tenterhooks for Connor's answer.

"I mean, Ellie is a pretty girl," Connor says. "And if she calmed down a bit, she'd be really nice. I can't say I agree with everything *you've* done in the past few weeks — I really don't think you've been yourself. But … well, you've got the looks *and* the personality, Daisy. You're the full package."

"Really? But what about my tiny, little boo—"

"Quark!" I bark at him from inside my room, but with loud and unmistakable authority, "for the last time: if you say that out loud to Connor, I swear I will haunt you from now until the very end of time!"

But Connor laughs. "I thought it was boys who obsessed about boo— bodies," he rejoins, blushing still deeper.

"See what you've done to him, Quark — he's got a one-track mind, thanks to you!" I could curl up and die of embarrassment, but, rendered motionless — and wordless — I have no choice but to listen, cringe inwardly (well, where else?), and wish myself a long, long way away from the inside of my own head, where I am being afforded a ringside seat for this stratospherically embarrassing conversation. I wish I was anywhere else right now — like the other side of the galaxy. Suddenly, Quark's threat to break me into my constituent parts and distribute me throughout the universe doesn't seem so bad!

I don't know what on earth (excuse the pun) Quark's doing here, but I am lost; just totally all at sea and adrift on a blushing sea of self-doubt. My head tilts down again, my eyes focus low, and I just know that Quark's now glancing up at Connor through the curtained fringe of my cinnamon hair. And … OMG! He's going all demure and flirty with Connor again!

Wait! I just missed a bit there, so stunned was I by Quark's repartee; did PQD just mention the 'L' word?! "Quark! %£@*%$!!!!!!" I mutter angrily in my mind what I'll never get the chance to say out loud to him. I'm mortified by what I think Quark's just said. I'm furious because he is so far over-stepping the mark — and there's no way it could be true: all I ever wanted to say to Connor in the first place was that I liked him and wanted to go out with him … okay, *really, really* liked him and *desperately* wanted to go out with him. But 'l_ _e'? Nah. I'm only fourteen. I love Mum and Dad — and Luke too, I guess. And I love Amy, obviously. But they are my family and my best friend in the entire world. To love a boy, though? I'm too young. I'd wanted to spend time with Connor to see if he's as great as I think he might be. I wanted him to be my friend. And only then — *maybe* — my boyfriend.

"Thanks — it's been lovely talking to you too, Daisy," I hear Connor say. Oh, thank goodness! I thought I'd missed 'myself' voice love for Connor, but apparently I only love *talking* to him. Phew! It's such a relief that Quark hasn't, for once, put his foot in my mouth and blurted that out. If I ever use the "L" word, I want to say it from the heart. From *my* heart. Not to have it flung out into the unknown by an uncomprehending entity.

"I've really missed talking to you," I hear Connor say. "But, Daisy …"

My head turns to face him and my eyes look deeply into his; my goodness, how blue they are! I've never been this close to Connor before, virtually breathing the same air as him — although, technically, I'm not actually breathing.

Connor's generous lips curve into a smile that doesn't reach his subdued eyes, "lose the act, huh?"

"What act?" My voice betrays Quark's confusion.

"This bad-girl thing you've got going on. Clever-girl, that's you. Funny-girl too." This time the smile is the full, knock-out works — even as the blush deepens again. "Yeah — and pretty-girl. But there's no need to play to the crowd like you have in the last few weeks. It doesn't suit you at all. It's like you're trying to be someone you're really not."

His deep blue eyes plant themselves on 'me', as if he's looking deeply into me — the real Daisy — buried deep within the fake that he's so gently reproached.

I thought Quark's behaviour as 'Daisy' was ... not passing without notice, because I've had detentions and failed tests and been told off and all that, but was just being put down as abhorrent teenage behaviour and nothing more. Apparently not. Both Amy, who knows me *really* well, and Connor, who seems to know me *way better* than I thought (and intriguingly seems to take way more *notice* of me than I thought), have gotten right to the point and have seen that I have genuinely not been myself recently. Of course, they'd never guess that I have actively been someone else!

"It's like ..." Connor struggles to put into words how he's feeling. "Yeah. Not since —" He pauses, "I wondered if maybe you blamed me."

"Blamed you? What for?" I get it immediately and can't believe that Connor should be so sweet as to think I'd blame him, but Connor's words baffle Quark.

"I mean, blame me for what happened to you," Connor explains.

"What happened to me?" Quark's still confused, but then *he* is what happened to me, so it's understandable that he's slow on the uptake.

"Well, you know: the fainting, the bump on the head, the ... personality change," Connor's abashed at this last statement.

"I have changed?" My voice has lost the obsequiousness it had when Quark spoke to me the other day; this stupefies him like

194

Hermione Granger's finest spell — as if he's stunned anyone could think he's been anything other than the ultimate teenager recently.

"Yeah, you've changed. This is the first time we've talked properly since then and … it's good. It's really is good to talk to you again. You're always good to talk to; well —" his smile widens, crinkling the corners of his eyes, "I guess listen to, really. But you're still not like you were before the bang on the head, and I wondered if you blamed me for that."

"No, not at all. You did nothing at all. I think I am just learning what it is to be a teenager. I am … trying things on for size, if you understand what I mean." Quark's not usually quick on the uptake, but he understands he must let Connor off lightly, and for that I'm grateful.

"I do, Daisy, but remember some bits of you … quite a lot actually, doesn't *need* to change. You're just per —"

"Connor! Hi!" Aaagh, it's Ellie Watson, with particularly 'Icky' timing! "Oh, hello, Daisy," she adds in grudging acknowledgement of my presence. "Sorry, didn't see you down there." She sighs deeply, expanding what she has in abundance and what I sadly lack. Despite Quark's attempts at snuggling up, Connor can't have missed the absence of anything much to press up against him, just as he can't miss what nature has seen fit to bestow upon Ellie.

"Remember, Connor we're all meeting up, aren't we?" She indicates over her shoulder to Sue and Claire, plus Steve and a few other members of the football team. "Our little *group*." She emphasises this as clearly not including me. "And now here you are." She grasps his arm and pulls Connor towards her. "And, er … there you are," she adds, emphasising the distance between me and 'her' group — now including Connor. "Really good to see you again, though Daisy," and her smile does have a teeny bit of warmth. Not enough to invite me to join 'her' group, but it's there nonetheless.

"Yeah … great to speak to you again, Daisy," Connor's intense gaze focuses on me. "Let's talk soon." He continues to look back at me as he's all but dragged away by Ellie and her crew.

"He likes us." Quark speaks inwardly, just to me. "I think he always did, Daisy. And you should stop obsessing about bits of you being too big or too small. It's you he's interested in — you the person. The full package, that's what he said."

"Yes, but —"

"No buts."

"Quark … "

"Yes?"

"That did not go as disastrously badly as 99% of the rest of your interference in my life."

"Is that a compliment?"

"No."

"Well, I think it went very well, and Connor is right about one thing."

"What's that?"

"I clearly have not gone far enough yet. There is much more teenage life to explore. He thinks I have not been myself *enough* just recently."

"Wait, Quark — no! That's not what he said!"

"So we will progress to the next stage: Total Teen."

"QUARK!"

196

Chapter 44

YOU CAN'T ALWAYS GET WHAT YOU WANT

Quark's angry. Everyone's sticking their oar into Daisy's — HIS! — life. He felt in his soul, well not *soul*, obviously he doesn't have a soul, but he felt deep inside — and this was difficult to admit — they were right. Daisy's mum and dad, Amy, Connor, even Ellie and Mrs Griffin all knew, not what had happened to Daisy, obviously, but they knew she wasn't herself. Something was seriously wrong with her. Quark is sure his plan to take Daisy to the next level of angsty teen will settle things once and for all: everyone would realise this was a new Post-Daisy era. Her body seemed to recognise the fact — it reverberated with a new chemical balance he didn't understand. He felt slightly nauseous and yet positively buzzing with energy. Energy he'd use to make sure New Daisy was here to stay!

He'd arrived on Earth and entered Daisy's mind and body with absolute textbook perfection, thinking the connection to her would end almost before it had begun. Every single *becoming* had been instantaneous. But this time the union had continued for hours and days and was now stretching into weeks! And while this was barely the blink of an eye on his timescale, it was significant to Daisy — and was increasingly so to Quark himself. The ancient, primal Quark was weakening. Hence his sudden haste to make a real mark; his reasoning being that if Daisy became more Quark-like, she'd soon *become* Quark.

The connection to her was so intense that he lived in a state of perpetual discomfort. With other beings, there'd never been time to emerge into consciousness, experience life or lay down memories. Now though, recollection of recent incidents rose vividly in his mind. Yet he struggled to come to terms with the fact that these were memories he shared with Daisy, or at least memories he was imprinting on her mind. He's no longer sure where *he* ends and Daisy Jacobs begins …

"Everyone's confused about who they really are. But trying to figure out *who* I am, *where* I am — or *what* I am — and what currently inhabits my body is really extreme!"

Quark's so surprised by Daisy's statement that he doesn't realise she's somehow eavesdropped on his private musings. "Everyone is also someone else?" He's confused. "But there is only one Quark; there are no others like me to be within everyone."

"*Yet*," Daisy takes his statement to Quark's ideal ultimate conclusion. "But, in a way, everyone already has many people in them."

"How can that be? *You* are just one person. Amy Porter is one person. Your mother and father, your brother. Each of them is a separate person. One person in each body."

"I am *literally* one person," Daisy replies. "And until you came along and really messed me up, I was *physically* one person. But I'm a different person at school to the one I am at home. And I'm not the same with Amy as I am with Ellie. I behave differently with Mrs Griffin and the other teachers at school than I would if I met … the Prime Minister, for example."

"So, you are the same, but different?" From deep within her head, Daisy signalled agreement. Quark pressed his point, "is that not confusing?"

"Not really." Daisy pauses. "Knowing this is part of growing up, part of being human. When you're a kid, you're always the same, always open, always 'on'. You might tell complete strangers about really personal things. But as you get a bit older, you learn what's acceptable or desirable with certain people, or in certain situations."

"Such as shouting at a teacher or saying something upsetting to your mother …"

Quark hears a strange sound like a distant tinkling deep within his mind. He realises it's Daisy laughing. He can almost hear a smile in her voice as she continues, "and what you say to people can make them like you … or not. Make them feel better, or worse. You can help them understand how you feel or help them feel more comfortable when they're with you."

"This is confusing!" He realises this could be useful for his plans of advancement. "How does it work?"

He felt Daisy laugh again. It was strangely comfortable to be with her this way. And interesting to be educated by her. Too comfortable! He shakes it off and focuses on the big picture. "Your head is full of chaos, Daisy Jacobs."

"Then you should have invaded a grown up, rather than a teenager."

"No."

"No?"

"I am pleased I selected you for the first human *becoming*. It is fortunate for me."

"How can that be if I am so difficult and confusing for you?"

"Because you have taught me what it is to be alive. I have *become* many, many times. I do not know how many because the process washes away the memory of each being. There have been countless forms and creatures and beings, but in them I existed for the briefest moment. Just an ephemeral snapshot … and then gone. From the whole population of each place, I have a slightly more detailed picture, but even that is blurred and distorted. And I am *in* those beings, I am not actually *them* — in the way I *am* you. I am there for a purpose. To *become*. They are … fuel."

"Like the food my parents' cook for you."

Looking in the mirror, he sees her words bring an amused, yet almost sheepish curl to her mouth. But if Daisy sees this, she makes no comment. For once she does not make a dig about him being a psycho-killer. "True." He looks away from the mirror, feeling weirdly embarrassed, ashamed, almost. "So before now, I never learned what it was to *be*."

He pauses again. He's still looking away, so he doesn't see that Daisy's eyes are as pale as a grey-green ice flow. "You are a frustrating and perplexing girl", he mutters, his voice a barely audible whisper.

"I'm interested in a lot of things and I like to dig into subjects and find out all I can about them. And I love life. I love being alive."

"Yes, you *are* alive."

"Well, I am for the moment, for as long as you'll let me live."

Despite the troubling subject, Quark's intrigued by this conversation. He's gaining a greater understanding of humanity; a situation that will help him become a more complete teenager — and as a by-product, bring about the demise of the entire human race.

A premonition of sadness almost overwhelms him, a sense of unease at the step he's now taking. The sentiment is as brief as the glimpses he'd had into the lives of those beings he had helped *become*. But it's discomforting. His connection with Daisy clouds his judgement. In the end, no matter what he feels, the reality is simple: only one being can occupy this body.

He finds comfort in knowing he's finally on the verge of success. Against impossible odds, Daisy has delayed her inevitable downfall. But she doesn't know what's in store for her. This will change her. This will *break* her …

Chapter 45

PINK!

I feel so self-conscious! So uncomfortable, so *not* me — I mean, I know I am very much *not* me right now, but this … this is extreme. This is hardcore. I feel as though I have an enormous flashing neon sign on my head saying 'look at me' ('Please Don't Look At Me!'). Over-eating was bad; detention was awful; insulting my dear mother and upsetting my best friend — they were ghastly. But this … this is going too far. This is —

Well, this is pink.

That's right: pink!

Need I say more? Can you imagine what I look like clad from head to (near enough) toe in inglorious technicolour pink? And even worse, I'm not wearing pink sitting alone in the dark in my bedroom with the curtains closed. I'm not in the kitchen where Dad and Luke could do nothing but stare at me, utterly lost for words and barely able to find their gaping mouths with their cereal spoons as they goggled at my sheer pink-ness. No, being at home and pink was one thing, but this is uncompromisingly, shout-it-from-the-rooftops pink. This is Mainline Pink. This is me, the teenager formally known as Daisy Jacobs, walking down the High Street, bold as brass and ten times as pink, on a Saturday afternoon to meet up with my friends.

And before you say it, I know what you're thinking. Does it really matter what Quark does when he is wandering about living *my* life; when he is being *me*? Get a sense of perspective, right? That's what you think. I'm still alive and (sort of) okay. Yes, I inhabit what is effectively a tiny box that's smaller than a USB flash drive, but, hey — I'm not dead yet, yeah? But I take this as the ultimate sign of my sheer helplessness. My inability to do anything very much at all to influence what happens in my life. My inability to be even a smidgen less pink. So as Quark sashays me down the street, I pretend I can't see through my eyes, and try to avoid the glances, looks and open stares as most of the population of Braedon get their Saturday afternoon entertainment from this alien version of my true self.

I am wearing a candy floss pink baggy T-shirt, a hot-pink blazer from Mum's wardrobe, which *I* (read Quark) did not ask permission to borrow (and for which I may never forgive either Mum *or* Quark), a champagne pink micro mini skirt that is so blush that I am (almost) more embarrassed about its brevity than its sheer pink-ness, and rose-pink sparkly tights. The only saving grace is that black Converse high-top pumps complete my outfit, but that sop to normality is more than offset by my flamingo-pink, spangly Alice band. Even my fingernails are pink!

The blazer is Mum's fault; the pumps are mine. My godmother bought the T-shirt for me; she clearly felt guilty at ignoring me for so long and over-compensated with this beautifully cut designer item which Quark rescued from the back of my wardrobe where it's been ever since she bought it, on account of its overpowering, all-encompassing, sunglasses-inducing *pink*ness. Where everything else came from and how and why Quark obtained them, he refuses to tell me. If I wasn't in a not-speaking-to-him huff, I'd tell him exactly what I think of him. And I wouldn't use the special swear words that Amy and I created either!

And, yes, I know we all care too much about what other people think of us. So what if Quark makes me dress in pink and wear too much makeup — I forgot to say that Dad could have plastered the spare room with what Quark smeared all over my face; it makes a clown's stage makeup look understated! It was scary seeing this happen at the mirror: my usually cosmetic-free face becoming doll-like with blusher, baby-pink lipstick, mascara and eye-liner pancaked across my features like the shoutiest of advertising hoardings.

Does it matter if Quark makes 'me' talk to the wrong people? Or if he, say, suddenly makes me swear like a sailor on shore leave? Does it really matter if I get detention? And fail a perfectly trivial Maths test? Or walk down the High Street looking like Barbie's mortified little sister?

Does it? Yes, it flamin' does!

When I'm not in school, I wear the earth colours that suit my complexion. That's me. That's who I am. I love being a girl. I'm thrilled to be a girl. I'm *proud* to be a girl. But I am not and never will be a girly girl. Even if the skirt I'm wearing was a decent knee-length, rather than a totally *in*decent barely-there belt, I'd still hate it, because outside of school and my Aunt Julia's wedding when I had to be a bridesmaid (in *peach*, not pink!) I do not wear dresses. I wear jeans, or dungaree shorts, or leggings, or jeggings. I'll wear a long smock top with leggings or tights. But not skirts. Not dresses.

So, yes, it matters.

Pink matters.

And suddenly it's obvious: to get out of this I have to *go* out. I have to leave my room. I must get out of this cage I've seen as a castle and get back to being me. Truly, 100% me: Daisy Jacobs. And Daisy Jacobs is not and never will be *pink*!

Because did I mention? I HATE PINK!

Chapter 46

BLACKBOARD JUNGLE

Quark is pleased. His ploy had been worth it just for the expression on Amy Porter's face on seeing 'Daisy', a vision in pink, flouncing towards her. But the thoughts voiced by Daisy herself, which he'd pretended to ignore, proved he was on the right track. He even caught a glimpse — just the barest peek, but a sighting nonetheless — into Daisy's previously impregnable citadel, with its crappy little TV. It was literally like a door left ajar with light leaking out into a normally dark area of her brain. She'd briefly left herself wide open and if Quark himself hadn't been so caught up in the moment, he'd have taken full advantage of her mistake.

All it had taken was for Daisy to be completely out of her comfort zone. Quark can't believe he hasn't tried something so simple before!

There were two things for him to consider here; first — why had wearing pink caused Daisy such an emotional kerfuffle? Was she really so averse to pink? Or had the drip, drip of Quark's control *of*, and interference *in* her life broken through her stubborn resistance?

Second — why had he been slow to react to the opening that could have ended this once and for all? In every previous existence, such openings happened swiftly and were the beginning of a whole cascade of *becomings*. But this time he'd hesitated, almost as though he hadn't wanted to end this particular existence …

In any case, his own distraction caused him to miss an open goal. So his human journey continues, for a short time at least. And

Daisy's life still hangs by a precarious thread. But soon there'll be another chance. And this time there'll be no more vacillating, no more debates.

He's pressing ahead with the end of teenage-lite as he enters the blackboard jungle of Scuttleford Secondary. He senses it as he walks down the corridor. He's like a spaceship in a science fiction film that has a fuzzy protective shield around it. He's keeping the rest of the world at arm's length. And until he's ready to turn every last one of them into space dust, that's the way he likes it.

From talking to Daisy and from living an approximation of her life, he knows that although she was never Miss Popular, she wasn't *un*popular. Now though, even more than the pink-stravaganza on Saturday, it's like gravity affects what Daisy calls Post-Quark Daisy differently. (Given what's currently inside Daisy's body, who knows, perhaps it does!) It's as though Quark's own version of gravity repels rather than attracts. Lots of people who used to nod to and talk to Daisy, look the other way or pretend to be busy when PQD passes by.

Overnight Quark has turned Daisy into a minor league bad girl, emitting a loud and clear signal not to mess with her or push her around. Rules are now for other people. Reason is a thing of the past. And Daisy's trashed reputation has by no means reached rock bottom.

Even Mrs Griffin, passing Daisy's classroom a while later, thins her lips and gives a sad shake of her head as she hears the cacophony from within. It's the suffocatingly intense racket only a covey of teenagers can make. And the loudest voice is one that only a few short weeks before she wouldn't have dreamt of hearing in such circumstances.

The class is studying the history of slavery. Their teacher has just read aloud a statement from a person struggling against repression — "They can take everything from you, but they can't take your mind". Mrs Griffin hears Daisy scoff at that. "Ooooh — the space creature is coming to eat your brain!" And, standing at the door, she sees Daisy lurching from her chair, arms curved above her shoulders in classic monster pose.

Mrs Griffin feels forced to step into the room to intervene. "Miss Jacobs, if you have quite recovered your equilibrium …? A little more self-control, please." Remarkably, Mrs Griffin's voice is steady and calm, as if absolutely nothing at all untoward is happening, and it seems to have exactly the same effect on PQD as it has had on a whole generation of children at Scuttleford Secondary School. The head teacher waits for a moment in silence and then the wind seemingly vanishes from Quark's sails and Mrs G sees Daisy return quietly to her seat.

She looks cooly at Daisy Jacobs, her head tilted, one eyebrow quirked and just the faintest smile on her lips. "So, are you yourself again now, Miss Jacobs?"

"Yes, Mrs Griffin," says Quark, levelly. Inside, Quark hears Daisy scream, "No, Mrs Griffin!" He adds, before he can stop himself, "… and no." And it's like something inside him shifts as a plug disconnected. Suddenly his bolshiness drains away, leaving behind a smirk like the Cheshire Cat's. For now he's done enough.

"It is *so* hard being a teenager!" says Quark later as his class gather their belongings before heading home.

"It is," Ellie Watson replies. "I think the hardest thing is dealing with other teenagers." She pauses and looks frankly at Daisy, before adding, "being criticised."

"Being ridiculed," Quark replies quickly.

There's a silence that's definitely awkward on one side, as each regards the other frankly. Finally, both nod as if in acknowledgement of past deeds.

"It is confusing when things change all the time," Quark says with unusual frankness. "I feel like the ground is constantly shifting beneath me." He grins, "I don't even know my own mind anymore."

"It's not just the ground that's shifting!" Ellie holds her arms out wide, shakes her head and looks down at her own body. "Nope, it sure isn't!"

Quark stares at her, frankly. "You are beautiful, Ellie. And you have a *most* attractive body."

Ellie flushes and puts her hand to her mouth as if trying to hold back a laugh. "Thanks … I think."

Quark thinks he is handling this rather well, but realises (for once) that he may have misspoken.

"I did not mean —"

"Oh, bless you — you're blushing! Wait — you're not …"

"I am not what?"

Ellie's eyes twinkle with mischief. She's headstrong, clever and maybe just a *little* sharp-tongued, and she's always held herself apart from Daisy. She's seen Daisy as the competition, but even before Daisy's bump on the head, she'd found herself softening towards her; and there was a wildness in her now that intrigued Ellie, but which she felt impinged just a little on her own territory. But it surprises her to find that she's once more enjoying a conversation with Daisy. "It's hard *knowing* you get things wrong sometimes." She pauses and then adds, with a giggle, "especially when you're equally certain you're always right!"

"I know — and us teenagers always think we are geniuses."

"Sometimes I think you *are* a genius!"

"What?!"

"I wish I could be like you."

"Me?! But Daisy's al— I mean, *I* have always wanted to be like *you*!"

"Why would you want that?"

"Because you are clever *and* funny; beautiful *and* popular. And you look like a real girl — with all those curves and great hair and perfect make-up."

Ellie looks frankly at Daisy, as if considering whether to be truly honest with this girl. She finally sighs and shakes her head ruefully. "I wear make-up because I'm insecure, Daisy."

"Why would you be insecure? You're gorgeous!"

"I feel like I'm running to catch up all the time, you know? And sometimes, along the way, being a little mean to others to take the attention away from how I'm feeling."

"That is why you use name-calling?"

"Mmm." Ellie nods and purses her lips, letting out a barely audible, "sorry."

"Me too."

"We do say mean things to each other, don't we?" Ellie speaks with warmth and a hint of regret.

Quark examines Daisy's memory, trawling for an example of a hurt that Ellie had caused Daisy. He finds one: "'Hold still Daisy, I'm trying to imagine you with a personality.'"

Ellie grimaces and shakes her head, sadly. "Yes, but then there was — 'Too bad the closest you'll ever come to a brainstorm is a light drizzle.'"

"Dais— I said that?"

Ellie nods, "yes. And — 'There's two things I really hate about Ellie: her face!'"

"Really?"

"And — 'I would never enter into a battle of wits with an unarmed person.'"

"I think Daisy Jacobs gives as good as she gets!"

"You sure do! I can't really compete; I know some of what I say is … well, a bit hurtful and insulting; it's just simple name-calling, really. But what you say is actually often *so* funny."

"Yes?"

"Yeah!" Ellie shakes her head, ruefully, "or at least it would be it wasn't aimed at me!"

"I sound quite nasty."

"Nah. It's legit, some of it at least. Anyway, I guess I usually start it."

"I am pleased we had this conversation, Ellie Watson."

"Me too … Daisy Jacobs. I wish we talked like this more often."

"Me also. You are not quite as bad as people say." Being an awkward teenage rebel is definitely *not* going quite as Quark expected, but he is still capable of Quarkiness.

"Thanks a lot! Quite a compliment. So … no more 'Icky'?"

"No. I promise."

Quark could not understand what was going on: for him this was practically charming. His mood during the day had been so up and down, veering between extremes of happy and sad, naughty and — he genuinely couldn't help himself — almost actually nice. The mood swings were becoming extreme!

Ellie spoke again. "We'll cut the misery in our lives — at least a bit! — if we're suddenly nice to each other. And everyone'll be freaked by us suddenly being friends!" She pauses and looks down. "Maybe we'll both feel less isolated too."

This amazes Quark. "But you have so many friends! Your Satellites are always orbiting you! You're a popular girl."

Ellie laughs, "first we try out-insult each other and now we try to out-compliment each other!"

Quark smiles too, a sad smile that does not reach Daisy's eyes. "But you are alive — I mean popular!"

What's happening to him?! First he sucked up to the head teacher, now he's making up to Daisy's worst enemy; some rebel he's turning out to be! It's almost as if instead of turning Daisy into a teenage rebel PQD, it is he who was being changed — into PDQ!

"I'd rather be brave, like you." Ellie says.

Quark nods, as if understanding something for the first time. "We want what we don't have." And maybe that's what's going on inside him: he wants what he can't have; what's he's never had. Maybe he missed his chance to pounce on Daisy as she left her lair because he wanted to live as much as she does? He realises he is becoming as reluctant to end her existence as he is to terminate his own.

"Yes, and we want it NOW!" Ellie laughs, "life's like that — everything's about extremes."

"Yes," Quark mutters sadly. "And you oscillate between the extremes: it is wonderful, it is terrible; I love you, I hate you. I want to live!" I don't want to die, he adds silently to himself.

This time Ellie lets out a full-throated laugh. "I never want to see you again, I want to be with you forever!" Her smile twinkles again, "but seriously, Daisy, that clever analysis is so typical of you. And what a word to choose! 'Oscillate'. It's perfect. I just love how you express yourself."

"I speak funny sometimes."

"Recently, maybe. Since your … accident."

"Now I sometimes I feel I don't fit in."

"Yeah! Like you're a mutant or something!"

"What?!" Just for a moment, Quark thinks she's seen through him.

Ellie chokes back a guffaw and covers her mouth with her hand. "No! Sorry — I didn't mean *you*; I just meant we *all* feel as though we don't fit in. I was just teasing …" she adds quietly.

Quark nods. "It is so hard; everything feels so intense. Sometimes …"

"Yes …?" Ellie encourages.

"Too intense to cope with. There is so much going on."

"With your body?"

Quark nods. "And in my head."

"Yes, it's so draining!"

"It certainly is!"

"It's all like: 'who am I?' 'What am I doing?' 'How will all this end?'"

"Yes," Quark says, "that is exactly it: how indeed …?" It must end, he thought, and soon. Because it was becoming too much for him!

Chapter 47

AT LEAST IT CAN'T GET ANY WORSE

"Quark, you practically made a pass at Ellie Watson! You know she's a gossip, and even the slightest hint of trouble becomes a fully-fledged scandal by the time she's finished with it. She gets a kick out of being vindictive." But otherwise she's just so perkily perfect!

"First, I did not 'make a pass' at her, I spoke to her —"

"You said she was beautiful and had a great body."

"We sorted that out — and anyway she knew what I meant; and it was *not* a pass."

"Well, you spoke to her, and that's enough."

"And second," Quark went on, completely ignoring me, "as I have told you before, Ellie is a nice girl. There have been faults — on *both* sides — and you have given as good as you have got from her. You have misunderstood each other's motives. "Plus," he continues, "why are so obsessed with the way you look — with your face and your figure?"

"What? I never said that!"

"No, but you thought it and I can read you like a book. This openness cuts both ways, you know. What's the point of wishing to look different? You are still growing and I think we look just fine just now."

"Again with the 'we'! *We* are not 'we'! Let's get this straight once and for all: me, Daisy Jacobs, you, body-snatching alien."

He ignores my sniping. "Anyway, you cannot change things simply by wishing it."

"Of course you can!"

"Nonsense! By thinking alone?"

"Yes, you can. If I am cheerful and happy and positive that I can influence how other people react to me. I can make them feel better. And making other people feel good makes me feel even better."

"But it does not change things on a quantum level. It does not have a fundamental effect."

"I disagree."

"What scientific theory is that based on?"

"Feelings and emotions."

"You oppose the theory of Quantum Mechanics based on 'feelings and emotions'?"

You have no idea how irritating it is to hear your own voice go all sarky-snarky when it's used by an obdurate alien to talk down to you! "I didn't say that, you're just putting words into my mouth." Like your invasive thoughts in my head, I think.

It's difficult to read him well when I can't see my face in the mirror and at the moment we're moving — outside I think, because I can hear street noise as well as the sound of my voice. I can't make out where we're going, Quark's masking it somehow, but that makes his thoughts easier to understand and 'my' low voice (that he's muted to prevent passers-by thinking I'm nuts) easier to hear. We're good at this communication lark now; I mean, seriously good. It's virtually seamless. But then I guess it should be as we're both inhabiting exactly the same space in the universe. However, Quark's focus is on stopping me from seeing where we're going for some reason — as if I could stop him, anyway!

"No, I'm telling you that merely being positive, being 'happy-clappy' will get you nowhere," he continues.

"That is just bleak. Quark, you are a sad individual."

"Daisy, being positive will not set you free."

"Again, I disagree. I find it hard to be glum and down-in-the-dumps for long. I'm cheerful, I'm an optimist — I just can't help looking on the bright side. Even with you in my brain, I still think my glass is half-full! And I live a happier life simply by feeling happy. If you smile, people smile with you; if you expect the best in people, you'll often find it. Although I find it hard to see it in you …" What I can see in him is the blurry outline of some plan or trap he has in store for me.

"Optimism will not set you free either."

"Well, being negative certainly won't! If I'd not been an optimist, this would have been over long ago and we'd all be dust floating in space by now.

"And you can be as cheerful as you like, but you're still stuck in that little room in your head."

"And you can be as miserable and misanthropic as you like, but I *will* be here, which means you are stuck too!"

Quark pauses and gives me another one of those 'you sad, sad thing' sighs which he's become really good at (and which I may keep for future use when I evict him from my body and regain the use of all my faculties).

After what Quark said a minute ago, I'm careful to shut down the links to other bits of my brain so that my thoughts don't leak out to him. Despite my talk of staying positive, I'm finding it difficult to do just that at the moment.

During the day I'm in my 'room'. I'm shut away in this barely used bit of my brain. My guess is that way back in pre-history it probably did something useful — maybe tracking prey or avoiding predators; that may explain why I can usually follow and avoid Quark and often work out what he's up to. Anyway, this is a safe space. But each morning when I wake up, or come to or whatever happens to me after I have shut down to recharge, my room feels more like a prison than a refuge. Because every day I'm reminded that, even though I hold the key, I *am* still locked in here.

My room started off as barely functional. Gradually, I've furnished it with some of my own stuff. Now there's a copy of my bed and a sofa. I had schoolbooks for a while, but Quark won't let me do any homework, in case I get good marks and wreck his reputation-wrecking plans! Life's so dull without homework!

There are no books to read either, as I can't remember whole books and so replicate them in here. I have limited access to other parts of my brain, but most of my research now involves physically leaving my room and exploring. And opening myself up to danger.

Of course, none of this is real — there's not really a sofa in my brain. But I 'see' these things as being here in the same way as I see my door — and my lock. Imagination is a key life skill!

Now, I look around — at the dark, dank, dreary world of this imaginary refuge and see that it is as much a cage as anything else; it's a prison of my imagination. And I realise I'm hemmed in by shadows of my lingering panic, as much as because I'm suffering my own, personal, alien invasion. Yes, I've shut Quark out, but equally, I've locked myself in. And, in a way, I always have.

I feel young and small and very much alone. And I'd be lying if I said I'm used to the lack of connection to my real life, to existence and context and human interaction. I really miss the physical day-to-day contact with my family and friends; the hugs and little touches that we all take for granted but which say so much.

The 'images' I carry round with me, or store in some minuscule part of my tiny room are not actually all visual images, some are kind of 'smell-o-grams' and some are like aural emojis. I can recall the heady, floral fragrance of Mum's perfume and almost taste the sweetness of her home-made Seville orange marmalade — 'Mama-lade' we call it. I can hear the calm, solid, reliable tone of Dad's voice, the sheer unflappability that helps me centre myself and remain steady even in moments of intense crisis. I can bring to mind Luke's gangling awkwardness, his happy smile and infectious laughter; and Amy's wit, her focus, the extraordinary positivity that makes even me seem like a pessimist ... and the overwhelming comfort she brings me just by her presence in my heart.

I don't have space in my room for all my memories, but there's some natural data retrieval system at work, so that even in my locked-in state I'm not word or face blind, or thrown by everyday events and situations. I know who I am and where I am (most of the time) and I seem to be able to bring into my room any piece of information that I, Daisy Jacobs, could ordinarily recall. But the memories, thoughts and images that mean the most to me are with me all the time and help sustain me.

Quark is still in his garrulous mood though and won't let me feel alone for long. "And I am not sure how to moderate my behaviour. Sometimes, I do not know how to act when I am with other people."

He needs sense talking into him; even fourteen-year-old sense. "Don't worry, no one does. Don't let actors on TV fool you; don't believe the cool people at school; deep down, no one has any idea what they're doing for most of the time — we're all just making it up as we go along."

"I try to take a lead from my — our — friends."

"What, Amy and —"

"Ellie Watson too — and her charming group of friends. They have been most helpful."

"Not 'Icky' Ellie again! No — you can't believe anything that lot tell you. It'll end badly. Ellie's not charming by any rational definition; and anyway, don't forget we're trying to make you more believable — a real teenager would not say 'charming'."

"I found her charming — and she's impressed by some recent changes in your personality. A big improvement."

Well, that tells you all you need to know, I think, but do not say. I also noticed "some" — maybe Quark is going too far, even for Ellie!

"And Connor too."

"Connor? But I — I mean you — I mean ..." What do I mean? I grit my metaphorical teeth, "*we* haven't seen Connor today."

I can't see it, but I can feel the way he twists my lips into what passes for a smile where he comes from. "Why do you think *we* are sitting here in the coffee shop? We are meeting Connor."

"We are?" It's like he's been blindfolding me, or forcing me into the blinkers that racehorses wear to stop them from being spooked by their surroundings; suddenly, they're removed and I can see. I've just been congratulating myself on my amazing 'Spidey' skills and all the time Quark's been tricking me. That's why he's been so talkative!

"And here he is." I see Connor approach, a smile curving his lips as he sees 'me'. Then I feel my body stand and tilt as Quark leans in to hug Connor as he reaches our table.

Then I'm looking at Connor. But not like before: not like his smile and his dreamy eyes and his — okay, okay — his delicious butt, *but* in a new and entirely unsettling way. Not at all in a yearning, admiring, teenage-crush sort of way, but in a more covetous — no, *avaricious* way. I can feel *it*/me *wanting* him. That makes the real me, in the secure environment of my locked room blush the brightest scarlet, but I really don't mean *wanting* as in wanting his body in the one-track-minded way that teens would think of; I mean literally 'wanting' his body — in an almost vampire-like way! Connor Wheeler's body. His ... form. Even weirder, I want Ellie Watson too. Ellie-too-good-for-the-likes-of you-Watson! And Steve Cooper. And Sophie Lewis. Even Mrs Griffin. I want her too. I want them all, each and every one of them. I want their ... forms. They should all *become* — that's what they should do! They should give their forms to me! Connor and Ellie and Steve and Sophie and Mrs Griffin and all of them; the whole school; the whole town; the entire world!

It's like suddenly *I* am Quark, and not vice versa! *His* 'door' is open and I truly feel him. Unequivocally sense him. I understand how he operates; I can sense the *becoming* he has so long desired and how I/he/we would *be* Daisy just a fraction of a second from now if I let him; and then, not even moments later Daisy Jacobs would be history — everyone in this room, in this town, in this county would go. And in minutes Earth would be less than a memory, because there'd be no-one left *with* a memory. I see this

216

with absolute one hundred percent clarity. It almost literally blows my mind, the sheer enormity of it ... the beauty of it. And I do mean 'beauty'. From Quark's perspective, I see and fully appreciate the neatness and perfection of becoming.

These thoughts are powerful and exciting; I'm inordinately, overwhelmingly powerful. I'm ancient, vast and overwhelming, yet small and vulnerable and THAT WRETCHED GIRL WILL NOT JUST ROLL OVER AND DIE!!! WHY WON'T SHE DIE? WHY WON'T SHE *BECOME*? I WANT IT; I WANT IT; I WANT IT —

And, like that, I snap out of him and I'm back; I'm me again. He's still here, Quark's still here; still in my head. Still me. But now I know him. Who and what he really is. It's like some horrendous game of inter-galactic tag: I'm *it*! How have I held back this force, this all-encompassing immensity for all this time? What on earth has curbed such ferocity? Although I'm still me, for that brief moment I saw behind the mask. This force can overwhelm me in the way an armoured tank rolls over an ant. So ... is this it now? Am I *becoming*?

I try to ground myself — difficult when I don't have a body to ground. I imagine coming home to my body; to my mind, my own locked room ... and somehow I convince myself that all is well. And the fear melts away like I don't have space for it in my life, which, in a way, is true!

Meanwhile, back in the real world, Connor's staring at me, his hand still in mine, one arm clasped awkwardly around my shoulder, his mouth open, a touch of dribble at the corner of his generous lips. My eyes, *Quark's* eyes, gaze into him. Did I, did we just ... did I just nearly *become* Connor too? Does he, on some level sense what nearly happened? He looks as though he's been tasered to insensibility.

There's something more going on here, something to do with the closeness between Quark and myself and a physical, almost chemical reaction to Connor and ... something else I can't quite grasp that's happening inside me, making me more open; making both Quark and I more open … and more vulnerable.

It's like there's not enough brainpower between us to control what's happening in my body and in my head. It seems we have one too many drivers!

Then I see a flash of what's coming; it's almost like a vibration in the air. I *know* what will happen. This is — maybe — what I wanted from the very start. But not now! Not like this. Please — no! Not when I'm not really *me*.

But Quark doesn't care, and Connor looks stunned into insensible oblivion. His smile is almost sad, his face serious as he closes his eyes, leans in to me … and presses his lips to mine. It's the briefest, slightest moment of fusion. I've thought about this and if you are or have ever been a teenage girl; I think you'll get exactly where I'm coming from: I mean *really* thought about this; and while I've always imagined this kiss would have my brain fizzing, I now feel only the anguish of an experience, a *life* stolen from me.

Yet I feel a flicker of consciousness, a hint of the *real*. Emotionally, his kiss gives me none of the depth of feeling I expected and hoped for. But there is a touch. Our lips meet. I *feel* his mouth meet mine! Not quite how I wanted, but I do feel the slightest touch of his lips — I feel it *physically*; his lips/my lips — I don't imagine them coming together, I *feel* soft flesh meeting soft flesh.

For that moment, I'm back: I'm Daisy Jacobs in Carlo's Coffee on the High Street, with my arm around Connor Wheeler as we lean awkwardly into one another. I feel his warm breath on my mouth, taste the mint he had before he arrived here — was he expecting to/wanting to kiss me?! I feel the texture of his soft blue sweater, I hear the clamour of voices as the other patrons get on with living actual lives, rather than existing in imaginary cages in their heads, I smell the heady aroma of coffee, and as the lady I see over Connor's shoulder brings a muffin to her mouth I want to run over and snatch it from her, so I can taste its blueberry yumminess. I can't believe it! I want Connor to kiss me again, so I can feel it properly. Or I can—

Except I can't. Because I'm instantly snapped right back into my cage, as though I'm one of those swing ball things you played with when you were a kid. I don't have legs to walk over to steal the lady's muffin. I no longer have a nose with which to smell the coffee, and the din of other patrons' voices mutes to a background murmur. I'm no longer a co-pilot; I'm the prisoner being transported again.

I return to the reality of now and notice Connor's frown. He's cupping my chin, his eyes pained as if wondering what the hell just happened. "I've wanted to do that for *so* long, but I waited and waited because I thought you weren't interested in me. I think I waited too long." He shakes his head, as if trying to clear a path through the clutter in his head, the contents of which I've just had the briefest glimpse into — sorry Connor! "I think … this … what just happened was for the other Daisy." His frown deepens, as if even he can't figure out what that means. "Not for the Daisy you're … *becoming*." His full mouth thins as he fights his way through the fog of confusion that Quark — and I! — have inflicted upon him. "Not for the Daisy you are now. I don't understand what's going on, but you must know you don't need to change to fit in, or to *become* someone you're not." That word again — does he have even the slightest hint of its significance?

Then, like a dog shaking itself vigorously after 'accidentally' straying into a large body of water, he shivers, straightens and breaks out of the spell he has been under. "It's not right, Daisy."

"What do you mean?" Quark trills, his hand — my hand! — running up Connor's arm and cradling his elbow. Awkward! His supreme Quarkiness is back with a vengeance and I although I can't see my face, I can sense him at the deepest, most instinctive level now, and he's flirting. Not in the natural, easy-going way that you'd want to imagine yourself doing, but in the cringey, drunken aunt at a party way that makes you want to curl up in embarrassment. After three weeks experience of being a teenage girl, we'd all probably struggle with the finer points of human interaction, but there should be positively NO flirting until you really *are* fourteen … or fifty — oh, God no, just had a flashback to my aunt again! "You don't want to kiss me? You don't like me anymore." He's using a pathetic put-upon voice I never would.

"I like you and I *do* want to kiss you." Connor's looking right into my eyes as he says this. "Or at least I want to kiss Daisy Jacobs." He nods his head, "it's Daisy I want to kiss. Not this … whatever it is you're trying to be now. To kiss you now would be wrong. It would be like taking advantage of you. I couldn't do that. I like you, Daisy. But … well, sorry, I like the other you more. Way more. This … this," he points at me, "all this is fake. Not real. Not *you*."

The words hang heavily between us in the silence that follows. Inside, I'm screaming — strangely enough with joy rather than anguish. I've come so close to being back home in my body, to my life with my family and friends and to a potential boyfriend on the horizon. And then it's snatched away.

But Connor's seen through Quark! He's rejected that version of me, just as Amy did before him. Both of them are still fighting for me; still trying to get me to *be* me.

Connor's words and the intensity of his gaze are like blazing sunlight warming my heart; and I can *feel* that — even in the isolated place of danger and torment where I'm trapped!

Chapter 48

HANGOVER

Quark is sick and dizzy. Weak, almost — although that's a ridiculous word to use in connection with an entity controlling the fate of entire galaxies! This weakness is … ugh! — *positively* human! He can't comprehend how one weedy little girl has reduced him to this condition of inefficiency. He feels powerless and inadequate; he's less than perfect and this is not acceptable!

One drink; that's all it was. He hadn't even been able to finish the second. He thought rum and coke was a sophisticated alcoholic beverage. However, he's not sure which was worse: the staggeringly sweet, syrupy concoction or the dark, musky rum. Separately they were both awful. Drinking them together, in a tall glass, he had not passed Go, he'd not collected £200 he'd just gone straight to HELL!

Now, Daisy's heart-rate is elevated, her cheeks flushed, her lips dry, her head pounding. And Quark is hiding from an issue which he should have faced, but that he'd decided he could just as easily avoid. He'd read somewhere that there was no issue, no problem, that was too large or too complicated that it could not be effectively run away from. So instead of problem/solution, he'd done problem/rum and coke/head down toilet. And that had been *no* solution. Apparently, singularities and alcohol do not mix!

The slightest movement now sets off an explosion in his head, and for once the resultant headache has nothing to do with Daisy's persistent, nagging chatter.

He occupies most of Daisy's brain. He's effectively closing her down, ever-reducing the space she has to exist in, the places she has to hide from the inevitable. At first, she saw what happened around her and heard what was said. Now he wonders if Daisy can see much at all. Does she have a paralysing headache too? Is her vision blurred? Does she realise her mouth tastes like Quark imagines the bottom of a budgie cage does? This, for those of you who have wisely avoided the rum and coke solution to life's vicissitudes, is not at the top of TripAdvisor's list of great gourmet tastes.

Before Quark had a teeny bit too much to drink, he'd been effectively blocking Daisy. Ironically, his connection to her, once very close, was now becoming cloudy and dim. He'd got her to the coffee shop for the entirely successful meeting with Connor without her knowing where her body was going. Then he got Daisy her first kiss. For obvious reasons it would also be her last.

Then he'd felt *her* presence within *him*; and it was ... like an over-stepping of the mark; like an invasion. Quark temporarily lost himself in a hormonal teenage moment, and suddenly *she* was in charge! It was just the briefest instant, but it had been the single most intense — and terrifying — of his entire existence. It was as though *she*, Daisy Jacobs, was the one who was *becoming*, and he, Quark, was about to become nothing but a memory ...

So, when he poured the first drink, he hadn't been exactly celebrating a victory. His once in a lifetime — and absolutely *never* again — experiment with alcohol had been in order to avoid thinking too deeply, rather than in honour of his doubtful performance as a human teenager; although he guessed that some very much older teenagers did very occasionally have a little drink.

A gentle tapping interrupts Quark's musings. No, actually, not a tap, a *banging*, a *hammering* with a force that is utterly unjustified this early on a Sunday morning. Quark reluctantly folds back one corner of the duvet and peers at the digital clock on Daisy's bedside table: 11:28am! It's practically the crack of dawn! What gives anyone the right to disturb an alien entity at this unearthly hour of the morning?! His head hurts and he will not come out from under these bed covers for any reason at all. Ever. In fact, just for the briefest microsecond he almost wished the head was still Daisy's — then she'd definitely have the headache. *She'd* have to cope with her bedroom spinning slowly around her. And also deal with some lunatic battering the door down when it's still practically the middle of the night.

"Daisy, it's a beautiful sunny morning," says Daisy's mum, who then checks her watch, "just. You're not planning on staying in bed all day, are you?"

"Yes!" Quark growls.

"Oh, sweetie, don't you want to come out for a walk with me?" Her voice is altogether too cheerful, and stabs like needles deep into the brain Quark is, at the moment, in no rush to take greater control of.

"No, I do not!"

"Come on … it's ages since we've had some girly time. We can walk along the river and go to the cafe by the weir for a lovely big Sunday lunch."

Lunch! Food? Now?! Ugh, the very thought makes Quark remember the head-down-the-toilet result of his avoidance tactics of the previous night. "Go away and leave me alone! I want to die in peace," he whines.

He hears a muffled guffaw from Daisy's father. "Oh, dear! I think we're having another teenage moment." Quark harrumphs loud enough to set off more loud parental giggling, but the laughter, muffled voices and footsteps finally move away.

He's alone. Alone to mourn his fate as history's first-ever hungover quantum singularity. And to contemplate how he got himself into this sorry predicament.

Death, that's the problem. The death of Daisy Jacobs. And as a result, the death of PQD. He knows his endeavours will be rewarded — maybe just hours from now. Because Daisy's changing. He can feel it, can feel the chemical balance of her body altering radically. Something big is about to happen. That much is obvious and to Quark this can mean only one thing: Daisy is *becoming*.

And that's good — no, it's *great!* After all, that's what he's here for: to pulverise her and every single one of her kind. And yet ...

While Daisy Jacobs herself will cease to exist, the entity we call Quark will go on forever — until the very end of time. But when Daisy dies, in effect he'll die too. He's been around for well over thirteen billion years and may be around for at least that again. But the big question for him at the moment is what will he exist as?

Now he's had just over three weeks of life. He's tasted Mama-lade and breakfast-strength coffee; pizza and pancakes and many other food types, including the dill-pickle, blueberry yoghurt and left-over curry combination that he'd like to erase from his memory as easily as it had been expelled from Daisy's body. He's watched people buying houses and auctioning plant pots on daytime TV; become hooked on Love Island and the best Netflix has to offer. He can list "interesting" facts about volcanoes, glaciers, and the many wives of a weirdly woman-hating Tudor king. He's made a new friend or two; he has (just barely) kept Daisy's old friends. And he's kissed a boy.

But soon he'll be dust again. He'll be exactly what he's been for thirteen billion years. He won't even have to think of doing homework, it's true, but he'll also never get to eat a bacon sandwich again. (Daisy will be happy about that; or rather, she would be if she actually existed, which, of course, she won't ...) And when Daisy *becomes*, Quark will not learn what happens to Steffie and Dan on Bake Off; he'll never have to drink rum and coke again, but equally he'll never get a hug. Imagine that: all eternity without a hug! He'll never see a flower again or inhale its sweet scent; will never hear the latest tunes on Spotify. And he'll never kiss a boy — or a girl — again. In short, Quark as he has got to know himself, will be as bereft of form as Daisy Jacobs.

And Daisy herself will be no more. No two ways about it, call a hand-operated soil-moving implement a hand-operated soil-moving implement as Daisy herself had said (or words to that effect), she would be d-e-a-d. And the fact is, though he would admit it only reluctantly, through Daisy's own gritted teeth, he lov—

Well, let's not get carried away! She's okay ... for a teenage human girl. Quark reluctantly admits he feels something not unadjacent to fondness for her.

But now he's had a drink to get his courage up, and her body chemistry is changing — clearly in his favour. This is it. The end is nigh for Daisy Jacobs!

Chapter 49

OBLIGATORY CHASE SCENE

"You love me! I heard you! You didn't say it out loud, but you do and that explains why you haven't killed me yet … because you can't bring yourself to do it. You can't kill the one you love."

Quark gets up quickly from my bed and rushes to the bathroom. I think he's going to be sick again, but instead he just stares at the mirror through red-rimmed eyes. He seems to be steeling himself for something. A big announcement maybe? But he says nothing; just stares at me with brooding bitterness. My arms are crossed as if that way he can fend off the me that's still inside. Me *and* my pesky emotions.

The silence stretches until finally, through thinned lips, he speaks. "*I* love you?!" he grinds out. The expression on my face is unreadable because my eyes are now cast down to my hands which grip the sink so tightly that my knuckles turn white and claw like. "How dare you!"

What's going on in his luxuriously appointed part of my mind right now? I thought we were on a firmer footing. I've been getting weaker, but I thought we were reaching an understanding. And I believed he'd come to really care about me.

But no — from one moment to the next, something changes. There's a shift in the atmosphere between us. It's as rapid as the flipping of a switch. He looks up, eyes filled with a seething malevolence that's straight out of a Hollywood horror film.

Ugh! Seeing myself in the mirror … I'd had nightmares about that mirror! About one day seeing my face warp into something monstrous and beast-like as the thing within me distorts my

226

features into a true reflection of what passes for its personality. How did I forget this? Forget what he — IT — really is? The way he looks at me now proves that beyond any doubt.

The image on the TV screen in my head is suddenly clear and without interference. I realise with a kind of stunned amazement that the TV's not a virtual antique anymore; now it really is that 56-inch OLED and every single pore of my own face is up there on the screen, in sharply detailed, richly coloured, perfectly pixillated clarity. And I know Quark's done this … in *my* room.

"What's wrong, Daisy?" he sing-songs in a voice like a harsh growl. I see my lips pull back over my teeth in a distinctly unpleasant vampire-like grimace. He grins. "Cat got your tongue? Nothing to say for once?" I notice my teeth are not evenly spaced with that cute gap between the top two incisors anymore; now they seem to consist entirely of sharply pointed canines — as though I'm looking into the mouth of a Great White Shark!

On the high-definition screen, my expression hardens. It's like I'm seeing the movement of a glacier in time lapse photography, so the action is speeded up and what was once warm simply ices over. And it's Daisy/not Daisy looking in at me on the big screen. The millions of pixels that make up my face rush apart and then implode into a darkness from which a screaming, shrieking shadow emerges. A huge black, wolf-like claw with long, sharp talons smashes through the screen —

And that's when I look around and audibly gasp. I shake my head, trying to clear my vision. But it's not a dream. This is my nightmare made real. I'm not in my room. I have no idea where I am! A wave of despair strikes me and for the first time in all of this, for the first time in a life filled with what I now realise were trivial panics, I know what true terror is.

Then the claw grabs me by my school tie. "Got you, you bitch!" the flat lizard voice says.

I'm choking and the pain is intense; more real than anything I've felt in weeks, because I can actually *feel* it. This isn't my imagination, it's not a 'what if', arm's length, distant memory of a feeling. This is claws gouging at my throat and hot, stinky breath on my face. Quark's eyes, red rimmed and sunken rear up out of the darkness and stare directly into the depths of my soul. This is not life experienced at second hand, through a mirror anymore, this is up close and personal with a creature from the inky blackness at the heart of the universe; this is life literally red in tooth and claw!

My face is no longer mine, now it's all him, all it, all dreadful, inscrutable darkness. But a darkness made real, a darkness given terrifying form. Its breath is putrid, its grip vicelike, its gaze unrelenting and without mercy or even the vaguest remembrance of humanity. The sometimes playful, almost childlike Quark is gone and in his place is something dark and malevolent. There's a low, hoarse growl in its throat as it throttles the life from my own.

"'Ur hurtin' 'e," I rasp out. "Quark, tha' 'urts!"

"I do not so love you!" Quark/not Quark screeches, each word punctuated by a shake that jiggles me like a rag doll. Just for a moment, as if down an ever-lengthening corridor, I catch a glimpse of him — a Frankenstein-like echo of who he'd been when he'd been me. Then that window into the soul of an ex-human slams shut. Quark is gone. With swooning horror, I realise I won't see him again.

"Now I'll fix you," it grunts. It shakes me by the throat again. "Now I'll end 'ou." Its' voice becomes harsher, less lilting, less human. It's holding tightly on to me. Crushing my windpipe. Crushing the life out of me.

My consciousness wavers and my vision blurs as I stare up into those baleful eyes. Through them, through the creature's wraithlike corruption I see the distant glimmer of one tiny pinprick of light — like the first star to appear at twilight — shimmering at first faintly and then with increasing brightness. One teeny dot of light and then another and another. But it's not the light of hope, it's not a beacon calling me home, it's eternity calling to me — and you. It's the end. I'm becoming.

"'Fix oo, 'ix oo. Now I'll 'ix oo," it mutters in a barely audible, entirely inhuman growl.

I can smell the sour odour of sweat and death. My own sweat and the death that's coming.

"'Ix oo, 'ix oo now!" Shake, shake. I see its blood red lips form into a parody of a scary clown grin as my head rattles side to side. My breath comes in bare gasps. "Now I'll 'ix oooooo!" The hand, the claw tightens its grip.

Even my panic is gone now and my breath is a memory.

Not real. Not real. Not real. I chant to myself, in time with each violent shake of my head. I try to force the vision away, to dig in my heels and stop the slow drift down the long tunnel of darkness becoming a headlong rush. But the blackness is in me. The darkness overwhelms —

I find myself unable to look away from its red eyes. They're soulless. Depthless. No longer mortal. I hear it again, "'Ix ooo now! I'll 'ix ooo now."

There's a guttural sigh, as if from a great distance, and I can't say if it comes from me as my life drains away or from what had been Quark as his goal finally comes to fruition. But now it sinks in. It's such a small thing. Such a tiny, tiny glimmer of hope: inside it, deep, deep inside, I know there's still the slightest spark of humanity.

I allow myself to sink for a moment longer and then dredge deep for the last remaining particle of energy to power the weakest of all sucker punches. It's barely a slap at the creature that has me, but I catch it off guard, so sure is it of imminent triumph. The half step it takes back is enough for me to gasp in another lungful of air. "No! No! No!" I scream, refusing to succumb to the everlasting night that has all but entombed me. The scream echoes around my head, drowning out the enticing murmur of eternal darkness.

I force my arms up under the hands that loosely hold me by the throat, twist away out of its grasp, its claws raking my arm as I pull back. Waves of pain from my raw throat and gashed arm cascade through my puny, under-resourced system. But the pressure loosens and I draw a scratchy breath. I hug my arm to me, grasping it with my other as I take another step away. My vision blurs, my arm is an agonising open wound, my throat painful and my breathing ragged as I stumble away. I turn and almost trip, clutching at the last moment at a rail on the wall that I hadn't noticed before and just managing to hold myself up.

And, like that, I'm running. Running down corridors, blindly turning corners, hurtling over obstacles to get away from it, all the time searching for a familiar landmark to allow to me reorient myself. You know those play centres in family-friendly pubs you were taken to when you were a kid? Full of brightly coloured bouncy cushions and ball pits? This part of my brain is kind of like that, except the colours are more muted — greys and cloudy pinks: whole corridors and crossways of pink squidgyness. I'm still in school uniform and have thick, clunky soled school shoes on my feet and I'm scared I might damage something by falling against the wrong synapse or whatever and giving myself a headache. Hang on though: wouldn't this be a good thing? I pause briefly, listening out for footsteps behind me, and kick out at a dark red sticky-out bit low on the wall next to me. No idea what function it serves, but neither that or the thump I aim at the grey blob higher up has any noticeable impact.

I set off again, thinking about my destination — the room that has protected me for so long from the monster that's been within. Its door has always had a physical key rather than a combination that Quark could steal from my mind. As I'm gasping for breath, struggling to pull air into imaginary lungs that suddenly feel all too real, I change that. While I hurtle down corridors that look more like my neighbourhood, I change the lock in my head so that my door is now secured by a remote access system. Instead of a key, I imagine a clicker like the ones people keep in their car to open remote controlled garage doors. I look down and it's there in my hand.

I'm still gasping for breath, struggling to breathe. But so intently have I been focussing on the new lock, that I realise I've missed a turn. Again! I now know the inside of my head almost as well as the back of my hand, because of the cautious night-time expeditions I've taken, trying to find a way to outwit him. But now it's Quark who's led me into uncharted territory. Somehow, I'd fluked my way back to familiar spaces, recognising bits of my grey matter as though they were street signs. But so intent had I been on avoiding the whole throttling thing that I focussed too much on escape and not enough on the direction I'd been heading. I tried to compensate by taking a shortcut down an alleyway between a couple of nerve endings. This was a bit of a backwater, not so illuminated by the flashes from synapses as signals zipped around my brain with a thrum that vibrated through the soles of my feet. The area clearly wasn't used much — maybe it was the bit used by our Neanderthal ancestors for night vision or where my fashion sense would have been stored, had I possessed any.

I take a turn and lean back against the wall, peering round the corner to see if I can double back and return to the area I know. But the floor vibrates with heavy steps and in the distance, down the narrow alley, I see the shadow of towering, louring monster with red laser eyes that look not *at* me, but *into* me with a gaze so intense it threatens to stop the heart I can somehow feel pounding away in my chest. The creature's face, moving in and out of shadows cast by lightning-like bursts of electricity, still bears the cold expression of my nightmares.

I'm hurt in my arm, in my throat, in my heart — in fact, I'm hurt in my everywhere! I'd been close to home, but now must take the long route if I am to make it back to the safety of my room so we can live to fight another day.

Chapter 50

~~THE BIG KILL~~ HE'S BEHIND YOU!

This chapter was supposed to be called " ♫Duh - Duh - Duh - Duh♫ " after the famous theme to Jaws, a firm favourite of Quark's for some reason, but it was thought the reference to a film from the 1970s would be too obscure. And "The Big Kill" is wrong as it gives away the ending; it's right there in the word *"kill"*. Quark's clearly had enough of tiptoeing around the issue and wants us left in no doubt: Daisy is for the high jump and this is the end of the road for humanity. This time there's no escape for our hero. If you're quick, you may just have time to say a few farewells, but don't bother packing for a last-minute holiday. (And actually, I think this whole paragraph may have given away the ending — sorry!)

Anyway, everyone was overruled. In the order of precedence that's been set, this is a Quark chapter, but Quark's not really up to the job at the moment. He's reverted to baser instincts — and a series of guttural grunts, even prettily laid out and set between the covers of a book is considered too "out there" even for a story as barely believable as this. The publisher feels that all credibility will be lost unless the author takes a firmer grip at this late (and potentially terminal) stage of proceedings. So, here goes —

***

The human sets off racing down corridors, bouncing off squidgy walls and rounding corners as fast as her imaginary legs can carry her. Clearly, the sound of heavy feet thudding after her doesn't encourage her to stop and smell the roses. She slips, stumbles and almost falls as she takes a particularly sharp turn, just managing to keep her feet. She pauses momentarily, but knows she has to keep moving, otherwise her fragile mind, hanging only by the thinnest of threads, will be lost entirely. As she begins to move again, she looks down and sees without too much surprise that the school shoes she'd been wearing on her few scouting trips out of her room have been replaced by her trusty well-worn Nikes. The extra grip provided by the running shoes she'd unthinkingly visualised back onto her feet had saved her.

But at a price: she'd had to ride the skid and take the turn that opened up immediately before her. It was the wrong turn. Focussing so intently on staying upright, she'd gone left, rather than taking the right turn that led straight to her door.

She's running for her life, sobbing at the unfairness of it all. The injustice of it ending like this. Her arm, cradled to her chest, throbs painfully and when she glances down, she sees the sleeve of her school jumper is soaked in blood. So much blood! The cut had been deep, but had seemed superficial, so where has it all come from? Someone has blood on the mind!

She grits her teeth, trying to bite back the pain, yet aware that her pain is not a distant, muted, second hand feeling, but a visceral explosion that threatens to overwhelm her. Her arm *actually* hurts and it's *really* bleeding. Her throat is sore where the creature tried to throttle her. Her chest rises and falls as she pulls air into her overworked lungs. All of this is happening to her while she is escaping from a monster from deepest space inside her own mind. The extreme suffering may be what *becoming* feels like, but while she can feel anything — even intense agony — she knows she's alive. And while she's alive she'll fight the creature with every fibre.

Until the very end, Daisy thinks she can rectify her wrong turn. A different route, a door, an opening, a side passage, a tunnel that will lead her back to where she needs to be. Instead, the spur on which she finds herself takes her deeper into uncharted territory, seeming to veer further away from her intended destination with every hasty step, before finally sweeping round in a long curve back towards the security of home.

Too late, Daisy realises the pounding footsteps that relentlessly followed her down the byways of her brain have finally stopped. As she turns that last corner and sees her door ahead of her, she sees why.

She comes to a halt, hands on hips, gasping for breath, with the pain in her throat and from her bleeding arm forgotten in the face of a more immediate and overwhelming problem. The creature is there, outside her door, blocking the way to her impregnable fortress. It's between her and salvation. She's trapped with nowhere to go. And so finally they're face to face: the slight human girl and the entity from deep space.

Her tank is empty. She has no strength left. The stereotypical monstrous shadow is before her, towering over a tiny, helpless female form. She's left with nothing but her courage.

But it's not the creature from the Black Lagoon anymore. It's still a semi-monstrous brute, but it's warped and stooped, face twisted away from her.

She glances back down the corridor, along which she's so recently had to flee from him. She could still run, but where would she go?

There's silence. Then the sobbing begins and the shrouded figure slumps to the floor.

This is her chance! Daisy edges slowly closer to the thing that's now nothing but a formless, quaking shadow. "Quark?" Her voice is a bare whisper and there's no response from the keening spectre. The girl hesitates, but she has no choice, she must think of herself — and of you.

She clicks her door open and steps quickly over the creature. With one hand resting on the handle of her door, one foot raised, ready to step into safety, she pauses again and looks down at the prone form at her feet. Flight will save her, but it seems fight has left *it*. Just yesterday she'd considered herself safe, a negotiation away from freedom. Was this another sign of what Quark would see as her weakness? Or a sign of the strength that was her humanity? She sighs and shrugs away the question. She turns and stoops down to him.

"Quark?" she whispers again, and takes a bare half step towards him, her arm reaching for the creature's shoulder.

It looks up as Daisy's fingers touch. She lets out a long hitching gasp: all the faces she'd seen in her nightmares and on the face of the monster as it chased her down the twisted corridors of her mind — the wolf man, Frankenstein's monster, Dracula, the mean clown, the stooping, long armed, clawed fairground monster of horror films — it's none of these that stares up at her. As she stands, hands clasped to her chest, mouth open in shock, it's her own self that lies there. Her own tear-streaked face that stares up at her! This time Daisy's not looking into a mirror, she's actually face-to-face, inside her own head with her doppelgänger, her nemesis, her kidnapper, her would-be killer. Pale, wan and completely vulnerable. Just a slight teenage girl. Herself.

"Daisy," it grinds out, "help me." It reaches for her and then stops, a frown on its pained face as another tear runs slowly down its cheek. A red tear. A tear of blood. The frown deepens and the expression swiftly changes from confusion to horror as its mouth opens … and blood gushes out of that gaping maw and the creature screams and sinks to the floor in a dead faint.

Daisy shrieks with every ounce of breath that remains in her lungs. It's a loud and long scream; a scream for the ages, for the nightmares we all dread are real; a wail for the life she thought she'd lost; a bellowing, deafening, yell that she both feels and hears — in this room in her head in which she sees and feels herself standing and yet also in the head of the Daisy that's standing there, staring down at her twin self. It's caterwauling whoop that careers to the very edge of insanity and then stops as suddenly as if a door has been slammed on it.

She pulls her hand away from the prone, bleeding thing that is her and not her, quickly enters her room and slams her imaginary (but real) door on it.

Chapter 51

CODE RED!

B ack to back, with the door between them, Quark and Daisy are panting and out of breath.

"Daisy, what's happening to me? What was that thing?" Quark pauses and tries to square Daisy's shoulders, tries to sit up straight, but he feels more like crying than being the strong, silent bogeyman of moments before. "I'm scared," he whispers.

"That was you and me." Daisy's voice is unwavering, even though she's hurt. Even though he — *it* — had hurt her. "That was the other side of us. The flipside. The dark side."

Daisy's just left behind the personification of every childhood monster from inside the wardrobe, under the bed ... and the darkest recesses of her mind. Now beauty and the beast are back in one body. He — Quark — is in charge, although he feels anything but, having all too recently met those monsters himself.

It's the end of his most wretched day on Earth. He's *so* tired, and Daisy's body aches abominably. Just minutes before he'd been in touch with every nerve ending, every atom of her being. He can still sense the chemical imbalance in her body. And a greater discomfort. He's acutely aware of how small this body is. Yet in the moments after the monster departs, he's more human than he's ever been. More truly alive than ever. His very vulnerability in this small person's body is strangely moving.

He feels, in his last moments of consciousness, as though he's drifting towards a higher level of being. It's happening. Nothing now can stop it, he thinks ... almost sadly. He'll sleep now, then wake to the most glorious becoming of them all!

"I'm dying!" Quark thinks. It's the middle of the night. He woke feeling as though some … monster had crept into the room and placed Daisy's head in a vice, while he'd been asleep, dreaming of the blissful Nirvana that awaited him on the other side of the inevitable becoming.

But now, the serenity of being at one with the entire universe is the furthest thing from his mind. He can't focus his thoughts at all — the pain in the girl's head is so intense. But there's more — his breasts are tender, his back is sore, his stomach feels bloated and as for down below … well, this Daisy Jacobs body must be dying! That creature he dreamt of must have damaged her!

He needs to get out and find a new body as soon as possible! To become, to reach the state that he longs for, he needs an active, alert, alive host. He's (sort of) happy to be the source of her downfall, but she can't die before he becomes, otherwise all will be lost.

The headache reaches its zenith and, from Quark's perspective, feelings and emotions more intense than any sensation he's experienced in billions of years of, admittedly brief and intermittent, life, surge through him. He moans and rocks in discomfort.

Inevitably, his whining wakes Daisy. "Er, Quark?"

Silence, except for a low, plangent, almost bovine moan.

"Quark?" she repeats, sleepily.

"Whaaaaaaaaaat?" A bare, guttural whimper.

"What's wrong?" The girl doesn't sound sympathetic.

"The pain … the pain!"

"Er … it's just my period."

"Huh?"

"I'm menstruating. I get this —"

"You've had this before! And … lived!?" Quark can't really focus as waves of — to him — agony roll through Daisy's body.

He succumbs with as much fight as a dog rolling over to be petted. "Do we need to call an emergency doctor? An ambulance?"

"— every month," Daisy continues. She barely tries to suppress the grin in her voice, "So — yeah, welcome to my world. What was that you said about the full, multi-colour teenage experience?"

"But how … how do we suffer like this and survive? How can we cope with this agony?"

"Er, I'm a woman?"

"But — the pain!"

"Quark, it's a mild headache and a few stomach cramps. It's really no biggie."

"No biggie! It is like a crescendo of white-hot burning agony!"

"No, Quark, it's really not. I guess I'm lucky. Some girls do suffer quite a bit of discomfort and for a few it is really painful. But for me, it's a headache and a stomach ache. If it gets too bad, take a couple of paracetamol."

Her sigh infuriates him. "Paracetamol! I need a transplant! And as for …" He can't bring himself to go into detail. "We need expert medical advice immediately. Hah!" An idea strikes him. "Your mother is a doctor; we will seek her help."

"Quark, she was out on a call out last night and she has surgery in the morning, you will not wake my mother just because you've got your period!"

"Ha! Suddenly it's 'my pe …' — thing!" Daisy's shoulders rise and fall as he struggles to get the words out. "When things malfunction, then suddenly it is *my* body. My responsibility. Well, don't forget if I bleed to death, you will die too!"

"Quark, for goodness' sake; I'm not going to die. If you can't cope with a little cramp, then heaven help you if you stick around long enough to have a baby!"

"A baby!" Had Quark already been in the bathroom, what Daisy have seen reflected in the mirror would be one of those picture definitions that appear in children's early dictionaries. And the word Quark was defining would be "panic". If it had been a dictionary for an older child, a teenager, it would have been "sheer, unadulterated panic".

"A baby!" Quark repeats. "I will *never* have a baby!"

"Well, I might have one — or two — when I grow up."

"And go through pain like this! And blood and — ugh!"

"What you're feeling is mild discomfort, Quark. With the occasional shot or two of ouch-iness. It's nothing more than that, and if you'd been a real human girl, you'd never have reached almost fifteen without knowing that. And it doesn't even begin to compare to the literal labour of childbirth. You should ask my Mum about my birth; she said that —"

"I don't want to know!" Quark shouts. "Don't tell me, I don't want to hear it!"

"Quark, you're a mass-murdering psychopath, how can you possibly be squeamish over a little blood?"

"It's not a 'little', I'm … well, gushing — it's pouring out of me!"

"It's really not — maybe 10-20ml over four or five days."

"Four or five *days*! This will continue?!"

"Of course, don't you know anything about periods?"

"I'm a quantum singularity; why should I know anything about p—" Quark stops, seemingly unable to continue.

"Say it. Go on, at least you can say it."

Daisy's shoulders rise and fall as Quark psyches himself up. "About pe—" He stops again then slumps forward, "it's too horrible — I can't say it!"

"It's not nice, it's not my favourite thing — but it's natural and normal and if I got the chance to change, like that — I'm mentally clicking my fingers here — and was told I could become a boy and never have a period again, I'd turn it down because being a girl is absolutely fantastic and having a period every month," she raises the voice inside her head so she can shout at Quark, "BLEEDING for just a few days every month, is a small price to pay."

Quark ignores her. "And anyway, I am not a psychopath."

240

"You're wrong there too," Daisy responds quickly, "you are amoral, you don't care about anyone or anything except yourself — totally egocentric — you are incapable of love and you don't learn from experience. If that's not a psychopath then I don't know what is."

"I have been human for less than a month, what do you expect! My normal existence is as a cloud of dust."

"Well, anytime you want to go back to that, don't let me stop you."

"And I *have* learned and I *am* capable of feelings," he added, huffily.

"Really?"

"Yes, and right now they are hurt."

"Aw, diddums, is the ickle monster upset? Just imagine — blood and hurt feelings on the same day."

Daisy's hands go over her ears as Quark tries to shut out the sound of her voice from within her head. "Will you stop talking about it!" He sighs, and then said more quietly, "just stop."

"This is why you've been so moody, isn't it? You can't cope with my —" Daisy stops herself, instead choosing to tread carefully around Quark's sensibilities, "the changes in my hormones? That's what's caused your abhorrent behaviour ... in the last few days, at least. The rest of the time, of course, it's just been down to your sunny disposition."

"I noticed a change in the chemical balance in your body."

"Really?"

"Yes, the balance of what you call hormones changed and that affected your brain."

"Cool!" Daisy's inner geek will out. Despite herself, she's fascinated. "And you can just, what — sense that?"

"Yes, of course." He speaks as if it's the most natural thing in the world.

"But you didn't know why it was happening and you struggled to cope with what it did to you — to *me*, to my brain?"

"Maybe."

"Because it normally has very little effect on me. I don't have mood swings with my — at this time of the month. I'm sometimes a bit tired. I don't always have as much energy. And sometimes, if I have a bad cramp, I'll have a hot bath. That helps to soothe it away."

Quark sighs. "A bath?"

"Yeah."

"But what about the ..." Quark steels himself. "What about the blood?"

There's a silence and Quark can almost hear her thinking. "It really is no biggie; nothing to worry about. Come on, let's go to the bathroom," Daisy pauses and now Quark can hear the fond smile in her voice, "I sound like my Mum, but ... I'll help you sort it out."

Chapter 52

LADY BUSINESS

I'm stuck; middle of the night, half-awake, half-asleep, worn out by the chase and the injuries I'd suffered. The night that had seemed to presage the end of the world now faded back to the realms of nightmare — although the injuries I'd suffered proved events had been all too real. Certainly, the pain in my throat was intense, though because I no longer had to actually breathe through it, the effects were minimised. And the cut on my arm hadn't been as deep as I'd feared. All the blood seems to have been an echo of what Quark was going through …

Now I can read him better, it's obvious he's really shaken. He's overwhelmed by what he sees as the chaos of human life — of *teenage* life. It's too much for him!

If I was living my life, I'd know exactly where I was in my cycle. As far as what my Nan terms 'lady-business', I'm as regular as clockwork. I can say to the day, almost to the hour when it will start, but in here it takes me a moment to react to Quark's whining. I feel it too, but the pain is a dull, distant throb compared to what I normally experience.

I'd been wondering how Quark would take to the red-blooded reality of life as a female member of the human race. Not even remotely well is the answer!

As I ran for my life, I'd been distantly aware of the dull pain in the pit of my stomach and the muffled throb in my head — as though the discomfort related to someone else entirely, which, in a way, it does!

As Quark goes through his panicked reaction, my heart beats in a strange, excited way — but … it's *my* heart and I can feel it, distantly but feelingly. He hobbles to the bathroom, as if he's recovering from major surgery, and my legs feel lead-like — as though they're unused to activity. But again, although I'm not actively controlling them, I sense the movement.

I'm still a passenger, it's not *my* body, but I have a greater sense of it than I've had for ages. My limbs seem reluctant to move — uncooperative to whoever's giving the orders. I'm only gently feeling my way back into being, and it doesn't yet feel as though my body is ready to be mine again, but I may soon be able to expand my territory — if not yet go for a complete takeover.

Quark is clearly floored by the physical and emotional effects of what's happening. I reckon the experiences of just living a life are gradually overwhelming him.

But he's also affected by the hormonal effects of my cycle. I mean, I know we're all basically sacks of water and chemicals, but Quark actually *is* just a bunch of malignant chemicals, so my hormones may have a greater proportional effect on him. I'm used to his swift changes of mood, but this chaos — literal and chemically induced — may explain his extreme behaviour.

Whatever's happening, I've fought like a demon to stay alive. I *enjoy* being alive and given the alternative, I'd like to just carry-on living. As far as I can tell, death sucks — big time. Whereas, despite its many ickies (as Amy would say), life has a lot to recommend it.

Quark has changed the person people see as Daisy Jacobs. My personality has lost even the echo of the sparkle Amy talked about. I'm colder, more distant; all pinched lips and wan complexion; it's like I'm made of stone. When I speak, there's no inflexion in my voice. It's as though he's no longer dangerous; it could be a ruse, and he may snap back at any moment, but he appears defeated. Especially after the events of tonight.

Before Quark arrived, I often worried about different things — the usual issues of a schoolgirl's life: friendships, bullying, boys, fitting in, getting less than 95% in Science or Maths — all the ordinary, mundane stuff of everyday life. Being swotty and having a passion for Literature and Maths and Science, I genuinely wanted to know a lot about things that most people my age have no interest in. All that set me a little apart. I didn't fit certain people's idea of the norm.

And then I was taken over by a 13.8-billion-year-old alien, who acted like a toddler in a toy shop. A toy shop that is the body of a fourteen-year-old human. I mean *I* struggle with what my body's going through. So, once the full experience hit *him*, he didn't stand a chance!

We're in the bathroom; all clean and fresh and sorted. But it turns out Quark's not at one with the programme. Even in the steamed-up mirror I can see that my sweet, innocent face is anxious; cheeks ashen with a pale red spot centred on each. The arrogance he'd put there has gone — for the moment, at least. The triumphant smile has shrivelled to a sad grimace that's painful to behold. Outwardly he's struggling to remain composed, but it takes one look to know he's fading rapidly. Weirdly, my heart echoes with pity for him and I almost find it within myself to surrender to him, even at this late stage, so he can fulfil his destiny. However, the urge to fulfil my own is stronger!

This isn't fair! I shouldn't even have to contemplate such things. All I want is dull, boring normality! Boring beats this any day. It's unbelievable that one girl should hold the fate of the planet in her hands (or head). But I know I have no choice. I clench my fist: I have to save the world, I— Hang on ... what happened there? Did I really just clench my fist? That wasn't Quark, that was me!

I'll do it again ...

I focus every ounce of effort I can summon. "Aaaaaaaaaaaghhhhhhhh!"

Nope — try again. I mentally grit my teeth and just concentrate on the fingers of my right hand. I picture my small, slim hand and 'see' the fingers slowly, ever-so slowly curve into a fist that I can shake in the face of fate ...

I almost think I can feel a twinge, a flicker of something, just at the very tips of the fingers of my right hand, but I can't make the fist. I'm sure I did it once though; and if I did, then I can do it again. I just need to find the right moment — and the energy to do it.

The steamy atmosphere in the bathroom is slowly dissipating, my image still as blurry as I feel, but I see my soft eyes, grey and mournful, whose slightest variation in expressiveness I'd become expert in interpreting. It's a weird way of deciphering how 'I' feel. But I see their lustre has faded and note how they stare vacantly out at me.

"You can still end this," Quark says. My voice is deeper, hoarse — drained of emotion; of conviction.

"How?" I reply in full neutral mode.

"Still time for you to surrender."

"Quark, you're going through the motions. Even you don't believe what you're saying anymore."

In the mirror, I see my head shake and my mouth open to speak. But before he can repeat his *becoming* mantra, I interrupt him. "Your eyes, Quark — I mean *my* eyes."

"What about them?"

"You forget, they are *mine*," I say. "I know them; I know *me*. You say one thing, but your eyes say another. Look at my face. Go on: really look at me now in the mirror."

There's a pause. "Okay, I'm looking."

"Is that someone on the verge of triumph? Someone on the brink of achieving their goal? Or more like somebody on the edge of a precipice? An individual overwhelmed by everything that's happened to them?" I give that time to sink in. "You can live without this."

"Without what?"

"Without killing. Without dealing in death and destruction. You can find form, find a body, a *soul* to exist within. There's no need to take their life. Why not just *be* them?"

"Because I need to *be*-come," he says through my gritted teeth.

"Why?"

"Because — well, it is complicated."

"What — and you think I won't understand? This is why you're here in the first place. The reason you invaded my body. You've told me repeatedly; but you have never actually explained it. So — come on, you've had enough time in school now to know how to make a case and explain it clearly. Tell me."

"Once upon a time —"

"Quark!"

"The universe was something very small," he continues without further prevarication, just the faintest ghost of a smile on my lips, "and then expanded incredibly quickly." I can see that the thought process, or maybe the focus on *this* fundamental point of his purpose, immediately brings more colour to my cheeks and a spark of life to my eyes.

"In fact, one of your scientists, a man called —"

"Einstein, yes," I interrupt.

"Would you interrupt a teacher like that?"

"No, Quark."

"You asked me to tell you this, so let me explain."

"Yes, Quark," I say, suitably chastened.

"He realised that the universe could not remain the same size; it must either expand or contract. This is where the 'Big Bang' came from. The fate of the universe rests on the notion that the universe will continue to expand ... forever. If it doesn't, then the opposite will happen, and the universe will contract. And the universe will end. Everyone and everything will be burnt to death in a fiery inferno; there will be a universal apocalypse."

I can't help feeling somewhat edgy at this notion.

He senses this. "You have something to say, Daisy?"

"Yes, Quark I do. I really don't fancy 'a universal apocalypse'."

"I can imagine!"

"I thought this was what you wanted; it's what I've been trying to stop for a month."

"I don't want to happen either. My lifetime's work is to prevent the end of the universe by stopping it from contracting."

"And your way of doing that is to go around decimating whole planetary systems and systematically eliminating countless races and civilisations?"

"I do not do this at random!"

"I know Quark, there is a system to your regime of mass murder. You are as organised as a Nazi."

He shakes my head. "You do not understand."

"No shit, Sherlock. Pray enlighten me."

My curse raises nothing more than an eyebrow. "The universe contains a lot of ... 'stuff'. You call this light and matter and suchlike. And that's fine — except if there is too much stuff."

"What happens then?"

"Gravity happens."

"Even out in space?"

"It's a fundamental force. It is everywhere, and if there is too much matter in the universe, gravity will have a bigger impact. Instead of expanding, the universe could slow. It could even contract."

"Leading to universal apocalypse."

My head nods.

"So, how is that prevented? How do you stop the ... stuff threshold from being over-stepped," I ask. But as I say the words, it suddenly becomes clear. "You eliminate stuff," I say, answering my own question.

In the mirror, my lips form a thin, but for Quark, warm smile. "You do see! You understand. You'll help?"

"Help?"

"You'll *become*?"

"What? No! Why would I do that?"

"So you can help me eliminate more of the stuff that is clogging up the universe. Before it is too late."

"We are not 'stuff'! We're human beings. This is our home, our planet. Earth will not cause the universe to slow down or stop."

"It might! Earth could be the tipping point!"

"So, by your reckoning, if you emulsify my planet, the universe won't reach that critical threshold and will continue to expand forever?"

My head nods.

"If you don't and instead let us all live, the universe ends up uniformly cold, dead and empty?"

"Yes. I knew you would understand and accept your fate, eventually."

"Piffle."

"Sorry?"

"Absolute piffle. I have never heard such a load of complete and utter codswallop in all of my life."

"This is neither 'piffle' nor 'codswallop' — whatever either of those things may be. This is science."

"This is mass-murder excused as housekeeping."

He shakes my head, but then reconsiders. "Actually, although I still disapprove of the 'murderer' tag, that is a useful analogy. Keeping things tidy, making sure the universe's mess doesn't get too out of hand — that is a useful and important job."

"And it's still piffle."

"And on what basis, oh mighty fourteen-year-old girl, do you refute this fundamental, self-evident scientific fact?"

"How old is the universe?"

"Thirteen point eight billion years — you know this."

"And how old are you?"

"You know this also — very slightly less than thirteen point eight billion years."

"And in thirteen point eight billion years, this is the best you've come up with? Mash planets and people into dust? That's it? That's your idea of 'saving the universe'".

"It has worked up until now! The universe is healthy." Quark rolls my eyes, as if I can't see him right there in the mirror.

I know I'm on the verge of something big. I've plotted to get him out of my head and body, but I've barely been keeping him at bay. But today I had brief control of one part of my body, and out-thought him too. Now I'm putting together a plan that might just get us both through this in one piece — or in Quark's case, probably several million pieces.

Chapter 53

WHAT ON EARTH IS GOING ON?

Q uark thinks in straight lines. He's serious and formal. He uses highfalutin' language, finds even contractions like 'can't' and 'don't' difficult — in fact doubly so, because he *can* and he *does*! He takes himself *very* seriously. There's a certain order to his existence. A natural rhythm that consists of — nothing, boredom, destruction, death, nothing, boredom, destruction, death, etc. The 'nothing' and the 'boredom' last for a very long time; the interesting bits — the 'destruction' and 'death' are generally over in the time it takes to read this sentence. And this routine is well-practised, ordered and familiar. Yes, there's an awful lot of nothing, but if you aren't sentient, that's not important. Only in those brief flashes of existence does Quark realise there might be more to life than death, but by that time he's usually … well, dead.

This has been the situation since a fraction of a second after the Big Bang.

So, you'll have noticed the key theme here — serious, formal, order, routine, boredom etc. And you've also seen Quark living Daisy Jacobs' life as a teenage girl. And trying to out-teen Daisy. She says her life is ordinary and the things she generally does, the things any of us do in our day-to-day life, are nothing exceptional — they're pretty mundane and average. To us.

To Quark it adds up to chaos. Chaos on the outside is a bad thing, although he's refused to face up to this. Even fifty minutes of History, followed by a short walk and then fifty minutes of Science, a bit of a break and fifty minutes of Maths is, to him, chaotic. An entire day of Science or Maths or English would be better. Or a week, maybe. Or a whole year: a year of double-double-double Science! Yes, it would be very, very dull, but he'd know what to expect: lots and lots of nothing and boredom. Almost no death and destruction, of course — unless Daisy keeled over with boredom, but then you can't have everything. There'd be structure. Order. And maybe, just maybe, Quark could cope.

But no. First, he has to do all the stuff to Daisy's body to get it ready to even go downstairs in her own house every day. Then the body has to be refuelled, while he interacts as little as possible with her meddlesome family — who are always interfering in his life and constantly asking Daisy what she's doing and how she's feeling. As if he knows — let alone cares! He can't understand why everyone is so obsessed with how everyone else is feeling. It's so random; he barely knows what feelings are, let alone how to put barely sensed emotions into words that anyone else can interpret logically. "Within parameters," doesn't give Daisy's mum much of an idea of where her girl is at. "A tolerable situation," (even when it isn't) doesn't make Mrs Griffin think Daisy is back with the programme. And "middling" doesn't assure her dad that his wife isn't right after all and Daisy *should* have therapy.

Quark is unsettled by what happens to him on a day-to-day basis and further upset by people's reaction to how *he* reacts.

To his cost, Quark has discovered that teenagers are supremely alive. They're just bursting with life and growth. And hormones! They have an entire world of possibilities ahead of them — and don't they know it. The world is their oyster. They still believe absolutely anything can happen. They're invincible. He finds it weirdly exciting … in a scary kind of way.

But the desire he'd felt to break out of the teenage mould turned to irritation as he became increasingly baffled by the disorder of daily life. He couldn't rely on a single thing being the same, or happening in the same way, or in the same order, from one day to the next. Instead, things went from bad to worse. That's why he was secretly relieved when Mrs Griffin told him to just stop it. He did so, immediately and with an almost audible sigh of relief.

But then the scary-killer-monster thing happened.

She's still shut away inside her head, questioning everything that's going on, pushing him, tormenting him. It's always a risk for her to come out fighting, yet she still does, every single day.

There's no stability and order, even here, in the body that should long ago have gone the way of every other body he'd ever connected to.

His plan hadn't worked even before her body blindsided him with hormonal overload. But then, instead of letting him wallow in pity, or suffer in helpless ignorance, she helped him. Just as she'd helped him several times before. This dichotomy confused him. He was bent on her destruction, so in a way it was natural for her to feel a degree of resentment.

She did, and frequently made him aware of the fact! Yet she didn't give up hope. She didn't give in *at all*. And she helped him almost as much as she hindered him. The girl was baffling!

Chapter 54

THE HERO INSIDE YOURSELF

This time of our lives is like one big fantasy, even without the odd alien invasion. We morph from one type of person into another — and sometimes back again — seemingly overnight. Anything can happen. Sometimes you just have to suspend disbelief at what's happening to your mind and body. Life is already throwing the kitchen sink at us, so what's happening to me is just a larger sink! What's to fear, really? I say go for it. Believe and *anything* is possible!

Quark's used the worst bits of being a teenager against me: the folly of fashion, the angst about others' opinions, the self-doubt, fears and fantasies about the opposite (or the same) sex. We affirm our right to be a close approximation of an adult when it suits us, while maintaining the priceless fallback position of being immature when we need to explain away some of the silly or childish things we do. It's a handy in-between state; being almost a grown up without having to take on all (or even *any*) of the responsibilities that come with age.

In return, I've used the best bits of adolescence to fight him. I've fought fire with teenage fire! I hope I've been true to myself in not just surviving, but in pushing back. After all, we live for a very short time, but we'll be dead forever …

And I remember what Dad says: if you can face up to one single issue in your life and work your way through that, then you can do anything at all. You can achieve anything you set your mind to. Don't run, don't turn your back on it. There's no need to panic, or see it as a big deal or "the end of the world as you know it" as he'd ironically put it — just imagine a series of manageable steps. Look at the problem and break it down one little bit at a time. Chip away at it. You don't have to be brave to do this. Just fearless. I can do fearless. Can't I?

So — here goes …

"At the moment, Quark, you're in a state of flux; you're neither one thing or another. You aren't really a teenage girl. It's like you're just playing a game."

"And you are neither alive or dead."

"I may not be technically alive, but I'm sure as heck not dead … unlike every single individual you've ever met. Just how many beings have you killed?"

"I —"

"How many planets have you destroyed?"

Quark sighs, but surprisingly plays along, shoulders slumped. "A lot."

"How many empty rocks have you pulverised?"

Another sigh. "A lot."

"How many comets?"

"Is there a point to this?"

"How many meteors? How many moons? How many uninhabited planets?"

"I don't know! Presumably you have a point?"

"Have you smashed enough?"

"Enough?"

"Yeah, you know — you said there couldn't be too much stuff in the universe, otherwise the effects of gravity could cause everything to contract. And then the universe could implode."

"That is correct."

"So — in almost thirteen point eight billion years, how many planets have you destroyed? And comets and moons — and all the rest."

"As I said, a lot."

"If that's the case, why keep smashing stuff up? Why not just let things be?"

"I am playing safe."

"Safe? I don't think that's how the Strathairns or the Vicia would see it; or the — what was it? — the Gnarg?"

I feel my head nod, but Quark says nothing.

"I bet, given the opportunity, they'd have a different perspective."

My body is slumped in a chair. Quark, exhausted by a long night with little sleep, being bombarded by turbulence from without and chemicals plus argumentative teenager within. I'll leave him something to think about, to see how much he's changed.

"Just consider that, Quark. Think about what you've done to all those people and how many more billion you'll eliminate in the future if you continue with this hunch of yours."

"Hunch? This is science!"

"You may think it is — and certainly the Big Crunch or whatever the collapsing universe concept is called, is an actual theory that actual live scientists, rather than loose conglomerations of matter, spend time thinking about, but it's just one theory. There are others. And no one suggests biffing a lot of stuff in case it causes the Crunch.

"But we're both tired now, it's the middle of the night, you're all clean and fresh and relatively pain free — why don't we get some sleep and talk about this tomorrow?"

"Are you going to leave me in peace now?"

"Don't I always?"

"Do you ever?"

"Goodnight, Quark."

"Good night, Daisy."

Chapter 55

I WILL DO NO HARM

I'm sorry to say, but Quark wants to make a brief statement. And to be honest, there's not a great deal I can do to stop him, is there ...?

I am Quark — don't be afraid! Don't flinch or try to run away! Running would be a) pointless, as I mean you absolutely no harm; and b) pointless, as I'll get you in the end, anyway.

Despite what you may have heard from certain people, I am NOT a raging homicidal maniac, or a death-dealing monster. I have been gravely misunderstood and have received an outrageously bad press. None of what has been said is fair or true. Unless it was me that said it, in which case it was both fair AND true.

In the past, I went to a planet and did the job I'm supposed to do: I destroyed it.

Now, I just linger here on Earth, within Daisy Jacobs. And I can feel *her* there, loitering inside with an intent so malicious it makes *my* head pound. It's uncomfortable, knowing that she's lurking, like a shadow or a poltergeist, waiting to strike out at me. She's digging away at the foundations of my control, as the basis of humanity's future teeters in the balance. I felt that twinge in my arm yesterday, felt the hand try to form a fist, but with the pain I was suffering, I was unable to prevent her from being so intrusive.

But she's always there, in the background, undermining me. And her skulking presence is adding additional layers to my already multifaceted headache. She's still there now, locked in a tiny corner of *my* mind, and I'm sure she's agonising about the 'pain' *I* am inflicting, the 'chaos' *I* am causing in the lives of those who care about her! Yet I'm powerless to do anything about it.

To an extent, I understand her discomfort with the broad outline of my plan, but we all have a job to do, a role to play; in this case mine is to destroy and yours is to be destroyed. But I know that, given the opportunity, you'd all like to be at one with the universe — after all, getting back to nature is very much the 'in thing' now, is it not? And what could be closer to nature than actually being part of it? Think of the satisfaction you'd feel in those microseconds before your mass extinction, in knowing you were playing a fundamental role in helping to preserve the long-term future of the *entire* universe! Everyone wants to have a purpose in life and what greater purpose is there than knowing that, according to a vaguely understood theory (one of countless competing theories) that may or may not be proved to be correct (only the passage of a few billion years will prove this, one way or another), you may — just may — play a part (a very, very tiny part) in helping the universe to thrive and prosper?! I mean, wow!

You know, that last paragraph didn't quite work out how I intended and I'm not entirely sure I sold my plan to you in the best and most effective way …

However, I hope I've convinced you to use your influence on Daisy. I've tried my best to help her see the light. I've even tried to make her popular, to make her stand out more from the crowd. Why didn't that make her happy? At least they least notice her now.

***

"I don't want *them* to like me. I don't care." Daisy interrupts Quark's direct appeal — to your relief, no doubt!

"You like them not liking you?!"

"Yes! No. I —"

"Well?"

"I don't like being disliked, but I don't really care what other people think. I want the people I *care* about and the people I *respect* to approve of me and the way I live my life."

"But *these* people are popular."

"For the wrong reasons."

"What reasons?" Quark's confused.

"Those who try their best and respect other people — they're worth my time, but —"

"But if someone gets into trouble because they are bored or they can't be bothered to focus or they make a mistake or because they are having a bad day, they are not worth your time?"

"That's not what I said."

"You are a snob, Daisy Jacobs."

"What! I am not —"

"You are. You think everyone has to be as clever as you are or as pretty as you are or as interesting and focused as you are. And you judge people if they don't meet your standards."

"What! Where's this coming from? How can you possibly —"

"I am inside your head and you are constantly looking over my shoulder and judging me — just like you are always judging other people."

"I'm not! I do my best to treat other people as I'd want to be treated myself."

"You tend to ignore many of the people at your school and in your village."

"Quark, you've got this wrong: it's not possible to be friends with everyone; I don't ignore people, I just spend more time with people I already know or with those I have something in common with. That's what everyone does. If I meet someone new, I'll talk to them and show an interest. This is how everyone lives their lives."

"So you ignore others and don't even try to talk to most people."

"How did you get to that from what I said? Quark, there are well over seven and a half billion people in the world; you expect me to talk to them all?!"

"You think your dull little planet and your teeny little galaxy are things of such wonder? They're not — it's all just random chance."

"Ah, I wondered where we were going with this; turns out you're peddling the same old, same old." Quark felt her sigh. "I disagree. I think Scuttleford is wonderful, and school is great and the world is amazing and the universe — and life itself — is simply astonishing, fantastic, glorious and beyond thrilling."

"You have watched *way* too much of that evil David Attenborough!"

"And you've watched way too little," she replies. "And you've been going round with your eyes closed all your life."

"Strictly speaking," Quark says, "I don't have eyes. Or life come to that."

"Well, with your metaphorical eyes closed. Life *is* amazing. And I'll fight for mine — and for everyone's. I'll fight for my 'dull' little planet. And for my 'teeny' Milky Way too!"

You'd think Quark would be diminished, almost broken, yet there's a quirk to Daisy's lips and still the faintest sparkle in her eyes. Quark sighs, but there's something that sounds oddly like — is that fondness in Daisy's voice as he speaks? — "I know, Daisy Jacobs, I know you will."

Chapter 56

DETENTE

"It's no good being mad at me, Quark, you may as well be mad with the whole universe you seem hell bent on protecting."

"You are made of cells, yes?"

I sigh. "Okay."

"Those cells come from other cells. One makes two, makes four, makes eight — etc, etc."

"Okaaaay."

"Every cell that is in you is made from other matter from other cells that existed before. Your life comes from other lives."

"I do seem to remember an awful lot of 'begetting' from my RE lessons."

"That's right; cells *beget* cells, *life* begets life."

"And your point?"

"You have always existed, Daisy. You'll go on existing, just in a different form."

"I quite like this form, thank you very much. Come back when I've finished with it and you can have it then."

"Daisy, it's not —"

"Hang on, why don't you do that?"

"What?"

"Come back later," I say, thinking that I'm onto something.

"But I'm here now."

"Yes, but you're not on a schedule, are you?"

"No, but —"

"Listen, Quark, there's a lot of life on earth. We're making a bit of a mess of it at the moment, I'll grant you that, but we've only had a few hundred million years really, and modern humans are just barely getting started — only a hundred thousand years or so. That's not even the blink of an eye to you."

"Daisy, really, I'm only doing my job. Fulfilling my function."

"Yeah, but no one's checking up on you. No one's keeping records. You'll be back this way, won't you?"

"Of course — in, oh, probably eight hundred million or maybe a billion or so years."

"So, there you are."

"Where am I?"

"Back here in a billion years. What's that to you?"

"Well —"

"I won't be here, and it's quite possible that by that time there may not even be life on Earth. There'll just be rocks and stones and … 'stuff' for you to hoover up. SLURP!"

My face had softened again after a day of Quark getting used to the new reality of life as a teenage girl. We'd talked for hours; just … talked. His smile on my lips now looks more natural. "For a little creature atop a little lump of rock that's spinning at hundreds of miles an hour while hurtling round a ball of fire at thousands of miles an hour … you have not done too badly."

"You are getting quite good at these compliments," I say.

"Daisy, you are forever," Quark replies. "You will *be* forever. That is a fact, that is how it is and how it will always be."

"Well, that's true for what I'm made of, but for *me*, for who I am, for the individual atoms that for this brief span of years make up the being known as Daisy Jacobs, that's not true."

"Billions of atoms propelled against one another in a luminous fireball of coincidence."

"Don't forget all that begetting," I add. "Who knows I may do some begetting of my own … " Inside, I'm blushing.

"Being inside your mind and seeing how *you* use what is in here," he taps the side of my head, "that has been … interesting. I like the way you see connections between things that are not necessarily connected."

"Like what?"

"Like between the people in your life, between cause and effect. Like with the equation your maths teacher put up on screen last week. He was showing the class the connection between what you are studying now, what you might study at A Level, and an equation you might see if you do maths at university."

"I didn't think you saw any point in 'wasting time' studying at school."

In the mirror my grin widens as my face becomes more meditative. "I can sense you, Daisy. You stopped exploring, stopped plotting inside there," he taps my head again, "instead, you focused on that equation. You could see the links, I felt it, you could see how that equation could work and more than that, I think you could see what it meant, what lay behind and beyond it. And I don't think seeing things like that is normal."

"No?"

"And there's a name for it. I think you are a scientist."

"I am just a girl."

"'Just'! Did you just say, 'just a girl'! I thought that was your superpower?!"

"I know in many ways I'm still a kid. I know I'm fighting you and fighting against the odds. I *am* a girl, but I want to grow up to be a woman."

"And how has it felt with *me* being you?"

"That's my point, Quark, you're *not* me. You're barely a pale imitation. You've taken me over. You're trying to push me out of existence altogether. You've made me less than a passenger in my own body."

"So?" There's still a defiant sparkle in my eyes.

"I'll let 'so' pass for the moment — but make no mistake, if we get time, I'll come back to the ethics of 'so'."

My grin widens and I know he's been teasing me.

I'm not letting him get away with that! But I have a bigger point to make. "What I mean is that *you* can be the passenger. Instead of being the invader."

Our connection is so strong and so close that he immediately gets the gist of what I'm saying. "Be a parasite within the host you mean?"

"No, not a parasite — that's malignant; the intention is negative. I mean an observer, an entirely benign presence. You have the ultimate opportunity; you are unique in the entire universe. You can go wherever you want to for as long as you want to. And this way you can truly live the life of any single being you come across. You can see them as they actually are; not try to kill them or try to manipulate them into being something they are not. There'd be no false images or misunderstandings. You'd be within them, you'd experience their language, their culture, their entire civilisation — for as long as you want. You can literally see both sides of an argument."

"What, and just leave you here?"

"Of course! After all, I've got a life of my own to live."

"Equations to study."

"Yeah. And any bare moons you come across, any useless comets or wandering bits of rock —"

"Pound 'em."

"Into their constituent atoms. Then no beings will be harmed in the continuance of your role."

"And who you are, *what* you are, will still be here, Daisy."

"Okay, so I'll see you again then — in what? Almost a billion years?" I see my internal smile echoed in the smile on my face in the mirror. "You know, in a weird kind of way I'd kind of miss you," I add.

"I'll miss you too."

I note with an inward smile that our long chat has brought about the return of Quark's ability to use contractions.

"I can't say I've enjoyed all aspects of human adolescence. It's quite a challenge at times. But it's been a pleasure to get to know you, Daisy Jacobs. I enjoy your company."

"Well, don't let me keep you — even though I do have a lot to say."

"You do!" He looks at me and smiles a wide, deep smile. "You always have a *lot* to say."

"And you enjoy it, don't try to deny it. You may not enjoy 'life red in tooth and claw', but you do get a kick out of this living lark."

He winces at the reminder, but the smile returns swiftly. "I do. I do. I don't think I will ever tire of listening to you, talking to you, *being* with you."

"I don't think an enduring friendship is possible, Quark."

"Oh, I don't know. I think a long-term relationship is very much on the cards. I think our friendship will last for a long time. A very long time."

And I thought I was getting somewhere! I thought I could help Quark to see sense and go off to explore the great outdoors. I thought I'd persuaded him to get a life. But I have a horrible feeling he's going for the one he's already got!

Chapter 57

THE STRANGER IN THE MIRROR

Morning again. The mirror again. Quark stares at the stranger in the glass. A sweet face, but once more subdued and serious. The once familiar animation that used to flutter between the bright eyes and the curved, rosy lips is absent. He misses that lively, animated girl. He misses … himself? He looks again, staring deep into 'his' own eyes. Looking for *himself*. Trying to see into the soul. But he doesn't *have* a soul. He is atoms and … he thinks of the T-Shirt in Daisy's drawer with the message — 'Never trust an atom, they make up everything'.

And at that thought, the eyes, now grey-green again, under their thick lashes suddenly fill with tears.

Who is crying? He doesn't even know anymore. Is this Quark? Or is the reflection in the mirror the true reflection of her? Am I crying? he thinks. Am *I* doing this?" And suddenly, he knows what he must do.

"Daisy, I am sorry." It's her voice, but *his* voice, deeper, huskier, with a rueful, almost soulful edge to it. "'Until you are naught but dust!' I remember that phrase, that threat. But you have to understand, this is how it has always been. I've simply existed. The conversations I have had with you are the first I have ever had."

"The first ever!" She replies, and the vitality, the energy, the *life* in her voice animates him immediately and he know he's made the right decision.

"Ever," he repeats.

"That's so sad!"

"There has never been the need before." He curls her lips downward in an exaggerated sad face.

"Aw! A grey existence. An existence without life or colour."

"I suppose from your perspective it is. It was. But there's never been the need negotiate, let alone actually talk."

"So, you've never really seen life and that's why you don't want to let go."

"I did not know what I was missing."

"And now you do."

"No, I did not know what I was missing until I met you, Daisy Jacobs."

"Is flattery the latest one of your tricks to try and wheedle me into surrendering?"

He laughs. "No. It's my way of saying I finally found the spark. I learned what life truly is."

"In all its technicolour glory!" This time Daisy laughs and he can hear the echo of it tinkling away inside her head.

He clears his throat, "yes, well — some parts of life are more enjoyable than others."

"That particular part may not seem wonderful at the time, Quark, but that is the *start* of life for us. From there we make the life that I've fought so hard to retain. From such a small thing — it's amazing when you think about it."

"Daisy, *you* are amazing."

"No, I —"

"Daisy, listen: you are extraordinary. In a few brief weeks — in just a tiny fraction of the briefest blink of an eye on my timescale, I have learned more from you about what it means to be alive than in all the eons of my previous existence." He pauses. "Now I hope to experience more."

"No more grey life?"

"No. Now I have seen what it is to be truly alive. Through your curiosity about everything, your thirst for knowledge, I have truly lived for the first time — briefly and vicariously, but I have seen what life is like. Through you, that grey existence has become full-colour. Thank you."

Daisy is touched, but Quark can sense her deep anxiety. "And so?"

"So?"

"Yes, what happens now?"

"I must fulfil my destiny. I must do what I came into existence to do."

Daisy sighs. "So my thanks for showing you what life's all about is for you to grind me into dust?" Her bitterness is evident. "It's all been a waste? You'll just gobble up all life on Earth?"

"I will. Eventually … "

"Eventually?"

"I have never had to wait this long. Never been forced — as I saw it — to actually live. After the first *becoming* it is always easy."

"And dull."

He continues as though he hasn't heard her. "Here, there are so many messages, so many stimuli bombarding you at all times: from TV, computers, radios, mobile phones, but also advertisements and news programmes, the barking of dogs, the songs of birds, other peoples' voices shouting and yelling or just talking incessantly, trains flashing past, cars revving and aeroplanes taking off, vans and trucks, the smell of exhaust from buses passing on the street, the colours everywhere, and every food tastes different — even the same recipe, cooked a second time, tastes different; the scent of soaps and perfumes and shampoos; the smell of people who do not use soap and perfumes and shampoos! The noise of children playing in the park, the leaking of other peoples' music from headphones and passing cars, the din of crowds at football matches, and people talking … talking and talking and talking — Daisy: space is totally quiet. Can you imagine absolute silence? Can you imagine days and weeks and years of seeing nothing and hearing nothing?"

"No. That must be awful!"

"It is bliss, Daisy. Silence. Nothing to see. No smells —"

"Good *or* bad."

"Yes! But every one of those stimuli reacts and interacts with what is going on in your own thoughts, emotions, feelings." Daisy's body sighs deeply. "It is overwhelming."

"And this is just Scuttleford, Quark. Imagine London or Mexico City, Tokyo or Mumbai."

"I cannot even begin to think about it."

"And then there's hormones ..."

"Don't talk to me about hormones!"

"But you've changed Quark. And I don't think it's just my hormones that did that. I don't think I need to *become* for you to get what you want. I'm already changing. So are you. People meet; beings meet. Entities meet — whatever. We change. You think in a different way to how you did when you arrived in me — on Earth, I mean.

"When I came here, I was not thinking at all!"

"Well, now you are. And the way you think has changed too. You make jokes! You use contractions. You kiss boys! You've not just been in my head, you've been in my shoes, living my life. *Living*, not *becoming*. You've had the chance to *be* me. To *become* more than atoms. More than mere matter. You experienced life."

"I have not enjoyed it all. Some of it, like when you —"

"Yeah, I get it, I get it! Some things about being human you don't like. It's not all a bed of roses, I'll agree. But lots of it — most of it — is pretty wonderful."

"Yes, but I make things more too. Make them bigger than what they were."

"No, you make beings into less than they were. You take away everything that they were and turn them to dust. Lots and lots of dust, maybe, but dust nonetheless."

"You are saying my life is pointless?"

"No, I'm saying you haven't lived at all, until now. Who knows, the theory may be correct and ridding the universe of matter could be vital, but there's plenty of useless stuff for you to work on, without getting rid of the good stuff, the inhabited planets, the suns that bring life."

"As I said, Daisy — you see the universe the way a scientist does."

"I've learned a lot about the world, about science, about myself — what I can do and what I'm capable of," she replies.

"You're capable of anything. Anything at all."

"And now you're learning from me!"

"Yes?"

"'You're' again! See, you're using a contraction!"

"And what does that say about me?"

"That you've become just a little human. That you've softened. You're rounder, less spiky."

"I've also learned about time."

"But you're practically as old as time!" Daisy says with a laugh.

"Thank you very much!" He pauses. "I mean, I've learned to value it more — to live in the moment rather than to see a great expanse of time."

"But isn't that boring? To imagine all those moments, stretching out ahead of you?"

"No. And that's the greatest thing you have taught me: to live. I will experience so many things in the time to come. I will actually live *in* those moments, not exist *through* them."

"But those moments will be within other beings?"

"Yes."

He can immediately sense the flare of anger within her. "I really thought we were getting somewhere! But you'll continue with all this senseless destruction of —"

"No, Daisy, you misunderstand me. I will live *through* the beings I meet, but you have taught me to share, and that is —" He pauses and her lips smile, "that's what I'll do: I will share periods of time with them —"

"So — periods again …"

270

"No — never again, I hope! But I want to experience life as the beings I meet experience it. I want to live like them; live *as* them. And pass on just a little of my experience to them. I will enjoy that for a while — before we meet again."

He knows her so well, that he smiles as he follows her thought process, from relief at her survival, to her own inward smile to — "Wait, what?! 'Meet again'!"

Chapter 58

DAISY JACOBS SAVES THE WORLD

"Humans have many good points."

"I'm pleased you recognise that." Obviously, he'll get to *his* point in his own sweet time and until then resistance is, as they say, futile.

"Strength, courage, determination — a stubborn inability or unwillingness to give in." Quark pauses before he continues. "And love is maybe the greatest strength. This is truly *your* superpower, Daisy Jacobs. You are like a love radiator. You are loved and your loved ones believe in you and fight for you. I admire that."

"I'm flattered, I think."

"You generate ... positive feelings in others. You make those around you feel better and those who care about you feel very much better."

I'm touched. "Thank you."

"I do not think that I have necessarily helped with this."

I laugh. "No, I don't think you have."

"Were you scared?" Quark asks.

"Of course I was — all the time! A constant panic!"

"Yet you continued to fight. And others fight for you, because you are worth fighting for."

"Quark, are you leaving?"

He continues as though he hasn't heard. "I do not consciously think about where I go. But *if* I leave Earth, I want to take a little something with me."

"Oh, Quark, I thought you were going to let us live! I thought you were building up to say you're freeing us from your nefarious, intergalactic plans."

"I do have plans to come back this way — remember?"

"Yeah, in a billion or so years, was it?"

"Yes … " Quark replies.

"Humanity won't be here then; not as we are now, anyway. But we'll have had our chance to grow, to maybe spread out to other worlds, to be more than we are now."

"Okay."

"What — after all that, you're just leaving?"

"No, as I said, I need to take something with me; well, two things, actually."

I mentally grit my teeth for what's to come. "Okay … tell me."

"I need you."

"Oh, Quark! First, you promise to free me, now you're going to — what? — use my energy to boost yourself away?"

"Something like that."

"But you'll leave everyone else alone?"

"I promise I won't touch a hair on their heads."

I take maybe one of my last, deep, inward breaths … and I give in. I finally surrender. "Okay then. Do it. Make me *become* and then go. Take me, but leave my world." I find the courage to simply end it. Weirdly, my lifelong edginess stills and I'm overcome with a sense of serenity.

"Daisy, I'm grateful for the offer, but I cannot do it. I cannot make you *become* … you are too —"

I interrupt. "See, I was right! I told you last week you loved me, didn't I? You can't make me *become*, can you?"

"No, I can't do that to you. I just need a little energy from you to boost me on my way."

"How are you going to get that?"

"I will tell you in a moment. But, as I said, there are two things I want."

"Is this the part where you change your mind and kill us all?"

Quark laughs, "no Daisy, there's no longer a part where that happens. Daisy Jacobs has saved the world."

"What then?"

"I want to come back for you."

"What? But I won't be here in a billion years!"

"Oh, Daisy you will. Don't forget, you are made of bits and pieces of the universe. Your very soul, Daisy, is made of stardust. You have always been here and what you are will still be here. But I won't wait a billion years for my return."

A humungous sensation, a feeling as big as a galaxy sweeps through me. "I'll be part of that."

"Daisy, what did you dream of last night?"

"Dream?"

"Yes, you dreamt, I *know* you did."

I'm surprised at his insistent tone; he must have somehow eavesdropped again. "Well, I dreamt about the stars, actually."

Quark nods, as though this comes as no surprise.

"It was incredibly vivid; like a 'highlights' tour of the universe. I saw the birth of stars; I saw strange worlds and extraordinary alien life. I saw planets, asteroids, moons and comets." Once I start my description, I can't stop. "Volcanoes the size of our moon. Planets with a dozen suns and others that were entirely made of water." I couldn't help it, the dream had been so real and my enthusiasm was gushing. "It was like the ultimate Grand Tour! And all so clear and ... well, *real* — profound almost. It was like I *lived* it. As though I really experienced these things; it felt like a gift of some sort."

"A parting gift," Quark whispers, but I barely hear him.

"And at the end, just as I was waking, I saw I smiling old lady, with soft grey-green eyes and a full head of wavy white hair. I think she was me — irrevocably changed by time. Maybe a future me, or a version of me, anyway, with my mind expanded to encompass limitless possibilities. 'See you again soon,' she said." I feel bit silly talking about the dream like this, but can't hold back. "The vision of the little old lady faded and left behind an ancient, tarnished stone, with the date blurred, but still just legible. As I woke up, here in the reality of my head, in my own bedroom, I realised that if I lived to the date on that stone, I'd be ninety-six."

The smile on my face in the mirror even reaches my eyes as Quark stares deeply into me. "A good life. A long life. And a great time to start a new adventure ... if I read your dream correctly, that is." And this time, I do hear him.

"What does that mean?"

"I feel such a close connection to you. I do not want that to end. You are correct — I cannot make you *become*. I do not want to lose the *who* of who *you* are."

For once, Quark renders me speechless!

"I will leave you, but I'll leave you knowing that I will see you again. One day, your molecules, your atoms, the essence of the being who is currently Daisy Jacobs will ... travel with me."

"What?!"

"*I* gave you the dream, Daisy. Like your TV show trick. I used the connection between us to show you what could be — in the, for you, distant future. We will wander from galaxy to galaxy — with strictly *low-level* becoming, just observing, experiencing life, not taking it. First you will live your life — your long and I am sure, happy life. Then we will set off on our adventures. And Daisy Jacobs will see the universe.

"I have learned a lot from you, Daisy," Quark continues. "I learned to be '*I*'; to be alive. Not a mere entity. I will take some of your energy, some of your life-force with me."

"Really?"

"You'll still be you, in your entirety. But there will be an echo of you with me, wherever I go."

"And then ... I'm going to travel the universe?"

"Yes, but first you'll grow and develop. And every atom will belong just to you. You'll —"

"Stop!"

"What?"

"What did you just say?"

"Huh?"

"You were talking about growing and developing."

"Yes, you are not ready. You are not mature."

"I know that, I'm a teenager; still partly — sometimes, mainly — a child. But you say I've changed?"

"Yes, you are open-minded. Your mind is growing, like your body is growing."

"Not quickly enough! Sometimes just I wish that my body would catch up with my mind."

"You're wishing your life away, Daisy," Quark said in a perfect imitation of Mum's voice.

"What? Was that a joke? Were you using my Mum —"

He smiles.

"See — you are learning too," I say.

"Maybe."

"And you say I'm changing?"

"Yes … ?"

"So, what's another way of saying that?"

"I —"

"I'm growing — yes? I'm developing … "

"Yes … ?"

"Quark, I'm becoming something more."

"Yes?"

"Aagh! Quark, you don't see it! Listen: I'm *becoming*." I giggle. "Quark … "

"Yes, Daisy?"

"This is weird, but part of me wishes you could stick around. A very small part, admittedly."

In the mirror, my face lights up and my mouth forms a huge grin. "Well, it's funny you should say that …"

"But Quark! I thought you were going to leave me. To give me back my body."

"And I will."

"I'm sensing a 'but'".

"I cannot cope with your extraordinary life."

"I wouldn't say extraordinary."

"It is and you are! You can cope with this chaos; with this life. And you held me at bay to save yourself — and save your planet. You have introduced the concepts of thought and observation, as well as the idea of self and of concern for others to a multi-billion year old, infinitely dense aggregation of matter. I'd call that quite an achievement: the very definition of extraordinary."

"Well … thank you. And so … "

"Can I observe you from your little *room* in your head, just for one day?"

"You're going to stay?"

"For a single day. We change places and I get to see how it is really done. Teenage life, as lived by an expert. And this one day … I think this one day, and the energy you bring to it — if you give it your all, if you try to live your life to the fullest, to the very best you can — I think that will give me the boost I need to leave you."

"And it'll be just one a day?"

"I guarantee it."

"No tricks?"

"Never! Your life is now yours." He grins again, "this will be a scientific experiment under controlled conditions. I just want the chance to see how it is done. To see how you cope with family and friends and being bombarded by so many impulses and stimuli."

"And then?"

"I'll go. But I will come back — and not just for your atoms, but for *you*."

"When?" I can't help sounding anxious.

"Don't worry, you will live your life. And a full life, I am sure."

"So — why?"

"Wouldn't you like to see more of the universe?"

"Yes, I think I'd like to be an astronaut, but —"

"Well, even if you do that, you won't get further than Mars. Together, we can go much, much further."

"And I'd be what?"

"You'd be Daisy. Or what was Daisy."

"Mmm. 'Essence of Daisy'."

"Yes, that's it; you'd retain the essence of who you were, who you are."

"But in a smaller package."

Quark smiles. "An even smaller package."

"Are you casting aspersions on my height?"

"No! I wouldn't dare insult my travelling companion!"

"When you leave ... I'll never be the same again."

"Neither will I, Daisy Jacobs," says Quark, "neither will I. And I can go now, I can leave you, knowing I'll see you again very soon. But meanwhile —"

"I get to live my life, knowing that each day that passes —"

"— will advance you toward your destiny."

"We are all a part of that, aren't we? All of us entwined —"

"— in the weave and weft of destiny. We are just —"

"— strands in the tapestry of stars that makes up the universe," I continue.

"But once your thread on Earth is cut, I know that —"

"— there'll be more to come. My ongoing existence will help to weave infinite new strands into that glorious tapestry."

"So?" Quark says, my eyebrow quirking in the mirror as he looks back at my reflection for perhaps the last time. "Are you ready?"

"You promise?" If I had lungs of my own, I'd be breathless after that mind-meld or whatever it was. The link between us has been clear since the beginning, but with both ends of the link open, he really is me and I can see into the stars and beyond. I see forever through him! We stand together, one body, one mind, both occupying the exact same space in the universe.

My head nods and through the windows of my eyes, I can see there is a big, full, Daisy-like grin on my lips; I look — *almost* —

like myself. "Yes, I promise I will not interfere; I will only observe. You can trust me."

"And then … then you'll return."

"I will. But not before you have had your time. *All* of your time. Don't forget, Daisy, your future — short and long term — is central to my plans. It is high time I had a travelling companion to share with me the infinite wonders of the universe. I will see you soon, but from your perspective, you will have lived a long life."

"And you won't interfere? You'll just let me live my life? And you'll show just a little self-control?"

"Please — just show me how to do it."

"Okay. I'll do it."

Tears flow freely down my cheeks — but who knows from whom they came. A multi-billion-year old heap of matter is not prone to sentimentality, after all.

"I will leave now," I hear my voice say, faintly.

And I suddenly feel … lighter.

Chapter 59

FROM HERE TO ETERNITY

"Amy!" Daisy Jacobs calls out to her friend. From this distance I see Amy Porter's shoulders slump; but she stops and turns to look at Daisy. Then, in a matter of moments, I see the expression on her face change from near blankness, to surprise, to amazement as Daisy hurtles towards her and launches herself into Amy's arms.

"Sorry! Sorry! Sorry!"

"Huh?" Amy frowns.

"I've been discombobulated for ages and ages. I've been a total artichoke, I know. But — "

"What did you say?" Amy interrupts.

"I'm back now, Amy. I'm me and I'm back." Daisy hugs her bestie and each holds the forearms of the other as they dance around in what might be seen, in some circles, as an excessive show of emotional exuberance.

Amy giggles. "Flying slugs, Daisy! What happened to you — was it that bang on the head?"

"Kind of. I'll tell you all about it another time. Maybe when we're older, because I think we'll both need a lot to drink for that story! But what matters is I'm here now and I love you and we have double Chemistry first thing! Yay!" Daisy lets go of Amy for a moment to punch both fists into the air and then pulls her back into a hug. And, finally, I understand what the big deal is with hugs.

My agreement with Daisy means my pass is 'access all areas'. I've promised not to interfere, but I can utilise the full array of human senses, as well as the extra plug-ins I'll leave for Daisy when I go. I feel Amy's body in Daisy's arms; I detect the delicate coconut fragrance of her cleanser and the raspberry and aloe of her shampoo; I hear the soft sigh uttered by both girls as they embrace properly for the first time in a month; I sense the release of oxytocin into Daisy's bloodstream. All that's true and I knew before — although I refused to truly feel them. But I realise that's not what a hug is. A hug is warmth and — Look, this might not be science at its purest and most demonstrable, but Daisy's right: I feel as though her heart has gone a bit squidgy and her head is utterly fuzzy!

"Hi." The voice is deep and faintly husky. And that one syllable causes a similar reaction in Daisy's body as did the physical contact with Amy.

She turns. "Hi, yourself." I feel her lips form into a smile as she looks up at him and note how his pupils dilate as he looks down at her.

"You okay?"

"Mmm-huh." She nods. "I'm just great, Connor." She pauses and I nudge her, just a teeny bit. Not pushing, not interfering, just very gently encouraging. Daisy holds her hands out, palms down in a gentle 'shushing' movement that I know is aimed inwards, at me. She clears her throat. "Actually, I was hoping to run into you."

"Yeah?" His head tilts as he stares deeply into my eyes — Daisy's eyes, I mean. His cheeks are flushed and from half a metre away I sense the turbulence that being half a metre from Daisy Jacobs is causing in Connor Wheeler's body chemistry. These two are a hormonal hotbed!

"Mmm-huh," she mutters again. And then, in an instant, her heartbeat settles, her breathing moderates and her temperature returns to optimal. Calmness settles over her as though she's donned invisible chain mail. Suddenly, there's steeliness about her — a determination to get her own way. She's serene. "I enjoyed our coffee the other day. Can we do it again — soon?"

"Yeah." Connor's flush increases. I can see he's happy. He's intrigued. Flattered. All of this is as readable on his face as if he were holding up cue cards. What's more interesting is what's radiating out from Daisy. It's like she's zapping him with pheromones and it's chemical, sure, but it's really even less tangible than that. It's like he's being charisma-ed!

This is the 'easy' target I saw when I arrived in this chaotic place! Daisy Jacobs: the vulnerable one. The puny alone-form in which I'd planned to seed the *becoming* of the entire planet. What was I thinking?!

Connor's smiles. "Tonight?"

"Don't push your luck, mister." Daisy grins. "It's a special occasion and I'm having dinner with my family."

"Oh? What's the occasion?"

"You don't know?" Her surprise is feigned. She punches Connor lightly on the arm. "It's Tuesday!" Why did she punch him? I want to ask her, but don't dare interrupt when she's in full flow. In any case, he doesn't seem hurt by her assault; instead, he simply laughs.

"Tomorrow, though?" She suggests.

"Yeah. Sure. Great." The tables have turned. I'm not sure how she did that, but he's the flustered one now. Daisy's the one who's in the driving seat. This relationship thing, this courting stuff, it's like a dance with one person leading and the other following and then there's a change of beat and the partners continue but with roles reversed. That's how it is with Daisy's parents, I realise. Are all relationships like this? Or maybe just the one that work well? The true partnerships.

We arrive at the classroom. Connor and Daisy exchange another look, full of the meaning that feels a bit like the hug with Amy, only without the touching.

"Pop quiz," says the chemistry teacher. I hear the groans from around the room even as my host lets out an exuberant "Yes!" and punches the air again. Really, this girl is simply fizzing with energy! I sense the release of yet more happy hormones from within the body of Daisy Jacobs. She actually wants a surprise test! She wants to be pushed to the limit. The challenge energises her. She thrives on the pressure these situations bring.

Daisy looks around the classroom as the questions appear on the whiteboard. Her eyes meet those of Ellie Watson and I lipread Daisy mouthing, "go for it," at Ellie. Ellie nods and mimes rolling up her sleeves, which Daisy dovetails into a quick one-two of shadow-boxing. Ellie's grin meets Daisy's.

As Daisy's father would say, "Of all the gin joints in all the world, she walks into mine." I had close to eight billion people to choose from to begin the take down of the planet, and this is the one I selected? Through Daisy's eyes I look around the room and then out of the window at the copper beech swaying in the breeze and the brilliant blue sky with softly scudding clouds. Thank goodness! This omnishambles of a planet, with its confusion and its teeming masses, its beauty and its endearing chaos would have been rubble by now, had it not been for this particular collection of atoms. And what a mistake that would have been!

"A*! Well done, Daisy!"

"Sorry, Mrs Griffin?" Daisy's taken aback by her head teacher's effervescing enthusiasm.

"Dr Theobald came to me at break to give me the good news. You scored full marks in today's test. Outstanding, Daisy. I'm so pleased for you. It's great to have the real Daisy Jacobs back with us!" She beams at Daisy and continues down the corridor.

"Well, I'll miss you, Quark," Daisy says inwardly to me, "even if Mrs G won't!"

I tinkle a laugh in imitation of the one I'd heard so many times.

"Oh, and Quark?"

"Yes?"

"Thanks for the boost; I got 100%, not just top marks." She pauses and grins. "I think you might have been worth at least a couple of marks!"

Luke blows a raspberry at Daisy.

Daisy looks sadly at her brother, then at her mum and dad. "Really, young people today." She tuts and shakes her head. "So immature," she continues, as she settles back into her chair at the dining table. Then she laughs, propels herself up and launches herself at her brother, who screams, leaps up from the table and races away. Daisy takes a shortcut, leaping over the back of the sofa and landing next to Luke, where she begins to tickle him.

"This, Quark, is how to relax at the end of the day," she says in a voice only I can hear.

"By torturing your brother?"

"No, by being with your family, or your friends or loved one. By opening your heart and letting them in."

"And not just trying to be the best all the time? Or worrying about what someone else thinks?"

She nods. "You're right. What you feel about yourself: that's what really matters."

It's the end. Not just the end of my day, but the end of my life. We're in the bathroom, but this time I'm staring out at Daisy Jacobs, whose sombre face stares back into the mirror.

"You do realise no-one will ever know what you have done for your world?"

She stands up straight and a slight smile quirks at her lips. "I saved the world. Me: Daisy Jacobs. It's tempting to shout it from the rooftops. But no-one would ever believe me, would they?"

"Nope. But what matters is *we* know. You did it. You saved your world … you saved me. And life goes on. Thanks to you."

The frown returns. "Go on, say it," she says.

"Say what?"

"Quark, come on. You can see everything that's in my mind."

"I'm only in your tiny mind now," I joke.

She growls. "Quark! You know what people say at times like this."

"Cup of tea?" I smirk.

She sighs.

"Ok, Ok." I pause, dragging it out. "My work here is done …?"

She squeals with delight. "Thank you, Quark!"

"Thank you, Daisy Jacobs."

She rocks backwards and forwards.

"Are you that keen to be rid of me?" I ask.

"I'll miss you. But you're coming back, aren't you?"

"In the blink of an eye."

The farewell sadness shines in her eyes as she squares her shoulders. I smile (inwardly, obviously) as she gathers her familiar strength and courage to face me one last time. She nods.

And like that, the bond is gone.

I leave her and look back to see her standing, alone. And I realise I can see her; I've left, but my existence continues. I relish the feeling of being the sole inhabitant of my own space. I feel energised, excited, *alive*!

Epilogue

I wake in my own bed. I yawn and stretch. I sit up and look around my bedroom. My *actual* room. I'm surrounded by the familiar, but the very first thing I notice is the faintest hint of Mum's perfume, lingering like the ghost of love.

There's a soft knock and Mum's actually here, peering round the door.

"Daisy?"

"Morning, Mum."

"You okay, my lovely?"

"Mmm."

She comes closer and looks down at me. "Sure?"

"Mmm. I am." I reach up to her.

And she knows, as only a mum *can* know. "I thought this Daisy had gone," she sniffs and takes a deep breath, "I thought my Daisy had left me." She practically glows as she sits down on the bed next to me, and with a sigh I rest my head on her shoulder as I've done so many hundreds of times before. I feel I'll explode with bliss as Mum puts her arm around me and eases me into the oh, so familiar embrace.

I am alive; I feel it in every one of my billions of atoms. A smile, like a flower unfurling, curves my lips.

THE END

AFTERWORD
by the author

To any scientist reading this — in fact to anyone with any understanding of science at all — I am sorry! Sorry, sorry, sorry! I like science fiction and those bits in end-of-the-world disaster movies where actors playing at being scientists spout nonsense in an effort to make us believe that speaking pseudo-scientific babble very rapidly will convince us that what they are saying a) makes sense and b) could really bring about the end of the world as we know, it.

I am very sorry to say that the science used in this book should come with inverted commas — 'science' — and should carry a health warning; it *easily* science-y enough to warrant the prefix, 'pseudo'.

However, though I glaze over and start to dribble when things get too complicated, I do love science as well as science fiction. And I strongly encourage anyone interested in finding out the real science (rather than the totally made up 'science') behind the ideas explored in this story (death, destruction, hormones, love and the end of the world as we know it) to read a book, watch an Alice Roberts or Brian Cox documentary or speak to a science teacher.

ABOUT THE AUTHOR

Gary is a husband, father, house husband and now author. In personality, he's somewhere between Quark and Daisy — not quite as geeky (or brave) as Daisy, but considerably less misanthropic than Quark!

After a failed career as a Civil Servant, he's worked in publishing, advertising and in other creative jobs that have always been in some way connected to writing. Writing for others is a great career, but making stuff up is the best job ever! Daisy Jacobs Saves the World is Gary's first and far and away finest novel.

Connect with him on Instagram @ghindhaughwriter

A BIG THANK YOU

Thank you so much for reading Daisy Jacobs Saves the World. We really hope you enjoyed it and would be so grateful if you could leave a review on Amazon or GoodReads (or both!).

Reviews are vital to a book's success and really help independent authors who don't have the power of an intergalactic publishing company behind them. You can share your review on social media too, so others can also enjoy Daisy's story.

Thanks again!

Printed in Great Britain
by Amazon

62097512R00167